MURDER IN RETRIBUTION

ANNE CLEELAND

KENSINGTON BOOKS
http://www.kensingtonbooks.com

KENSINGTON BOOKS are published by

Kensington Publishing Corp.
119 West 40th Street
New York, NY 10018

All Kensington titles, imprints, and distributed lines are available at special quantity discounts for bulk purchases for sales promotion, premiums, fund-raising, educational, or institutional use.

Special book excerpts or customized printings can also be created to fit specific needs. For details, write or phone the office of the Kensington Special Sales Manager: Attn. Special Sales Department. Kensington Publishing Corp, 119 West 40th Street, New York, NY 10018. Phone: 1-800-221-2647.

Kensington and the K logo Reg. U.S. Pat. & TM Off.

Library of Congress Card Catalogue Number: 2014934220

ISBN-13: 978-0-7582-8797-7
ISBN-10: 0-7582-8797-6
First Kensington Hardcover Edition: August 2014

eISBN-13: 978-0-7582-8799-1
eISBN-10: 0-7582-8799-2
First Kensington Electronic Edition: August 2014

10 9 8 7 6 5 4 3 2 1

Printed in the United States of America

For Father John, a kindly convert; and for all others like him.

MURDER IN
RETRIBUTION

PROLOGUE

*D*R. TIMOTHY MCGONIGAL *LET HIMSELF INTO THE FLAT HE SHARED with his sister, and was pleased to see that she was still sitting up at the table, working at her laptop even though the hour was advanced. He had experienced a very eventful night, and it would have been a shame if he had been forced to wait till morning to tell her about it.*

"Hallo, Caro." Suppressing a smile, he considered how to go about it; he rarely had the opportunity to be the dispenser of big news—he was rarely in the spotlight—and tried to think of a clever hint to drop so as to draw out the moment.

Caroline glanced up, the glow of the laptop glinting off her glasses. "Hallo yourself, Tim; I had nearly given up on you. Did you have supper?"

"No, and I am hungry—I've been very busy." This with a great deal of meaning, but she was frowning at the laptop again, her brow knit and her fingers busily tapping. Something had been kept warm in the oven and it smelt wonderful—she was a very good cook. He thought—and not for the first time—that she would make an exemplary wife for some lucky man if she would only make an effort; she certainly took good care of him. He felt guilty, sometimes, that she was so devoted to him. "How does the enzyme?"

Caroline's mouth quirked up even as she continued typing. "The bugger is driving me mad, thank you very much. Give me a mo' and I'll keep you company while you eat."

"I have been visiting Acton." He glanced at her sidelong, and quickly deposited the plate on the table next to her because it was hot on his fingers.

This caught her attention and she paused to look up in surprise. *"Have you indeed? I worry about him—you know how he is. Is he recovering, do you think?"* Caroline was referring to the recent death of their mutual friend; Fiona had been murdered—shot while walking to her car in the parking garage at work. It was one of those senseless, horrific crimes that make a man reconsider all his firmly-held precepts, and Timothy inwardly flinched to remember it again; it was still a bit unreal to him. Fiona had gone to school with him and Caroline—and Acton, too; she had been a forensics scientist at the CID in New Scotland Yard, and Timothy had loved her for years, although he'd never embarrassed her by speaking of it. Fiona knew, though; he was not very good at hiding his feelings. The fact she'd never treated him with anything more than warm friendship told him that she did not return his regard. And now—now, all vestige of hope was gone.

With a mental shake, he brought himself back to the present. *"I'd say Acton is recovering nicely."* Very pleased with this version of a clever hint, Timothy smiled to himself again as he settled in at the table and poured them both a glass of wine—the pinot, which was one of his favorites. Caroline knew her wine, which no doubt came with the territory; she was a genetic engineer and could always spot the best blends.

His sister drew up her legs to clasp them, and sipped the wine, eying him over the rim of the glass. *"Tell me, then; I'll be happy to hear it."* Michael Sinclair, Lord Acton, was a member of their circle of friends, if he could still be called such. He had a brilliant intellect and—as was often the case with such men—he was a bit odd. He had become more and more reclusive in recent years and Timothy had struggled to stay connected to him, with only limited success.

Unable to contain himself for a moment more, Timothy paused in the eating of his dinner so as to watch her reaction. *"He introduced me to his wife."*

Her reaction was all that he could have hoped for. "His wife," she repeated slowly, staring at him. "Never say Acton has married—I won't believe it."

"Believe it." He grinned. "Nearly dropped my teeth."

"Acton. Has married." She paused between saying the words, as though to impress upon him the foolishness of such a thought. "He couldn't have—not without telling us."

"I don't know if anyone knows," he cautioned her, belatedly alert to this fact. "Best not say anything as yet."

Setting down her glass, his sister gazed at him in wonderment. "How can no one know that Acton is married? Tim, I believe you are drunk."

"Caro," he returned, smiling at her consternation, "you have not yet asked me what she is like."

His sister brought her legs down and sat up. "I'll need more wine, if there are more shocks to come."

Obligingly, he poured. "She is young—no more than twenty-three or twenty-four, I would say."

His sister gaped, and he laughed aloud. When she recovered her voice, she asked, "How on earth did he meet her?"

"He did not say." Timothy did not tell his sister that he had been visiting in his professional capacity and that it was clear Lady Acton had been shot in the leg at very close range—some things were best kept within the bounds of professional discretion. "I had the impression that she is also with the police." He paused, thinking about it. "She is attractive, in a delicate-boned sort of way."

"You astonish me." His sister leaned back in her chair and regarded him. "It is the eighth wonder of the world."

"And," Timothy built up to the final revelation with a dramatic pause, "she is Irish."

"Good God, Tim. Irish!"

"An accent as thick as your hand," he assured her.

But this was apparently an absurdity too far, and Caroline's manner suddenly became concerned as she leaned forward. "Oh, Tim—he has been taken-in. Poor Acton."

He shook his head, certain of his ground. "I don't think so, Caro; he seemed very fond of her." He thought of the way Acton had watched his wife—unsuccessfully trying to hide his deep concern. "It was rather touching, really; you know he's not one to be fond."

"She must be pregnant," his sister concluded in dismay, unconvinced by her brother's testament.

"I don't believe so." The doctor had asked this very question before starting treatment, and the patient had disclaimed, blushing furiously. He had surmised at the time—gauging from her reaction— that the wound had been accidentally administered during sex play. They were police officers, after all; to each his own.

had an innate ability to read people, and she could usually tell when someone was lying. Presumably, this ability was inherited from some Irish ancestor—hopefully one who hadn't been burned at the stake as a result—and it was a mixed blessing; it was no easy thing to be constantly aware of the currents of emotions that swirled around her at any given time. Acton guarded his own emotions very closely but she knew on this occasion he was speaking the pure truth. It was a huge relief, all in all.

Fearing she would disgrace herself by being sick during what should be a sentimental milestone in married life, she stood and backed away a step, taking in a deep breath and trying to settle her stomach. Acton rose to stand alongside her and the SOCO team took this as a cue that the visual inspection by the detective staff had now concluded—although there had been precious little detecting done, thus far. As Acton nodded permission, the examiner moved in to bag the corpse's hands and conduct preliminary tests for trace evidence before the body itself would be bagged and removed. After the man moved away, Doyle continued, "And do not pretend this blessed turn of events is not *completely* my fault."

"Oh? I feel I may have had a hand in it." He cocked his head, trying to tease her out of the sullens.

For whatever reason, this attempt to humor her only succeeded in making her more annoyed and she made a hot retort. "I am well-aware that you have no self-control, my friend; mine is the burden of keepin' you at arm's length."

"You failed miserably," he agreed.

She had to duck her head to suppress an inappropriate smile; it wouldn't do at all to be seen giggling while this poor mucker's mangled body was supposedly under examination. Faith, her husband was a treasure; a lesser man would be giving her the back of his hand after having to listen to her sauce. He was relieved by her reaction—she could feel it—

and the tension between them dissipated. Face facts, she thought; what's done is done, and in this case it was your husband who had the doin' of you. She'd been trying all morning not to dwell on the consequences of that fateful night some weeks ago, and what it might mean to the future that she had a hard time picturing to begin with. Due to her intuitive ability, Doyle had managed to carve out a useful position as a detective at the New Scotland Yard CID and she especially loved the fieldwork; interviewing the witnesses and gathering the evidence that allowed her to untangle the latest wreckage of human conflict. Now the future was once again uncertain; her life was going to change dramatically and she couldn't help but think it may not necessarily be for the better. As she eyed her new husband, she reflected that, in truth, she was not yet fully recovered from the last dramatic change.

"It is not as though we didn't want children."

Again, she hid her surprise. The subject had never come up, which was only to be expected as their courtship had not commenced until after they were married; she and Acton were still feeling their way and it was not what anyone would characterize as a normal marriage—they were not your average mister and missus.

Feeling considerably relieved—now that the dreaded moment of revelation was behind her—Doyle made a mighty effort to right her ship. As they were no longer on a level with the corpse, her stomach seemed less inclined to rebel and she seemed less inclined as well—grow *up*, Doyle. "It's just that the timin' couldn't be worse, Michael."

"Do you not want this baby?" he asked gently, his tone neutral.

She met his eyes, a bit shocked and ashamed that such a question could even be asked. Faith, what on earth ailed her, that she was thrown so off-kilter by this unexpected turn of events? She was acting like a spoilt child and he'd be regretting this whole adventure in marriage if she kept this up. "Whist, man; don't be daft." She met his eyes with what she hoped was a message of reassurance. "Of course I do. I'm havin' a fit of the dismals, is all. And I'm not used to feelin' ill— I'm just that frustrated, Michael, and I beg your pardon fastin'."

She managed to convey a smile at him through the mask and rested a hand on his arm, even though it was in full view of the SOCO personnel. He covered her latexed hand with his own for a moment, and she could sense his relief. You should be ashamed of your foolish self, to worry him so, she scolded; but it was such a crackin' shame that this child was conceived on such a night. Nearly a month ago she had confronted a killer who had lured her to Acton's flat, and by a miraculous turn of events had managed to kill the killer and save the day. It had not been an unmitigated success, however, since in the process she had shot herself in the leg, and whilst awaiting the doctor's arrival she'd demanded that Acton make love to her amidst the carnage. It had seemed like a good idea at the time, and while she may not have been entirely rational, she had definitely been fertile. Although they were already secretly married at the time, this prompt pregnancy would only add fuel to the bonfire of speculation as to why Lord Acton, celebrated chief inspector at the Met, had married a first-year detective constable by way of Dublin in such a skimble-skamble fashion. *Please,* baby, she pleaded mentally; don't come early.

Silently, they stood side-by-side and watched the photographer take the final photos before the body was bagged and transported from the scene. Now the more tedious task of helping the examiners scour the area for clues would commence, and it would no doubt be a hard slog, considering the untamed vegetation on either side of the aqueduct. If this crime scene was anything like the others, there would be precious little to show for such a dogged search and Doyle sighed yet again; she was not one for meticulous by-the-bookings when there were better uses for her talents.

Acton glanced at her, assessing. "Would you like to go home?"

"No; truly, Michael, I am right as rain—I'm that sorry I snapped at you." Mainly, she was very sensitive to her new status as Acton's wife, and did not want to give the impression to the other staff that she felt entitled, and didn't need to earn her way.

Before he could respond, his mobile phone pinged, and he checked the ID and took the call. He listened, said, "Right; I'm coming," and disconnected. "Another one—Newmarket."

"Faith; we'll be runnin' out of crime scene tape at this rate." There had been a rash of underworld murders in the past few weeks, and rumors of a vicious turf war seemed to have merit, as the body count kept climbing between the two warring factions. "They're callin' you because they think it's connected?" Normally Acton's territory did not include Newmarket, but if the first responders thought it was part of a pending investigation, they would contact the presiding DCI.

He crossed his arms and surveyed the scene before him. "Presumably; we shall see. There is always the chance that an unrelated killer is taking the opportunity to use the other murders as a cover."

"A shadow murder; like the first one we worked together." She smiled up at him, mistily sentimental about their first bloated corpse—what a fine day that was; she had been terrified of him, of course, but it had all worked out. Or worked in, more like, which in turn had brought her to her current sorry state.

"I'll not soon forget." He returned her smile, which was as sentimental as he was like to get; he was not one for pretty compliments—nor was she one to expect them.

She offered, "There's a bright side, I'm thinkin'; if all the villains are to be killin' each other off, all the more time for us to be paintin' the nursery." She had the satisfaction of seeing a flicker of relief in his dark eyes; *shame* on her for fretting him so.

His gaze moved to the wooded banks on each side of the aqueduct, assessing the task ahead. "I will have Williams come to help you finish here."

Doyle was instantly cross again. "I don't need Williams to help me."

"Yes, you do." He found the programmed number on his mobile and rested his eyes on her whilst he waited.

Sighing in repentance, she observed, "It is a rare wonder, husband, that you don't throw me over in favor of a more worthy redhead."

He gave her a look as he spoke to Williams, and Doyle had to duck her head to control another inappropriate giggle; Acton had little choice but to put up with her. A brilliant and eccentric man, he was suffering from some sort of obsessive neurosis and the object of his fixation was her own fair self. He had interrupted a murder investigation to confess his status as a Section Seven—a stalker—and with no further ado had bundled her off into marriage; not that she had put up much of a resistance. She was not certain how long his condition had been in existence or how long it would last; she only knew that she was right for him, and he for her. Thus far, she had no regrets—well, she was bitterly regretting that she had hysterically demanded sex after her first kill, but that wasn't really his fault; men were not known for standing firm in such a situation.

Acton finished his conversation with Williams and rang off. "He will be here shortly. If you would allow him to be of service, I would appreciate it."

He was teasing her in his dry way; she was professionally

jealous of Williams and tended to be territorial. "Be off, my friend," Doyle replied with as much lightness as she could muster. "We will see you later."

Smiling at her use of the pronoun, he squeezed her arm gently and then left for Newmarket.

CHAPTER 2

RELIEVED THAT ACTON WOULDN'T BE A WITNESS IF SHE WERE indeed to be sick, Doyle crouched down again to study the conduit where the body had been found while the SOCO examiners began to systematically scrutinize the area in ever-widening circles. She could guess what they would find; absolutely nothing. For a turf war, there was remarkably little evidence.

The scent of decomposition still lingered on the ground because the body had been there for a time, and she took deep breaths to steady her midsection, annoyed with herself because decomp had never bothered her before. Acton had already known she was pregnant, of course. She should have said something before this, but she was hoping her symptoms were built upon nerves and not upon the presence of the Honorable whomever who had been conceived the night his or her mother had killed a man and then accidentally shot herself for good measure. Nothin' for it, she thought in resignation; this is exactly why the nuns warned you about sex.

Struggling to hide her irritation, she called to the SOCO photographer so as to double-check that the woman had taken some close-ups of the maggot activity on the corpse. Doyle was irritated because the photographer had been emanating equal parts amazement and derision when introduced to Doyle earlier, even though her outward manner had been all that was correct. The general consensus—which Doyle could sense in resounding waves—was that Acton had lost his mind. Nothin' for that, either, and this was exactly what she deserved for stepping into the center ring at the circus—not that she would change a thing; best get on with it, the circus was soon to have another act.

After hearing the photographer's falsely-respectful assurances, Doyle crouched again, unable to shake the feeling that she was missing something, here. Acton was right; it was cooler in the conduit and time-of-death could more exactly be established by the insect experts, who could opine to a remarkable degree of certainty how long the body had been dead by gauging the life cycles of the various insects feasting on their grisly windfall. The body had no identification on it, but she had little doubt the victim had a record, and they would know who it was very shortly. It was odd that the man had been shot in the face; ordinarily, a professional did not face his victim and there seemed little doubt this was a professional hit—unless, as Acton had suggested, someone was using the excuse to conduct a little murder on the side. She wondered if he suspected as much—that might explain the shot to the face; it was the work of a nonprofessional trying to look like a professional.

Leaning back on her heels, she decided she was relieved to have the subject of her pregnancy out in the open, despite the fact that everyone at the Met would be counting to nine on their fingers. Acton said it was wonderful news, and it was, of course. It was just that she'd spent a rather solitary life—it came with the territory, knowing the things that she knew. Acton had been famously reclusive in his own right, and now the both of them were to make a go at family life when it wasn't in their respective natures. She looked up at the trees, shifting in the breeze. He loves me, she thought; so much that he is willing to put his hand to this particular plow and I am balking like a donkey at the hitch. Shame on me.

In this repentant frame of mind, she managed to greet Williams with good grace when he arrived on the scene. Doyle was conferring with the SOCO team about the dearth of evidence when she spotted him and mustered up a more-or-less genuine smile. "Williams."

"Doyle," he acknowledged, returning her smile. Williams was several years older than she; tall, blond, and athletically handsome; he was what her late mother would have deemed "proper English," which was not necessarily a compliment. Intelligent and reserved, he was favored by the powers-that-be at the CID, which led some lesser beings to criticize him as arrogant. Doyle was not one of them; Williams had been unfailingly kind to her and although he was a rival for advancement, she considered him a friend. It was true that her faith in him had been shaken a bit because during the last investigation, she'd entertained a shrewd suspicion that he had manipulated some evidence at Acton's request. Manipulation of evidence was the closest thing to a mortal sin in this business, but she had no sure knowledge and besides, she couldn't really send her better half off to the nick.

"Congratulations on your promotion," she said to Williams with a fine show of sincerity. "You deserve it." Williams had recently been promoted to detective sergeant, and he now outranked Doyle, who remained a lowly detective constable. He had done some good work on the recent Leadenhall murders when Acton had pulled Doyle off the case because he feared—correctly, as it turned out—that she was in danger. Unfortunately, no one could ever know this was the reason, and so she had been stuck doing very dull research work at headquarters whilst Williams had snatched the palm from her, and had been covered in glory as a result. Nothin' for it, my girl, she thought, trying not to grind her teeth; it appears you are in need of a fine lesson in humility.

Williams contemplated the ground for a moment. "I didn't deserve it more than you did," he acknowledged frankly. "There were other forces at work."

Doyle could see that he was telling the truth and not merely being kind, which was interesting—perhaps they were reluctant to promote her due to her new status as Acton's wife.

"Oh?" She gave him a glance that invited confidences, but he did not elaborate, which was very like him—Williams was very much by-the-book, and not a gossip. "Ah well; rather you than Munoz," she teased, and was rewarded by a small smile. Munoz was another DC in their unit, and oftentimes a thorn in Doyle's flesh. Williams was not the type to say something unkind, however, and instead he turned the conversation to the recently deceased.

"Let me guess." His hands on his hips, he took a survey of the area. "No evidence."

Doyle conceded this unfortunate fact with a nod. "We'll be seein' if trace can give us hair or fibers—his hands have been bagged—but no, it appears another blank wall."

"I'll search with you, if you'd like."

She accepted the offer, although he was now her flippin' superior officer and therefore had no need to ask her flippin' permission. "Fine—I'll take right if you'll take left." Acton would be very pleased to witness her willingness to cooperate; she could be less donkey-like if she put her mind to it.

They began carefully combing the floor of the cement aqueduct to see if the SOCOs had missed anything and then, coming up empty, proceeded to the vegetation on either side, which was dusty and fruitless work. It occurred to Doyle that Williams hadn't asked about cause of death, which would help him in his search. She called out across to him, "He was shot in the face—large caliber."

"Good to know," he called back. "Time of death?"

"Days, but it is unclear—we'll have to wait for the insect report."

After they were finished, they came together again on the floor of the aqueduct and Doyle paused to contemplate the conduit again, her brow knit as she brushed back wayward tendrils of hair.

"What is it?" Williams was regarding her steadily, and Doyle remembered that she could never read him very well; people who were reserved or held their emotions in check, like Acton, were not as transparent to her.

She couldn't very well tell him that her instinct was acting up, telling her she was missing something important, and so she explained a bit lamely, "Presumably a professional hit, but it should have been two shots to the back of the head, execution-style, and it was not."

Williams surveyed the scene alongside her. "Perhaps there's a connection to the Kempton Park murders."

"Perhaps," Doyle agreed, carefully noncommittal. It was true this murder could easily match the recent spate of murders connected to the Kempton Park racecourse near London—although in those, the only face-shot victims were women. That case was officially closed, as the supposed killer had in turn been supposedly killed by his supposed henchman. Doyle knew, however, that she had shot the true killer and Acton had disposed of his body with no one the wiser. The killer had been a trainee—a temporary detective constable named Owens, and the revelation of his murder by Doyle's hand would have come at too great a price.

Glossing over that subject, she continued, "It just seems odd; Acton suggested that perhaps it was an attempt to commit a shadow murder; an act of rage like this doesn't fit with the lack of forensics."

"It is certainly a paradox."

Doyle was not strong on vocabulary, and since she wasn't

certain what the word meant, did not respond. "What's next, then?" As Williams now outranked her, he had the lead in the investigation, but she couldn't quite bring herself to call him "sir" just yet.

"We return to headquarters and research our victim; look for motive."

They turned and began the climb back up to the roadway, the soles of Doyle's boots slipping a bit on the loose gravel. Williams took her arm to steady her. "Are you feeling all right?"

Doyle blushed. "I'm a bit under the weather," she admitted. "Is it that noticeable, then?"

It was his turn to be embarrassed. "No, not at all; I just wondered."

Grand, she thought as they clambered up to the cusp; I must look like something the cat dragged in.

Williams gave her a lift back to headquarters, and as he drove through the traffic they spoke of possible leads to pursue. Doyle was still trying to decide what she was thinking about, and so made a summation aloud. "By all appearances, this one—and no doubt the Newmarket one, too—are connected to the turf war; although Acton thinks the jury is still out on this one."

"Oh? Did this victim look Irish or Russian?"

Doyle bristled. "People don't *look* Irish, Williams."

He gave her a glance, and she amended, "Well, most times." She had auburn hair, fair skin and was a caricature, herself.

"We'll find out," he continued diplomatically. "If he's connected to the turf war, he'll definitely be in the database; the victims have all been Watch List types."

Doyle frowned and looked out the window—she truly wasn't feeling well and it helped to look out the window at the horizon. "Why do you suppose the villains are goin' at it? What set off this particular turf war, d'you think?"

"Unclear—although it always comes down to money; or the power that leads to money."

"You don't think it's personal, then?" She was thinking of the shot to the face—it took a rare breed to face another person and shoot them, large caliber, in the face.

"No," he replied. "Not for these characters. Usually a turf war is exactly that; rivals fighting to control a lucrative rig. We should take a look to determine if something has changed so that there's suddenly a lot of money to be had."

She nodded, as this did make sense; Williams had a superior intellect to hers and she respected his opinion—she was more a leaper-to-conclusions than an analyst, and was always acutely aware that she did not have the book-learning that the others did. Luckily, detective work centered on people and their interactions—not just the forensics—and this allowed her to solve cases by using her perceptive ability. Detectives like Williams and Acton took an opposite tack, and carefully analyzed the evidence as though it was all a mathematical equation. She glanced sidelong at her companion, and then wished she hadn't, turning quickly to look out the window again. In his own way, Williams was almost as smart as Acton; by the time he was Acton's age he could well make DCI. He will go far in the CID, thought Doyle with a sting of jealousy. I, on the other hand, will be raising red-headed children. She chastised herself yet again for her poor attitude; red was a recessive gene, after all.

There was a small silence. "I haven't had a chance to congratulate you," said Williams in a level voice.

Thinking of her pregnancy, Doyle forgot about looking out the window and stared at him in dismayed surprise.

He glanced over at her. "On your marriage," he elaborated.

"Oh," she said. "Thank you."

"I hope you will be very happy," he said firmly.

This, interestingly enough, was not true.

CHAPTER 3

Doyle sat in her basement cubicle at the Met, preparing a report on the aqueduct murder. The victim's fingerprints had identified him as Yuri Barayev, a Russian businessman who was surprisingly not featured on the Home Office's Watch List. Acton's theory that this was a shadow murder—someone taking advantage of the cover that the other murders would provide—may indeed have merit. The current turf war had claimed as victims several unsavory characters who could be loosely characterized as Russian mafia, for want of a better term. Some of them were former KGB—and former KGB personnel always made the Home Secretary's people wring their hands—but the problem with pursuing the Russians was that they tended to be clothed in respectable corporate guise, courtesy of the pervasive corruption back home. Usually they were bankers, laundering money or running a protection racket and—because it was sometimes a fine line between robust free enterprise and sharp dealings—the police were often frustrated.

The Russians were warring with an equally unsavory group of troublemakers known as the Sinn-split; an Irish terrorist group that had refused to comply with the Sinn Féin cease-fire but instead continued to cause trouble—not necessarily with bombs and violence, but with black market dealings and other economic sabotage.

The Sinn-split people were notoriously attracted to race-courses, and two months ago a horse trainer had been murdered by Owens, Doyle's attacker. The murdered horse trainer was Irish and himself on the Watch List, so it would behoove the fair Doyle to check for a connection, as Williams had suggested. Owens had admitted that he worked for a syndicate just before he tried to kill her, and in his more impassioned moments, a trace of an accent had appeared—but it was difficult for her to identify accents, as everyone who wasn't Irish had a very strange one to begin with. Closing her eyes, she tried to remember what he'd said—the raving lunatic; she didn't like to think of that night, but now she'd have a permanent souvenir. Not your fault, baby, she noted fairly; but nonetheless, you're a mixed blessing.

At the time, she hadn't thought Owens was Russian, but he definitely wasn't Irish, either. He'd said the murder of the trainer was business, and intimated that he had inveigled his way into becoming the man's lover as part of an assignment. Perhaps he wasn't Russian-Russian, but one of those other nationalities in the former soviet empire; it seemed evident he was somehow involved in all this, since now the Irish and the Russians were going at it, hammer and tongs. She opened her eyes and gazed thoughtfully at her reflection in the laptop screen, wondering why she couldn't seem to convince herself of this. With a sigh, she moved on; she'd learned long ago that she had no control over her perceptive ability; the intuitive leap would come when it wished—if it came at all—and she had to possess her morning-sickened soul in patience. Only now it was afternoon, so her soul was afternoon-sickened, which did not bode well. I should try to eat something, she thought, and then made no effort to do so.

The two bodies found today were the Russian in the

aqueduct—Barayev—and a Sinn-split associate named Rourke who was found lying in the heath near the Newmarket race-course. By all appearances, they were tit-for-tat murders, and it certainly seemed as though the two groups were at war, vying for something having to do with the racecourses—faith, it was a turf war in the truest sense of the word. The only flaw in this working theory was that Barayev had no obvious con-nection to the Russian group. Therefore, as Acton had hinted, she should be open to the possibility that he'd been killed by an unrelated third party who was taking advantage of the carnage to commit a shadow murder.

DC Munoz, in the cubicle next door to Doyle, popped her head over the partition, shaking back her hair and glower-ing—although to be fair, she had an attractive glower. "When are you going to take a break, Acton?"

Doyle had decided to maintain her maiden name at work, as it was too confusing to be another Acton. Besides, she was sensitive about the whole title issue; she had married far out of her element and didn't want anyone to think she was putting on airs. Munoz, naturally, did not comply with her re-quest, but Doyle was consumed with guilt; Munoz had also been passed over for promotion and Doyle had the sneaking suspicion that this was Acton's doing, just so Doyle wouldn't feel as badly. Munoz, giving the devil her due, was a very good detective; she was also to be avoided because she'd fancied Acton for herself and, as the reigning beauty of their unit, had no idea that Doyle was even in the running. Therefore, Munoz was now a crackin' blowtorch of bitterness and disap-pointment, which made it difficult for Doyle to be anywhere near her and she half-wished Munoz would be promoted just so she would be transferred out of Doyle's orbit.

"It's still Doyle, Munoz, and I'm at a stoppin' point. Want to get coffee?" Coffee actually sounded semi-edible.

"I don't think you can go to the lowly canteen anymore; there's no peeress section."

"Munoz," warned Doyle. "Be civil, or I'll be tellin' everyone you draw religious artwork."

This turned the trick; Munoz looked rebellious but made no further attempts to needle her companion as they walked together to the canteen on the third floor. Instead, she offered in a constricted tone, "I sell it for extra income, and I would appreciate it if you didn't mention this to anyone."

"Done. Such a tale would sound the knell to your fine reputation as an unprincipled brasser."

Stung, Munoz retorted, "It's easy to have principles when you are rich and married."

"And not necessarily in that order," Doyle agreed in a mild tone as they approached the coffee machine. "Have done, Munoz; I couldn't be tellin' anyone I was datin' Acton, surely you can see that." Best not to mention that her first date with Acton had been after they were married; it would only confuse the issue.

Munoz struggled with holding her tongue, and Doyle practically winced at the wave of rage and frustration that she could sense; Munoz was not accustomed to being relegated to an also-ran. Apparently everybody and his uncle fancied Acton; the reason Owens had wanted to kill Doyle was to make a run at Acton himself, the *raving* lunatic. Hopefully, Acton's marriage to her would now discourage all crazed pursuers—the man should thank God fasting.

"I don't want to talk about you and Acton." Munoz chose a table near the perimeter, so that the weak sunlight shone warm through the windows. "I want to talk about Williams's promotion."

Another potential minefield. Doyle said carefully, "I saw him this mornin' at the aqueduct scene and he was very gracious—no lordin' it over my lowly constable self." As you would have done, Doyle added silently. Munoz had once helped her out, but Doyle had no illusions about Munoz's character, religious drawings or no.

"Have you heard," Munoz asked neutrally, fingering her cardboard cup, "if any other promotions are in line?"

Ah, thought Doyle; that's what this is all about. "Acton doesn't talk to me about that kind of thing, Munoz. It wouldn't be right."

"You don't talk about it *at all?*" Munoz's fine dark eyes scrutinized her with open skepticism.

"We talk about the cases, but not about the politics." Doyle thought it over. "Acton is not very interested in the politics, I think." Munoz would probably be surprised to hear that she and Acton really didn't converse much at all. Before the marriage, neither of them had been very social, and on some evenings very few words were exchanged. Doyle found that she was perfectly happy not to feel the need to make conversation; Acton needed to be with her but he was very reserved by nature. This might change over time or it may not; it didn't matter; she loved her husband and was very content. And after all, the sex more than made up for the silence—she had no idea that marriage involved so much sex. You live and you learn.

With a guilty start, Doyle realized belatedly that perhaps she should disclose as little as possible about her marriage to Munoz—or anyone else, for that matter; quite the tangle patch, that. Munoz's next remark only strengthened this resolve.

"Do you have sex with him?" There was a faint hint of incredulity in the question.

That the question was even asked of a newlywed was an indication of Acton's reputation. The others had nicknamed him "Holmes" due to the obvious comparison, only they didn't know that the addiction in his case was to Doyle and not to cocaine, and anyone who wished to wait around a few more months would see proof positive. "That is none of your business, Munoz."

Munoz accepted the rebuff, and they sat in silence for a few minutes, each lost in thought. Others who passed by their table would glance sidelong at Doyle and exchange whispered remarks as they walked away. I'm world-famous, thought Doyle, trying not to look self-conscious; the DC who snatched up Acton—no one would ever credit that it was the other way 'round.

The whispered attention did not help Munoz's mood, which had returned to sullen. "It's so unfair; you won the husband sweepstakes, and then Williams is promoted before me."

"Your turn will come, Munoz. A little patience is all that is needed." Doyle reflected that their supervisor, Inspector Habib, would probably rival Acton in rushing his bride to the altar if Munoz gave him the go-ahead. "You're a heartbreaker, is what you are; be off, or I will think you are fishin' for compliments."

Munoz had to agree with the truth of this remark, and her mood improved as they made their way back down to the basement. Doyle reseated herself before her laptop screen and wished she could finish up her report; she was still waiting for the ERU photos, which seemed to be taking longer than usual. She decided she would complete it tomorrow; her conversation with Munoz had touched off a different train of thought. She sent a text to Acton that said, "Cereal?"

She waited for a response, which came with flattering promptness. "Done."

Smiling, she sheathed her mobile and, taking a quick look around, gathered up her rucksack. Time to make it up to her poor husband, who'd demonstrated remarkable patience with his balky wife.

CHAPTER 4

DOYLE HAD MOVED INTO ACTON'S FLAT AFTER THEY MARRIED, and the fact that it was also the scene of her attempted murder did not in any way dim the delight she took in their home. The flat was located in an upscale building overlooking the park and with a remarkable view of the city. Acton might be an acetic, but he had very good taste and spared no expense on the simple modern furnishings he enjoyed. Without a twinge of regret, Doyle had consigned her own rubbish to the bin, bringing with her only a framed photograph of her mother, who had died more than a year ago. She loved living with Acton in this tranquil space, and tried not to feel a stab of regret when she thought of how this idyllic existence was set to change in the coming months.

She arrived home first, and remembered with an inward sigh that this was one of the days their housekeeper came in. Marta had been a retainer at Acton's estate in the country where his mother, the dowager Lady Acton, still resided, and the housekeeper had moved to London to see to Acton, which she did very efficiently three days a week. Thankfully, she did not live in, but resided with her cousin a short tube ride away. Marta was German by ancestry, and Doyle would not have been surprised to discover she was bred by Nazis; although the housekeeper hid her feelings behind a façade of respect, Doyle knew she heartily disapproved of Acton's bride—Marta was an easy read.

Doyle explained to the woman that she could leave early today without preparing a dinner, and mentally chastised herself because she always allowed the housekeeper to see that she was intimidated, which only added to the other's disdain. Marta thanked her woodenly, and gathered up her coat and purse. When Acton was present, Marta referred to Doyle as "madam" or "Lady Acton." When he wasn't, she didn't. Doyle, however, was impervious to the snub—no one knew better than she that Acton had married out of his species. Mainly, she was a bit embarrassed because Marta no doubt guessed the reason that workaholic Acton was rushing home to meet his bride in private—"cereal" had become their code word for sex. It was nothing to be ashamed of, Doyle scolded herself; of course Marta would be aware of the goings-on in the household—privacy was a luxury, now. Still, Marta always made her feel as though she was a twopenny brasser and not Acton's lawful wife, which didn't help matters.

Determined not to dwell on Marta's subtle insolence, Doyle took down her hair and shook it out in anticipation. Despite the increasingly unmistakable signs that she was pregnant, Doyle had stubbornly adhered to their schedule of abstaining from sex during ovulation even though her temperature was no longer fluctuating. She'd been in denial, of course, and to make matters worse, she had been avoiding the subject with Acton, as though she could make the entire issue go away. Silly knocker, she thought, reviewing her pale complexion in the mirror; make it up to the poor man. After all, there was no point in closing the barn door; that horse is well away.

A short time later she heard Acton's key card in the slot, and she went to greet him at the door, dressed only in her robe. Almost instantly, his mouth was on hers, his hands pulling at the tie and his need urgent. He murmured against her mouth, "Marta?"

"She will have to wait her turn," Doyle teased. He said nothing further, his mouth moving down her neck, but she broke away for a moment, struck by a thought. "Oh—d'you think we should?"

"Yes," he said, sliding the robe from her shoulders. "I asked Timothy."

She tried not to think how embarrassing it would be to face Dr. McGonigal when next they met, and instead happily acceded to Acton's furious lovemaking. It had been this way with him from the first; he craved her. She believed it was a symptom of his condition, a means by which he could climb into her skin, so to speak. Today their first fevered encounter was on the entryway rug; the second a more leisurely tryst after they adjourned to the bed. At its conclusion, he moved his mouth along her throat, across her face; his weight pressed against her. "How do you feel?"

"Satiated."

"I meant," he murmured, his mouth near her ear, "—are you still queasy?"

"You have discovered the cure, thanks be to God." Best not to mention the rug burns on her back.

They lay quietly together, saying nothing, for quite some time. He liked to fold her in his arms after lovemaking, pulling her to him so that her back curled neatly into his chest—he was quite a bit taller than she. He would hold her against him and his fingertips would lightly move over her forearms and hands; slowly back and forth, repeatedly. She privately thought that nothing else he did to her was as pleasurable.

"I have a meeting tomorrow," he said from the pillow behind her head. "It is in Brighton."

Although it seemed an ordinary comment, it was actually quite significant; he did not do well if he was away from her.

"Is it overnight? I will come with you." As long as there was no unexpected fieldwork, she could always complete her report away from headquarters.

He thought about it. "I'm not certain how long it will last. It has to do with contraband; the latest developments and protocol. I may be back by evening."

"If it does not look that way, call and I will come."

"Ask the concierge for the driving service."

"Michael," she teased, "is the bloom off the rose already? I thought you would trust me with the Range Rover."

"I will have the Range Rover. You may drive me back home, if you wish."

"Brave man." She smiled into the gathering twilight; she was a new driver, and not very competent.

He was quiet for a minute, and then said, "I have been putting aside fungible assets for you."

Faith, here was a twist on post-coital conversation. "Tell me exactly what that means, my friend."

He continued slowly, "If I were to die, there could be a great deal of unpleasantness. The current heir to my estate is a cousin, and he and my mother could make your life very difficult."

"Michael," she said gently, "they may have your stupid estate with my blessin'."

"If the child is a boy, the estate belongs to him."

Doyle blinked in surprise. She hadn't thought about any of this. "Oh."

"I would like him to have it," he added quietly.

"Then he will have it, and no mistakin'." If Acton needed reassurance that she was a fervent supporter of primo—primo-whatever-it-was, she would give it to him.

"There are valuables and cash in a blind account at Layton's," he continued in his level tone. Layton was Acton's man of business. "Jewelry, gold—fungible assets that are anonymous and outside the estate. On my death, go to Layton and he will help you. If Layton has died, do not speak of it to anyone else, and I will give you the deposit numbers."

She was silent, trying to absorb what he had told her. Correctly gauging her silence as confusion, he continued patiently, "If the bank accounts are legally frozen, this will give you access to funds that no one else will know to claim. You will need to hire the highest quality solicitors—spare no expense."

"Right." She paused a beat, and then asked with what she thought was commendable calm, "Is there any reason you're believin' you'll be dyin' soon?"

"No." His arms tightened around her. "I am merely being cautious."

She was relieved; he was telling the truth, and was allowing her to read him so that she could see that it was the truth. It was a switch; he'd been very guarded around her lately, but then again, she'd been guarded, herself. Grow up, Doyle, she thought; you're not the first couple faced with an unplanned pregnancy, and there will be plenty of time to become accustomed. Only—only it was such a shame that the current turf war served to remind her of raving-lunatic Owens, and her pregnancy served to remind her of raving-lunatic Owens, and he truly didn't deserve another stray thought, the raving lunatic; the whole miserable incident was dead and buried and done with.

She paused, her scalp prickling as though she was on the verge of some intuitive connection, but the moment passed and she couldn't get a glimpse, mainly because she was so very drowsy—how lovely it was to be at home and abed with Acton early, not late at night when they were already tired. Faith, with all the recent murders it was a wonder he had managed to get away from work at all—she'd been so busy sulking about her pregnancy that she didn't know how far along in the investigation he was, he hadn't discussed it with her. He'd been guarded about these turf war cases.

She opened her eyes, wide-awake and her scalp prickling. Acton had been guarded about these cases. The last time he had been guarded with her about a case was because he planned on killing the suspect himself, and he didn't want her to figure it out.

Before she could continue on with this train of thought, however, he said, "Perhaps I should seek treatment."

She hid her surprise. Saints—what had gotten into the man, that he was willing to speak of his condition; he hated to speak of his condition almost as much as she hated to speak of her intuition. Then she realized it was more properly what had gotten into her; whilst she had been avoiding the subject and wanting to throw things, he had been quietly considering what needed to be done in preparation for this baby. She grasped his hands, which were still making their stroking circuit, and kissed them both in turn. "Michael, I am so sorry I've been actin' like a spoilt child. Forgive me, please."

"There is nothing to forgive. You have had a lot thrust upon you in a short space of time."

She smiled to herself at his choice of words, but let the opportunity to say something flippant pass. It was true; in recent months she'd married her boss out of hand, nearly been killed, killed someone, shot herself by accident, and had gotten pregnant to boot. For the love o' Mike, what could she possibly do for an encore?

Letting his hands go so they could go back to their rhythm, she thought about the question. He rarely referred in any way to his neurosis—or whatever it was—and he would surely hate having to speak of it to anyone else. "I am of two minds on the subject," she admitted. "You are not a danger to me—quite the opposite. It affects no one else. What would you have them do? Start feedin' you some vile drug, or try weanin' you away from me?" This had actually crossed her mind more than once; unthinkable that he may wake one morning to find his fixation gone as quickly as it had come—and that he would regard his better half with the same incredulous disbelief that everyone else did.

He gently turned her over so that she lay on her back, and leaned over her, his face very close to hers. Apparently, she had said something amusing. "You are remarkably foolish if you think I am going to leave you."

She twined her arms around his neck and broadened her accent, "Faith, m'lord, 'tis a sad, sad sight I'd be, what wi' me poor belly and you not willin' to do right by me."

"Knocker," he said in imitation, and kissed her.

CHAPTER 5

At first, he had been wary of her, even though she was just a woman, and not very strong. She was mganga, and although the new God said be not afraid, it was hard for him to forget what the old gods said, in the old country. After a few minutes, though, he decided she was good of the soul, and it was she who was wary—it was not easy to be mganga.

THE NEXT MORNING, ACTON PREPARED TO LEAVE FOR HIS CONference in Brighton and Doyle prepared to leave for work. Ordinarily, she was an early riser but in recent days she had been reluctant to rise from their bed, particularly because as soon as she stood on her feet she began to feel out of curl. She found if she took deep breaths and nibbled on a plain, refrigerated biscuit she could control the nausea, and tried to build some optimism based on this discovery. I'm to have a new attitude, she reminded herself; I'm to be a grown-up and not a balking donkey so that Acton will not be worried that I'm incapable of doing battle with the pretenders to the throne.

Marta came in early to make up for leaving early the day before, and Doyle explained that Acton would be out of town and no dinner need be prepared as Doyle would forage on her own; the last thing she wanted was to spend an evening alone with the disapproving housekeeper.

Marta replied, "Yes, madam," because Acton was present, and Doyle smiled to herself; judging from the pillow talk the night before, the poor woman would have a long wait of it, if she was thinking that Acton would come to his senses anytime soon.

"Timothy and Caroline would like to play cards on Sunday, if you'd like," Acton said as he kissed her good-bye.

Doyle smiled. "That would be grand, Michael."

She managed to dress for work, and then leaned against the back wall of the lift, fortifying herself as she descended to the lobby of the building. When the doors slid open, she straightened her shoulders and walked past the concierge desk through the revolving doors to catch a cab for work, because Acton didn't want her riding the tube. Technically, he wanted her to use the concierge driving service, but she shied away from it, still too sensitive about giving the appearance of flaunting her new-found wealth. As a compromise, most days she hailed a cab and as a result, one of the drivers had taken to waiting for her in the mornings. His license said he was Rwandan, and because his English was almost unintelligible, she felt a kinship with him, and appreciated his allegiance. As he held the door for her, he made a comment that she interpreted as a greeting. In return, she mustered up a wan smile and they were under way.

She raised the window, as the street outside smelt of gasoline fumes which did not aid in the settlement of her poor stomach. Mind over matter, she thought with steely resolve; I will think about other things. Acton must have made the plan for Sunday when he spoke with Timothy; he had called to ask the doctor to recommend an obstetrician. Truth be told, Doyle wasn't certain she was looking forward to the Sunday get-together. Acton was clearly making an effort to behave as a normal couple would behave in an attempt to please her, and as Timothy and Caroline were his oldest friends, it would seem the ideal way to make a stab at some sort of social life. The problem was that Doyle had never much desired a social life—for the obvious reasons—and didn't particularly want one just now, whilst she was still coming to grips with the other major changes in her life.

For the second time that morning, she gave herself a mental shake; this type of socializing may be just the thing to help Acton, as apparently he believed he was in need of treatment. I think that's the nub of it, she thought in all honesty; I'd rather no one else had a window into the relationship between us, especially a psychiatrist. Not to mention that neither one of them could be completely honest with anyone—faith, they weren't completely honest with each other, and with good reason.

They had gone to visit the McGonigal siblings for the first time last week, and Doyle had privately found it a little trying. She had first met Timothy when he'd deftly treated her—no questions asked, thanks be to God—on the infamous night she shot herself in the leg and managed to get impregnated. A few days later, she'd met his sister Caroline at Fiona's funeral. Fiona had been a forensics scientist at the CID morgue, and she was murdered by the same raving lunatic who had tried to kill Doyle, but no one else knew of it. Acton had given the eulogy, and the occasion was the first time that Doyle had made a public appearance as his wife. Her husband had spoken eloquently of Fiona's goodness and their friendship, but all the while the general congregation was covertly eying Doyle, rampant curiosity and shock battering her from every angle. So as to be a credit to Acton, she'd tried to maintain her poise, but would not have been at all surprised if her blush had become indelible.

On top of the general trauma of being revealed as Acton's unexpected wife, Doyle became aware of two things that day: Timothy had been in love with Fiona, and he was unaware that Fiona and Acton had once had an affair. Doyle was becoming accustomed to such interesting revelations, and was fast coming to the conclusion that the workaday lives around her were merely a dignified veneer, and that underneath it all were undercurrents of love and longing, some seething and some more circumspect. She had never paid much attention to them before Acton; jealousy and lust had been motives for crimes with no real application to daily life. Now, however, she was resonating like a tuning fork, picking up the fluctuating emotions all around her. It all came from having a certain husband shake her from her underpinnings, it did.

Last week, they'd spent an evening with the McGonigals in an attempt to teach Doyle how to play Brag, a card game the others had played together since university. Timothy was a kind man and liked her simply because Acton did. Caroline, by contrast, liked her only for Acton's sake. In truth, Caroline reminded Doyle of one of the nuns she had known at St. Brigid's; a woman who was doggedly determined to do good no matter the sacrifice, not aware that it shouldn't be a sacrifice at all, if it were done right.

"Not to worry, Kathleen; I will take you in hand," Caroline had said to her in a friendly fashion when they were alone in the kitchen.

Doyle was not certain how to respond, and had instead smiled her appreciation.

Caroline had lowered her voice. "And if you ever need advice about how to go on, you need only ring me and I will help you. All conversations will be kept strictly confidential, of course." She then had cast a speaking glance in the direction of Acton.

I think she meant well, thought Doyle—even if she was privately distressed by Acton's marriage. And I am glad I resisted the urge to tell her that the only thing I really needed to know was where the nearest available bed was—although a bed was apparently not always needful. Doyle smiled to herself at the memory of the heated session on the entryway rug, and the cab driver smiled into his rear-view mirror and said something friendly and unintelligible.

The card game had been a mistake. Caroline had explained the game in simple terms so that Doyle could understand, and they played some preliminary hands so that she could get the hang of it. The game was what her mother would have called a vying game, with each player given three cards to parlay as best they could.

Doyle kept trying to catch Acton's eye, but he didn't pick up on her problem until they began to play in earnest, for points. Then he met her eyes and realized what she had been trying to signal; she shouldn't be playing a game that involved bluffing. She won every trick she could, and relinquished the ones she could not, with the result that she steadily added to her lead. Timothy laughed and was pleased for her, Acton was amused, and Caroline—who was apparently a very shrewd player of cards—was annoyed. As a result, Doyle began to fold where she needn't, just to mollify the other woman, and then suggested they play Forty-five, a game her mother had taught her that was based wholly on skill with the cards. It went much better.

As the cab wound its way to the Met, Doyle entertained the unhappy conviction that Acton was going to try to make the card games a weekly event; perhaps he would introduce other friends, gradually. She should try to be a good wife and encourage him to socialize so that she was not the sole object in his universe, but she longed for solitude, and the days where it would be just the two of them were counting down. "Do you have a wife?" she asked her cab driver.

He nodded and smiled broadly, his white teeth positively gleaming.

Has no idea what I'm saying, she thought.

The driver then said something she could not follow, but

which contained the unmistakable word "baby," as he made a rocking motion with his free hand.

I stand corrected, she thought, and nodded to show she understood. "I'm to have a baby." The words hung in the air. Holy Mother of God, she thought; I'm to have a baby.

The driver grinned.

CHAPTER 6

Once at work, Doyle collapsed in her chair and drank deeply from the latte that awaited her as though she was an alewife at the tap. Although she'd lost her appetite, apparently her craving for coffee continued unabated and she leaned back, savoring her return to the land of the living. Acton arranged to have her favorite coffee concoction delivered to her desk each morning; before they were married, the gesture had been the first indication that she meant something to him, and she fingered the cup fondly. With a start, she wondered if she was allowed to drink coffee in her condition and reluctantly set it aside. I'll have to ask, she thought with resignation; it wants only this.

Detective Inspector Habib, her supervisor, appeared in the entryway to her cubicle. He was a very correct and self-contained Pakistani man who would occasionally unbend enough to give Doyle some good insight on her cases. Today, however, he was issuing orders to beat the band, the singsong cadence of his voice rapid-fire. "The chief inspector has asked that you work with Detective Sergeant Williams on the aqueduct and Newmarket cases. He asks that you take witness statements and coordinate forensics with the senior investigating officer."

"Yes, sir, I will," said Doyle, unconsciously speaking as rapidly in return. Acton was careful to respect the hierarchy, and despite their marriage, still delivered all assignments by way of Habib. As Habib was very keen on protocol, this seemed the right tack, although it was clear the man had been a bit thrown by the unexpected turn of events; he admired Acton, but he could not approve of inter-caste marriage.

"DS Williams will take the lead," Habib added, not-so-subtly reminding her that Williams outranked her now.

"Yes, sir." If Munoz was listening from the cubicle next door she would be fit to be tied; excluded from this plum assignment and reminded of Williams's promotion all in one fell swoop. After Habib turned on his heel and left, Doyle waited for the explosion, but it did not come, so she decided to tempt fate. "Munoz, have you dropped dead over there?"

Munoz's voice came through the cubicle partition wall. "I don't care, Doyle; Williams is not worth the trouble. You are welcome to him."

Doyle correctly interpreted this to mean that Williams had not succumbed to Munoz's lures, and so did not argue the point. "Ah well; his loss."

The other girl continued, "I'm too busy working on a project for Drake, anyway."

The hint of triumph in this announcement reminded Doyle that there had been some serious flirtation going on between DCI Drake and Munoz. *I hope she's not having an affair with him,* thought Doyle, remembering Drake as vain and self-centered. *Nothing I could say to her, of course; she would laugh in my face, what with my own history.* "What sort of project?"

"I'm supposed to keep it under wraps. It has to do with flesh-peddling."

Doyle idly reviewed her inbox and found herself drinking from the latte again—it was that forbidden-fruit effect. "Sounds dangerous, if you don't mind my sayin'. Look to yourself; you'll be sold to white slavers, else."

"I'm not white; they'll not have me."

"Spanish slavers, then," Doyle corrected. Hopefully she had teased Munoz out of a temper tantrum, but it appeared she had been only partially successful.

"They like Williams better because he is a man—it is *so* unfair."

This topic was a potential minefield; Williams and Munoz had vied for top honors at the Crime Academy, but Williams had topped Munoz in most subjects. She would not thank Doyle for reminding her of this irritating fact, and so Doyle turned the subject. "Whist, Munoz; you're an intelligent and good-lookin' minority female. Go out and exploit your fair self."

This comment was met with a few moments of profound silence. "You know, Doyle, every once in a while you have a decent idea."

"Don't be over-kind," Doyle cautioned. "You'll get soft."

But Munoz wasn't listening, instead thinking aloud, "I should make myself available to the public relations people; get my face shown about a bit."

"That's the ticket; Williams is nowhere near as politically correct."

Munoz made an appearance in the cubicle entryway, surprising Doyle so that she juggled her coffee. "Walk with me over to the deli; I'm sick of the canteen and I'm in need of a bagel."

After a quick weighing of Munoz's mood, Doyle acquiesced. She'd done precious little work thus far, but she decided she could use some fresh air, now that she was feeling more the thing thanks to the forbidden brew. It was a fine, sunny day, and besides, she was married to a DCI—they couldn't very well sack her, after all. With a guilty start, she made a mental note not to start thinking she could exploit her connection to win favors at work, or she'd soon be without one or the other—the work or the connection.

The two girls made their way upstairs and out the front doors to the street. Once outside, they ran into DCI Drake, who was headed in. "Now, here's a striking pair," he said with practiced charm. "Are you escaping?"

"Only to get a bagel," explained Doyle quickly, still feeling guilty for thinking she was immune from repercussions.

"Join us, sir," invited Munoz, with a smile that had enslaved many a man. "It will only take a minute."

He laughed and declined. "I am tempted, but I have too much work to do." He turned to Doyle. "I haven't had a chance to offer my best wishes."

"Thank you." He had, in fact—at Fiona's funeral, but must have forgotten. Or he was trying to get Munoz's goat, which was another possibility as Doyle could detect a gleam of amusement in his eyes.

Munoz, however, was too practiced to allow herself to be shown to disadvantage. "It is such unexpected and wonderful news," she exclaimed warmly. "I had no idea such a thing was in the offing; did you, sir?"

"No, Acton played his cards very close to the vest. Cut me out completely."

Doyle blushed and Munoz laughed in appreciation. "He who hesitates, sir."

"Carry on, detectives." He strode away.

Munoz stared at Doyle in abject astonishment. "Don't tell me *he* was interested in you, too?"

Doyle soothed the other girl before her ears started steaming. "Of course not; he was bein' gallant, you knocker. It's what men do when there is no chance they'll be held to it."

They continued on their way, and Munoz added after a moment, "It's not as though I don't have my own fish on the line."

Doyle recognized her cue and asked, "Faith, what has happened, Munoz? Have you met the anti-Williams?"

"Only that I have a date—a date with a man I met at the security desk." She pursed her full lips with a self-satisfied air.

"Truly?" Doyle gave this interesting announcement the response it deserved. "And how did this happy turn of events come about?"

"He was visiting on business from Belarus, and didn't know that you couldn't come into our building without an appointment. He was in the wrong place, anyway—he needed to inquire about tariffs. I overheard him as I walked in, and gave him directions."

"He was handsome," Doyle concluded.

"Yes." Munoz tossed her head. "I imagine he is rich, too—he's a banker."

"Send me a postcard from your castle in Belarus," teased Doyle.

Munoz shrugged, so as to make it clear she was above being overly-excited about any mere man. "We're going to some clubs tonight."

Doyle felt a qualm. "Be careful; you hardly know him."

Munoz gave her a glance that was equal parts amused and superior. "I know how to take care of myself, Doyle." This was probably true; Munoz had plenty of experience with men. By contrast, before she married Acton, Doyle had the sum total of none.

They purchased Munoz's bagel and began the walk back, Munoz's mood much improved after the Belarus banker discussion. She offered the bagel to Doyle, "Want a bite?"

Doyle took a quick look at the onion-flavored cream cheese and looked away again. "No thanks." Her heart sank; when Munoz was informed of her pregnancy she would leap to the obvious conclusion, as would everyone else. It doesn't matter a pin, Doyle reminded herself stoutly, and tried not to think about it. It was very wearing to have a new attitude.

Back at her desk, Doyle felt guilty enough about her lack of productivity that she decided to call Williams to ask for instruction on her assignment, thinking it was a little strange he had not yet contacted her—he was usually very much on top of things. He didn't answer his mobile, and a call to his desk resulted in the relayed information that he was out sick. Doyle hung up and frowned at the phone. He hadn't looked to be sickening yesterday, and he was definitely not a dosser, looking to miss work. Must have caught something, she decided, and hoped he was not feeling too down-pin; she had a lot more sympathy lately for people who weren't feeling well. She called again to leave a message on his mobile, and then picked up the threads of her aqueduct report, hoping forensics would send the missing information soon.

After working steadily for a time, she paused to tilt the coffee cup so as to retrieve the last, cold dregs, and wondered if she would go to Brighton tonight or if Acton would come home late, instead. Truth to tell, she was a little tired and would rather not make the journey, but if he needed her, she would certainly go—she could always sleep in the limousine like a Pharisee. She would wait and see; perhaps she would do some shopping after work, and get it behind her—she'd be needing some new clothes soon. New clothes, new attitude, no coffee, she thought a bit grimly; in all things give thanks.

CHAPTER 7

DOYLE INSERTED HER SECURITY CARD IN THE SLOT AT THEIR flat, tired but nevertheless feeling that she'd completed a put-off chore. Acton had phoned to say he would drive back that evening, and so in the meantime she'd girded her loins and made good on her intention to purchase some new clothing. Never one to care much about her appearance, she now had the burden of trying to convince the general public that Acton had not committed matrimonial suicide. To this end, she would try to appear a bit more polished than in the past without, she hoped, making the transformation too notice-able—no need to appear to be putting on airs.

She had stopped by the local shops on the way home and made some purchases with the aid of the shop girls who were remarkably helpful, once they saw Acton's title on her credit card. She bought two sweaters which would serve her well in the next few months, and trousers in the next size larger. Al-though it was too early to be thickening, she had discovered that she did better in the mornings if she wasn't wearing any-thing too constrictive around her middle.

She had also passed by the jewelry shop where they had purchased Acton's wedding ring, and on impulse, she'd gone inside and chosen a new tie clip for him. He'd lost his old one—she'd noticed that he had to hold his tie back with his hand when they were examining the corpse yesterday. He would be delighted with it, which was one of the advantages of his condition; she could do no wrong.

She pushed opened the door to her flat with her shoulder since her hands were full, and realized as soon as she entered that she had visitors. An older woman sat on the leather sofa, ramrod straight and regal. Doyle recognized her in an instant, and paused in surprise. "Why, you are very like him."

The dowager Lady Acton was indeed very like Acton. She was tall and lean, with dark eyes and brows. Her hair was colored silver, but Doyle imagined it was once dark like his. Poor Acton's father, she thought; he made little contribution, here.

Marta stood in the kitchen, making tea even though she was not supposed to be here in the first place, emanating a mixture of defiance and uneasiness. I'm to be outnumbered, then, thought Doyle grimly; we shall see.

Acton's mother did not rise or offer her hand, but scrutinized Doyle coldly and made no response to her comment. Doyle realized that she appeared to disadvantage, coming in laden with packages from expensive stores whilst her husband was away, but any thought of offering an explanation was dismissed; she knew she talked too much when she was nervous, and she refused to be nervous before this woman, whom Acton so disliked. Instead, she walked to the table and calmly set down her packages. "I will also take tea, Marta." Marta looked as though she expected a donnybrook, which, Doyle realized, was to her own advantage; if it came down to hand-to-hand, Doyle had the benefit of Academy training, even though the older woman outweighed her.

As she walked around to seat herself across from the dowager, she remarked, "If I had known you were to be visitin', ma'am, I would have been at home."

It was an implied rebuke, and if it was possible, the woman

stiffened even more. Good one, thought Doyle with deep satisfaction; perhaps I should mention that I recently shot and killed a man from the very spot the old dragon now sits. Unbidden, she felt a twinge of conscience; her mother's daughter should overlook all insults in the interest of family peace, and make an effort to be civil—perhaps this visit was an olive branch.

"I am here because I could not credit what I have heard," the older woman rasped in a dry voice.

Then again, thought Doyle, perhaps not.

"How old are you?" The dowager's tone indicated if Doyle had been fourteen she would not have been surprised.

"I am twenty-four," said Doyle, wishing she had put on some lip gloss; it was true she did not appear her age.

"And undoubtedly Irish," the older woman mused in extreme distaste, as though she hadn't been able to credit this report without verifying it for herself.

Doyle couldn't resist. "Aye, that."

They regarded each other for a long moment, while Doyle held her tongue and tried to remember whether the Fourth Commandment applied to one's in-laws.

Marta brought over the tea tray to set it down, and Doyle recalled that the Commandment definitely did not apply to traitorous housekeepers. "It's surprised I am to see you today, Marta."

The woman stood and crossed her hands before her; her expression wooden as she emanated waves of wariness and resentment. She is wary because she knows Acton will back me against all comers, Doyle thought; and she is right.

"My lady was in town and thought to make a visit; I saw no harm in it—" Marta hesitated, realizing that she was in a corner, but nevertheless added deferentially, "—my lady."

But this was an honorific too far for the dowager, who made an aristocratic sound of outrage and shifted in her seat

to address Doyle in an icy tone. "It is clear," the woman gave
Marta a sidelong glance, "—that you hold my son in some
sort of sexual thrall. Deplorable."

Holding on to her temper only with an effort, Doyle concluded that his mother didn't know Acton very well; she certainly wouldn't have made such a remark if she knew how
close to the truth it came, although anyone who took a gan-
der at Doyle would not mistake her for a sexual temptress.
"I'm afraid I'd rather not be bandyin' personal matters
abroad, ma'am."

At this additional implied rebuke, the other woman nearly
quivered with outrage. "You will mind your manners, child."

" 'Tis you who should mind her manners," Doyle retorted
hotly. "Have done."

After staring at Doyle incredulously for a long and ominous
moment, the dowager rose to her feet and pronounced, "It is
far worse than I could have ever imagined. I will await such
time as my son comes to his senses."

Although she was inclined to think this a very good plan,
Doyle realized that this person would be the only surviving
grandparent—although it boggled the mind to imagine her
baking ginger cake at Christmas. "Lady Acton, shouldn't we
be comin' to terms? We have a common interest, after all."

"I shall never have a common interest with you," the
woman declared with finality as she pulled on her gloves with
a jerk.

Wait eight more months, thought Doyle, and tried again. "I
will never see my own mother on this earth again, ma'am;
that is the terrible meanin' of never. Please think on it."

It was clear the dowager did not appreciate being lectured
on familial obligations by a miscreant, and made her stately
way to the door. "My ridiculous son has entered into a misce-
genation of the worst order. I have nothing more to say."

The words touched a very sensitive nerve, and Doyle's fury
was suddenly unchecked as she sprang to her feet. "You'll not

be comin' into *my* home and be insultin' *my* husband," she hissed through her teeth. "Out the door wi' ye, ye harridan." She took a threatening step toward the older woman, tempted to draw her weapon for emphasis.

So as to avoid bloodshed, Marta hurried forward to open the door, and Lady Acton exited with as much dignity as she could muster under the circumstances. After the door was shut, Doyle had to struggle with her temper for a moment before addressing Marta. "How did this come about?" She had no illusions; Marta had obviously contacted Acton's mother as soon as she realized Doyle would be home alone. Nevertheless, she wanted to hear what the housekeeper would say.

The other made no effort to concoct a story. "I do beg your pardon, my lady."

Ah, thought Doyle; when I'm in a fury, I'm "my lady."

"She is my old mistress, and I could not refuse her."

This was a lie, but no more than Doyle had expected. "You may go, Marta," she said coldly. She then retreated to the bedroom to lie down, still trembling with rage. As is human nature, she relived every word of the encounter, and thought of a good many things she should have said. Her mobile rang; it was Acton.

"I'm on my way; I should be home within the hour."

"That's grand, Michael," she replied, keeping her tone neutral.

"What has happened?" he asked immediately. No point in trying to hide it if something had upset her; his radar was extremely fine-tuned.

She sighed. "Your mother came to visit."

There was an astonished pause. "My mother?"

"Aye, that."

There was another pause. "Is all the crockery broken?"

She smiled, and felt better immediately. "I controlled myself, I did."

"Good girl. Should we talk about it now or when I get in?"

"It can wait," she replied. "I did not show to advantage."

"Impossible," he assured her, and rang off.

She decided she felt well enough to get up and make herself presentable, which meant taking off her clothes and brushing out her hair. If Acton was in sexual thrall, she'd best look lively.

He arrived a commendably short while later and kissed her as he came in, running his eyes over the area where her robe gaped. He was distracted, however, and wanted to hear what had happened.

"You may be needin' the scotch," she warned him.

"That's as may be," he said. "Let's hear it."

She realized that Acton had not been drinking as much these past several weeks, and she felt another stab of shame—another indication that he was the grown-up, between them. Trying to stay calm, as though she were giving a report, she described to him in general terms the battle between the Lady Actons, thinking to edit the more explicit insults. He listened to the recitation, making no comment. Although she put it off as long as possible, she reluctantly concluded, "I should mention that durin' the conversation she made a comment about our sex life." He would draw his own conclusion as to the nature of the comment, of course; they would probably qualify for an Olympic team, if there were such an event.

He was furious, as she knew he would be. "Marta?"

"I imagine so. They were both already here when I came in."

Acton looked grim. "She has no business letting anyone into our flat."

Doyle decided that she may as well make a full confession. "It does not surprise me, Michael; when you are not present, Marta is not always very respectful to me."

There was a pause while he struggled to control his reaction—he was most unhappy, was our Acton. "Kathleen, you should have told me; no one is allowed to disrespect you."

"Yes, I should have told you," she agreed.

"It is a reflection on me, after all."

Good one, she thought—he is trying to couch it in terms that may inspire me to change my non-assertive ways; good luck to him. "I see that now," she said humbly. "I'm that sorry, Michael; I should have thrown Marta out headlong—or at least put her in the stocks."

He ducked his head, and finally had to smile. "I am expecting too much, am I?"

"A little." She smiled in return. "I am still findin' my way in all this; give me another week to become accustomed to demandin' off with their heads."

He pulled her to him and rested his chin on her head. "No one has license to make you feel inferior. I will ring her up now, and fire her."

This was much appreciated; it was a fine thing to have such a champion, but she felt she had to warn him, "Your mother said she was goin' to wait for you to come to your senses."

Scrolling for Marta's number, he absently replied, "My mother will relent; in the end, she has no choice."

Deciding that she'd rather not ask him to elaborate on this ambiguous remark, Doyle listened in as Marta was given the well-deserved sack.

CHAPTER 8

DOYLE WAS WORKING AT HOME ON SUNDAY AFTERNOON whilst Acton sat on the sofa, reading the contraband manual from his conference and entering notes on his laptop. He seemed very interested in the new procedures the Home Secretary was instituting to counteract smuggling and black market trade, and Doyle had a very good idea as to why this was, although he didn't know she knew. She had a shrewd suspicion that he was running a smuggling rig with illegal weapons, which presented a fine dilemma for her; she was a policewoman, after all, with a healthy respect for the rule of law—it was a dangerous thing to be a rule unto oneself, there was no telling where it would end. Hopefully, not in some prison somewhere; she couldn't imagine Acton would do well in prison.

She was seated at the table, researching the Sinn-split information on file and cross-referencing the Russian mafia information. Her main object was to find a nexus having to do with racecourse crimes—such as doping, money laundering, or illegal gambling—because such a nexus could provide some insight as to what had touched off the turf war. Williams had suggested that something might have changed; some unsavory activity had suddenly become more lucrative so that the factions were willing to go to war over it, and this seemed as good a theory as any, if only she could find some hint. Thus far, however, she had found no indication that the long shots were winning when they shouldn't, or that more money was passing hands than was usual.

Another angle was to research the victims' biographical information so as to cross-check the Watch List with suspected racecourse activities. Strangely, the most recent Russian victim—Barayev-of–the-maggoty-face—did not fit the usual profile. He was by all appearances an ordinary businessman from Moscow—or as ordinary as one could be in such an environment; the high achievers tended to have unsavory connections due to the nature of the beast. That he was a high achiever seemed evident; the man's clothes and shoes were of the highest quality, and his fingernails had been manicured. His biography showed that he was on the board for several banks and import-export companies, and the majority of his time was spent as the CFO in a venture capital firm—or what passed for one in the questionable climate of the Russian oligarchies. Interpol had no record of him, and as far as she could see, he had not raised any eyebrows anywhere. Strange that he had wound up in a London aqueduct with his face shot off in the midst of this turf war. "I'm thinkin' that you may be right; it may have been a shadow murder," she mused aloud. Mainly, she was angling to make Acton take a break from his worrying interest in contraband protocols—it made her very uneasy, it did.

Acton looked up. "Barayev?"

"Yes. By all accounts he was just mindin' his own business. Perhaps someone not connected to the turf wars read about all the murderin' in the papers, and decided to seize the main chance."

Acton made the obvious suggestions involving the usual obvious suspects. "A disgruntled wife, or business partner?"

Doyle frowned with regret—the reason the usual obvious suspects were usual and obvious was because they were so easy to twig. Not in this case, however. "He was a widower, and it looks like he was mainly an advisor—not someone whose death would help anyone else out, financially."

Acton looked out the window for a moment. "Perhaps it was a message to another player."

This was of interest, and she looked over at him. "That's what you think, isn't it?"

"Yes," he admitted, and it was the truth.

Ah, she thought; now we are getting somewhere—when Acton came up with a theory, it was usually spot-on. But thinking on it, she frowned again. "That's a tangled theory, Michael; it's a shadow murder to send a message? How would the supposed recipient know it was a message as opposed to just another dead Ruskie in the turf war?"

"Keep digging," he suggested. "But first, what can I make that would tempt you to eat?"

She considered this as he walked over to gently click shut her laptop. It was true she had only nibbled on a dry biscuit that day; it was wretchedly hard to even contemplate taking a bite of anything.

He led her over to the sofa. "Does nothing sound appetizing?"

She thought about it. "Somethin' cold, I think."

"Timothy said ginger tea is sometimes helpful."

She was touched that he had asked for advice. "That does sound good," she lied.

He smiled, seeing right through her. "It's worth a try; if you can't do it, you can't do it."

"Do we *have* ginger tea?"

"We do now. I will brew some."

"Pour it over ice," she suggested.

After he prepared the tea, they sat together on the sofa while she valiantly tried to take a few sips. His arm rested on the sofa back behind her, and he held a strand of her hair between his fingers, absently rolling it back and forth whilst he watched her. Frettin', she thought; I am a sad trial to my poor husband. "It's the strangest thing, Michael; I have completely lost my appetite."

He thought about it. "Is there anything that makes you feel better, even if for a little while? A hot shower? Fresh air?"

"I feel best," she confessed, "when I am lyin' on my back with your weight atop me."

His fingers pausing on her hair, he gave her a glance that was openly skeptical. "Is that so?"

"My hand on my heart, Michael. I think it has somethin' to do with the heat and the pressure."

They regarded each other for a moment before he said, "All right, but you must eat something first."

This seemed counterproductive. "I'm to be blackmailed, then?"

"Choose," he said firmly.

"Toast," she decided. "I believe the ginger tea is actually helpin' a bit."

After she had eaten a half slice of dry toast, they experimented, lying on the tiled floor before the windows so that the heat of the sun was intensified. "Not too heavy," she cautioned, "I have to be able to breathe." He adjusted, and it did make her feel better, with the cool tiles to her back and the warm body pressed against her. She even began to feel a bit sleepy, but soon became aware that her husband was not at all sleepy and with a giggle, turned her head to nuzzle his neck as an invitation.

"None of that," he said sternly. "You shouldn't burn any more calories."

"You can't help yourself," she teased, moving her hips against his. "It's a sexual temptress, I am."

There was a pause. "Perhaps if you lie completely still—"

"Remove your clothes, husband; I shall lie as still as a stone." She put her hands on his head and pulled his mouth to hers.

Later, while she showered, she *willed* herself to feel better.

Two days hence she was to visit her new obstetrician, and she was dreading the ordeal, but perhaps it wouldn't be all to the bad; she would make a list of questions, including how to survive this miserable morning sickness which seemed—unfairly—to last all day. Closing her eyes, she let the water run over her head and sighed. Faith, how she'd love to put a stop to this foolishness and quit frettin' her man; he had enough on his mind as it was, what with the whole outfoxing the Home Office on the guns-running thing. At least he was finally discussing the turf wars with her—she'd been anxious about nothing, it seemed.

After she turned off the shower, she stepped out in her towel to find that Acton was leaning against the vanity with his arms crossed, watching her. This was not a surprise; when they were home he was drawn to her, and especially now, when he was worried. Stepping over, she raised up on tiptoe to kiss him, and then, teasing, rubbed her wet head on his shirt, making him flinch away with a smile. "I'm feelin' much better; Michael. Truly."

He continued to watch her in the mirror as she began combing out her hair. "I've been screening some candidates to take Marta's place, and I'd like to give one or two a trial."

"Aye then," she agreed, rather surprised that he'd found the time—usually when there were multiple connected murders like this he was frenetically busy at all hours. On the other hand, it seemed every time they got a lead, the witness wound up in the morgue. And there was no question that the general mood at the Met was not the exigent one that would have existed had the victims been young schoolgirls; justice should be blind, but no question she would turn a shoulder on those who'd chosen to lie down with dogs.

"If you would, let me know if you see anything amiss in any of the candidates." He was referring to her intuitive ability; he was intensely private, and with good reason. It was only to be expected that he would be very particular about anyone who would be given access into their lives.

She smiled at him in the mirror. "No one who answers to your mother."

He gave her a half-smile in response, but had already moved on to the next subject. "I spoke to Caroline, and I asked her not to patronize you to the extent she does."

With acute dismay, Doyle met his eyes in the mirror, but he continued in all seriousness, "I want to make it clear that I will tolerate no disrespect from anyone. You are my wife."

"Saints, Michael," she remonstrated gently, lowering the comb. "Perhaps not the best tack to take, my friend; if Caroline doesn't know how to get on with the likes of me it's because we hardly know each other, and the three of you are miles smarter." She paused for a moment, trying to put her instinctive reaction into words. "She'll unbristle once she becomes accustomed—and become accustomed she must. She is only being a bit territorial about you and you can hardly blame her; I am quite the shockin' surprise."

He looked as though he meant to say something, but thought the better of it.

Thoughtfully, Doyle resumed combing her hair. "And she may be resentin' that I've taken Fiona's place for the four of you—it's a new grief, after all. Be patient; she'll come about. Please say nothin' more."

"Right, then." He stood and kissed the top of her wet head. "And it was kind of you to lose; she doesn't like being beaten."

"No; not by me, leastways." He had twigged her, then—can't put much past this husband of hers; mental note. She turned to look up at him, fingering the ends of her hair. "No one ever married? Of the four of you, I mean."

"No. I was the first."

"Good one."

"Very good one," he agreed, and kissed her again.

CHAPTER 9

IT WAS CLEAR TO DOYLE THAT CAROLINE MADE AN EFFORT THAT evening to modify her behavior. When she arrived with her brother, she presented Doyle with a bottle of wine in a very friendly manner and suggested they share it, glancing at Acton to make sure that he observed this show of good grace. Doyle was forced to confess that she didn't drink alcohol, but Caroline laughed good-naturedly and promised to bring ginger ale the next time.

Once they advanced to the cards portion of the evening, Caroline insisted they play Forty-five, the game Doyle had taught them. She's to be killing me with kindness, thought Doyle, which is rather sweet and shows how much she values Acton's good opinion. The game commenced, and if Caroline was operating under duress, the only symptom was that she drank scotch along with the men and the wine went untouched.

Timothy did surgeries once a month at a charity medical clinic, and he related some amusing stories of the unusual conditions he was forced to confront because a large percentage of the patients were recent immigrants from third-world areas. Doyle found it very interesting and asked many questions, wishing she had some skill to offer those less fortunate—she couldn't very well offer to tell them if they were lying, after all. The clinic was funded by the local Catholic diocese and this led Timothy to ask if Doyle attended a church in the area.

"St. Michael's," she replied. They looked at her a bit blankly and she added, "Near Chelsea; not a very large parish, I'm afraid."

"We attend Holy Trinity," explained Caroline. "You must join us; it would be closer for you."

Doyle was not certain what to reply, as it had never even crossed her mind to transfer from her old parish.

"I am taking instruction at St. Michael's," interjected Acton smoothly.

"Why, Acton, that is wonderful," exclaimed Caroline in astonished surprise. "To think that Kathleen has managed such a feat—well, *well* done."

Doyle blushed with embarrassment; faith, everyone would be much more comfortable if Caroline took her new attitude down a peg or two. Deftly, she changed the subject by asking the other woman about her work.

"We are making *enormous* headway with enzymatic applications for nonregenerative cells," Caroline enthused as she looked up from her cards. "It is very exciting."

"That does sound excitin'," offered Doyle, who hadn't a clue.

But Caroline only smiled in good-humored acknowledgment as she made a discard. "It's very dry and dull, unless you're immersed in it, as I am. And so I'll say no more, except that I'm to speak at a conference next week, and I haven't yet been told what I'm supposed to speak about. I hope it is nothing I have to get up to speed on."

"Out of town?" asked Acton as he took his turn.

She laughed, as though this were a private joke, and said as an aside to Doyle, "He knows that I think civilization ends at the city limits, and I rarely set a foot outside." Playfully, she tapped Acton's arm with her cards. "You are not one to speak, Acton—you never go anywhere, either."

"There are too many people gettin' themselves murdered in London," Doyle offered, hoping to avoid a discussion of Acton's reclusive habits. "He's in dire need, here."

"Perhaps we should all take a trip together," the other woman offered with a friendly smile at Doyle. "I imagine if we put our minds to it, we could all find the time."

Doing it too brown, thought Doyle, who was well-aware that Caroline had not the smallest intention of going anywhere with the likes of her.

"Have you traveled much, Kathleen?" Timothy gathered up the cards to take his turn as dealer.

"Only the trip from Dublin to London, I'm afraid." And best not to mention that when she'd lived in Dublin with her mother, they usually walked everywhere because they hadn't enough money for bus fare.

"We will take you on a tour, then," Caroline enthused, including Acton in her glance. "The enzymes can mind themselves for a week—and so can the criminals, Acton."

"If only that were the case," said Acton mildly as he won the hand.

With a nod of his head, Timothy indicated his sister. "Caroline's being modest—she'll be the keynote speaker at the conference; she's making some huge inroads into paralysis treatment, and she's to be written up in the Medical Journal."

"How rewardin', Caroline," offered Doyle in all sincerity. "To be helpin' people as you are."

Shaking her head slightly, the other woman disclaimed with a smile, "It's purely selfish—I positively relish the work, and I'm lucky they pay me."

When she has the attention she craves, she can be gracious, Doyle observed; it's only when the attention is centered elsewhere that she acts up. I'll keep it to mind, so that Acton doesn't feel he must defend me at every turn, which only gets her back up. Her fond gaze rested on her husband for a moment. Knocker, she thought; I'm not so very defenseless. Feeling her gaze upon him, he lifted his head from his cards to meet her eyes. Ah, she thought; he is eager to attempt the cure again.

"May I fetch you something to drink, Kathleen?" asked Caroline with an abundance of good will.

Acton forestalled her, "I'll do it, Caroline—Kathleen, what would you like?"

"Water—or perhaps iced ginger tea." She saw Timothy and Caroline exchange a glance; Timothy must have told his sister she was pregnant—ah well, it would be hard for him to keep such news from his sister, and Doyle had the impression she ruled the roost. "There's the plate of cheese and fruit on the counter also, Michael." This was courtesy of the blessed concierge; neither Doyle nor Acton were handy in the kitchen, and most of the time they sent out for food; hence the dire need to hire another housekeeper.

"Is Marta off tonight?" asked Caroline as she idly played with the pack of cards. "I wanted to ask her advice about a recipe."

Acton was in the kitchen, so Doyle was forced to disclose, "I'm afraid Marta no longer works for us."

The other two stared at her in surprise. "Why—what has happened?" asked Caroline.

"We had a fallin'-out." Doyle hoped this bald announcement would discourage any interest in the details.

Apparently, this gambit was not successful as Caroline frowned. "Will she return to Trestles?"

"I do not know," Doyle replied, and offered no more. She could feel that Caroline was shocked and unhappy; but if she believed that the upstart bride had thrown out a devoted retainer, she was welcome to do so. After routing both Acton's mother and the disapproving housekeeper, Doyle was gain-ing some confidence, secure in the sure knowledge of her husband's devotion. The only good opinions I care about are God's and Acton's; in that order, she thought. And perhaps the CID's, if it doesn't clash with either of the above—her intuition told her that Acton was up to something, after all.

Caroline stepped into the awkward silence, saying briskly, "Then you'll need some help. Let me lend you our Kitty, or allow me to send over some meals; I do love to cook." It was apparent she was sorry she had reacted so negatively, and was trying to make up for it.

"Acton's handlin' it, I'm not sure what's to be done," Doyle confessed, which was not very housewifely of her, and probably only added to Caroline's ill-concealed dismay.

"I will speak with him, then," Caroline announced with a martyr's air, and rose to join Acton in the kitchen.

Doyle was thus left alone with Timothy. There was a pause, and then they both spoke at once: "I want to thank—" said Doyle.

"Let me say—" said Timothy. They both abruptly stopped speaking, and then laughed together. "Ladies first," offered the doctor.

"I wanted to thank you for all your help," Doyle told him in all sincerity. "You are a good friend to us."

The doctor blushed, which endeared him to Doyle, who was a raging blusher, herself. "My pleasure; happy to be of service." He then offered with a hint of embarrassment, "I only wanted to say that you have made a remarkable change in Acton. For the better," he added, as though this had not been made clear.

She smiled. "It is my own pleasure, and I am certainly happy to be of service."

He laughed in appreciation, and then added, "And more changes coming—I was so pleased to hear your good news. We can hardly credit that Acton is to be a father; it is wonderful."

"It is indeed," she agreed with some firmness.

They were shortly rejoined by the other two, and the card play resumed. Doyle nursed her ginger tea and began to wish the evening was over so that she and her warm and heavy husband could go to bed. They played a few more hands, then Acton announced he had an early morning and the McGonigals took the hint and made ready to depart. As they were leaving, Caroline asked Doyle if she would be available for lunch sometime.

Since she normally met Acton for lunch whenever he was free, Doyle cadged. "It depends on whether I am in the field, I'm afraid. Perhaps you can send an e-mail on a day you are available, and I can let you know."

"I'll do that," said Caroline. "I would love to share some meals with you—it would do me good to watch my weight."

Unsure as to how to respond to this, Doyle just smiled. She was slender and fast becoming more so; Caroline was slightly overweight.

After the guests had left, Doyle stood to help Acton carry the glasses to the kitchen. "I'll do it," he said. "Why don't you lie down?"

"Michael, you are makin' me crazy." She smiled to take the sting from the words, and put her arms around him. "If I don't want to help, I will not hesitate to say so."

He put the glasses on the counter and turned to return the embrace, holding her close. Ah, this was heaven. She stroked his back for a moment, feeling the lean muscle under his shirt and thinking that perhaps the dishes should wait.

He said against her head, "I don't think this should be a standing event, do you?"

Cautiously, she responded, "I don't mind, Michael; truly. And Caroline was so much nicer tonight, after her scold." It had been a false front, but Acton probably already knew this, he was a fair judge of human behavior, himself. "And besides, we have to take the Caroline with the Timothy; we can't separate the two."

He was silent, as though unconvinced, and so she added, "And we don't want everyone to think I'm one of those jealous brides, tryin' to separate you from your friends."

"I have no interest in what anyone thinks."

This was true, and she'd forgotten there was no point in making such an appeal. "Then we'll play it by ear, my friend; we can always tell her I'm feelin' down-pin, which would be true ninety percent of the time."

He bent his head to rest his mouth against the top of her shoulder and rocked her gently. "If I could take this away from you, I would."

Shame on her, for bringing it up. "Michael, you are frightenin' me—next you'll be recitin' poetry. Snap out of it, man."

He straightened up to smile down at her. "To bed, then."

She smiled back. "I am actually a little hungry." It was a lie, but she had decided she would force herself to eat so that he did not fret himself to death.

He sat and watched her silently whilst she ate a small bowl of her favorite frosty flakes, which sounded the least repulsive of the possibilities, and tried to pretend it was delicious. "How things have changed," she lamented as she crunched. "In the early days of our marriage—*so* long ago—you would not have allowed me to finish my cereal before carryin' me off to bed."

"Eat," he directed. "Things have definitely changed."

CHAPTER 10

She was a very nice lady. It was hard to understand her sometimes; she was not English. They said she was married to a rich man, a policeman. This was good; she would have care taken of her. She needed care to be taken, he could tell, and it worried him. Although the new God said do not fear death, she was mganga, and he was worried that it meant death. Sometimes it did.

DOYLE STRUGGLED OUT OF BED THE NEXT MORNING AND PRE-pared to go to work. Her joints now ached on top of the general queasiness, and for two pence she would have gone straight back to bed. It's a good thing you're to see the wretched doctor, she thought; you'll probably fall into his arms, weeping with gratitude. Doggedly, she ate some cereal and was glad Acton had already left; she would be hard-pressed to be civil to the poor man—although she was in desperate need of the cure. After debating, she decided to lie on the tile floor with a heavy book upon her abdomen, and this home remedy actually seemed to help. Not as well as a tall and heavy husband, but it would do in a pinch.

When she felt up to it, she dressed and tried to convince herself that she was feeling somewhat better; she was due to assist Williams with the turf war murders and the last thing she needed was to miss this prime opportunity for fieldwork. He had gotten back to her last night with an apology for not getting in touch sooner, and she couldn't very well take a turn at calling in sick—it would be crackin' unbearable if Munoz took her place on this investigation and was promoted to DS before she was; this was the type of high-profile major crime that could do it. Can't be quitting now, she rallied herself, examining her pale face in the mirror; although I wish I owned a dab of makeup.

After exiting the building, she was crossing the sidewalk toward her waiting cab when a short, slightly stout man wearing a rumpled trench coat approached; it appeared he had been waiting for her. "Lady Acton," he called. "My name is Kevin Maguire; may I have a moment?"

Doyle halted in surprise at being thus hailed, but the man spread his hands to show his harmlessness and did not appear to be threatening. Doyle thought of the gun she always wore in an ankle holster and was not alarmed; not to mention the concierge was within calling distance, if she needed reinforcements.

Maguire smiled in a friendly fashion. "I'm with the London World News," he explained, "—and I wondered if I could ask a few questions."

"No, you may not," said Doyle immediately, and began walking again. God only knew what angle a newspaper would take on her hole-in-corner marriage, and besides, she shared her profession's healthy distrust of the press; it seemed they too often took the side of the villains, just to flex their own power.

He pleaded with her, still smiling and walking backward so that her progress was somewhat impeded. "Nothing demeaning or scandalous, I promise you; just a page-seven article about the unlikely romance springing up at New Scotland Yard. It will be terrific public relations; the readership would eat it up, your husband being who he is."

Doyle had to bite back a smile at the irony. They wouldn't dare run the true story—it was too unbelievable, even for a

scandal-sheet. "No, thank you," she said firmly. Then she received aid from an unexpected source, as her Rwandan cab
driver came to her rescue.

"No, no," he said to the reporter, stepping forward and
wagging his finger. He took Doyle's arm to escort her to his
cab, saying something unintelligible to the reporter, the only
word Doyle recognized being "leddy." He made it clear that
she was not to be molested en route to his cab.

Maguire put his hands up and smiled in a gesture of defeat.
As they drew away from the curb, she looked back to see him
wave—he was no doubt used to being given the cold shoulder.

"Thank you," said Doyle, turning to the driver. "You are
very kind."

He turned and smiled at her, his white teeth gleaming, and
she smiled back. I am surrounded by champions who think
I'm in need of rescue, she thought with an inward sigh. I suppose I shouldn't complain. Thankfully, the driver didn't follow up with any conversation—it would be too draining and
she just wanted to marshal up her energy—*faith*, her joints
ached. Hopefully she wasn't catching the flu on top of everything else.

Williams was apparently eager to begin their assignment, as
he was lurking about her cubicle, making conversation with
Munoz whilst he waited for Doyle. Doyle realized they must
have been talking about her, because they lapsed into silence
as she approached. A nine day's wonder, she was; just crackin'
grand.

"Sorry I'm late," she said to Williams. "I'm ready to go." She
grabbed her latte as though it were a lifeline, and thought;
I've got to stop drinking this stuff—maybe tomorrow.

She saw that Munoz's mouth had a mulish cast, which she
nonetheless managed to make alluring. It was clear the girl
was unhappy that Doyle, who was taken, was to spend the day

with handsome Williams, who was not. To distract her, Doyle asked, "How is the Belarus prince?"

"Charming," said Munoz, throwing a glance at Williams which apparently was meant to remind him that he had lost his chance and should repent fasting. "I'm seeing him again tonight."

"I'll want to hear the details," said Doyle, although she was just being kind. She had no real interest in Munoz's complicated love life.

"Later, then," said Munoz, glancing up at Williams through her lashes.

As they walked down the aisle way, Williams leaned in to ask, "What do they call that kind of girl in Dublin?"

Doyle smiled broadly. "A brasser, she is."

"I see."

"I'm thinkin' you have met more than your fair share," she teased, and it was his turn to smile broadly. This seemed an auspicious start to their field trip, and she was cautiously optimistic that she wouldn't be tempted to sulk over his newly exalted status—she had always gotten along with Williams, and although he was a bit reserved, he was a good man. Acton seemed to think so, certainly, and again she thought it interesting that a straight-arrow like Williams would be willing to skirt protocols at the behest of her better half. She didn't know anything definite, of course, but her instinct was rarely wrong. Perhaps he had his own notions of justice, like Acton did, which was a bit alarming; she was too fresh from the Crime Academy to look upon such an idea with anything but disquiet. As they walked out to the utility garage where the unmarked vehicles were housed, she recalled that he'd been ill. "How are you feelin', then?"

"I am well," he replied in a clipped tone. "How are you feeling?"

So, he did not appreciate the inquiry. Touchy about it, he

was, and so much for their auspicious start. Which reminded her that she was to have a new attitude, and it was past time for the fair Doyle to face facts.

As she opened the door she asked, "Where to first, sir?" She could see he was taken aback at being thus referred to, but there was nothing for it; he outranked her and protocol was protocol. She had been petty not to call him "sir" the other day at the aqueduct.

He slid in and started up the car. "Newmarket; there's a witness who may have seen something. He owns a souvenir shop off the track and called in after reading about the murder in the papers. Dispatch says he was barely coherent, though—we'll see."

This was one of the hazards of having a sensational case; those odd members of the general citizenry who yearned for attention would call in false leads so as to feel a part of it. Although Doyle was well-suited to sort the wheat from the chaff, it nevertheless meant a waste of time and resources. Of course, sometimes the witness honestly believed they'd seen or heard something significant, which meant the lead had to be run down until it could be ruled out. Much of detective work, Doyle had discovered, was crossing out false leads, but although it was tedious work, it was necessary work—particularly in this type of case where the body count was mounting faster than the police could keep track. "Do we have a workin' theory, sir?"

Williams did, apparently. "Since the victim was an Irish national and killed at a racecourse, on the surface it appears to be connected to the turf war—perhaps a tit-for-tat for the latest Russian victim."

Doyle knit her brow. "But the latest Russian victim doesn't seem to be involved in any of this. Acton believes it was some sort of shadow murder, instead."

Williams shrugged his broad shoulders slightly. "We have to take the facts as they are, and see where they lead."

This seemed inarguable, and sounded a lot like something Acton would say. "Remind me about the Newmarket victim, do you have the case sheet handy?"

"Thirty-five-year-old Irishman named Todd Rourke. Not on the Watch List, and it appears he had no particular connection to the racecourse—not an employee, or a regular of any sort. His car was there, so ERU is going over it for prints, and we are checking his mobile records to see if he was visiting anyone in particular."

Rourke, thought Doyle; that rings a bell—who was it? She couldn't remember. Perhaps it would come, given some time. She wished she had Acton's memory for details—he could remember everything about every case he ever had, it seemed. He certainly knew everything about her. "Priors?" she asked, trying to jog her own memory.

He glanced over at her. "No convictions, but has known associates in the contraband business—weapons and drugs."

"Certainly sounds like the Sinn-split." Not to mention the man was probably a rival of Acton's if he was muckin' about in illegal weapons—faith, it was all too complicated for anyone with a queasy stomach and aching bones. In an attempt to focus, Doyle pulled out her occurrence book and started making notes—she could always organize her thoughts better when she wrote them down. After a moment, she suddenly stopped writing and looked up at the road through the windshield. She didn't feel very well. Desperately surveying the horizon, she breathed deeply. You're all right, Doyle, she thought—don't you dare. Think about something else; mind over matter. After another minute of furious concentration, she realized it was hopeless.

"Sir," she said in a strangled voice. "Would you please pull over? I am goin' to be sick."

Williams looked over at her in alarm and immediately pulled to the shoulder. Thankfully, the road was undeveloped along this particular stretch, and Doyle hastily alighted and walked behind a small clump of bushes where she was promptly sick as a cat. Grand, she thought; you are a tryin' little baby, you are.

CHAPTER 11

DOYLE SMOOTHED HER HAIR AS SHE RETURNED TO THE CAR, feeling better physically but mortified to the soles of her shoes. Williams was watching her as she slid in. "Shall we go back?"

"No," she replied, too embarrassed to look at him. "Sir," she added belatedly.

"Are you pregnant?"

"Yes." She was so taken aback by the bald question that she simply answered; he was one who ordinarily had more tact. He said nothing more, but started the car again. He was angry, she thought in surprise—or dismayed; something powerful. Perhaps he feared she would be of little use.

"I'll be fine now," she offered cautiously, with more optimism than was warranted. "I can do the work, you know."

"I know." He suppressed the emotion, but it simmered, just beneath the surface. There was an awkward silence for a few long minutes; she hoped she wouldn't be sick again for fear he'd push her out of the car; it would be a long and humiliating walk home.

With a visible effort, he began to discuss the case again in a level tone. "The chief inspector believes there are major players involved behind the scenes."

Considering this for a moment, Doyle dredged up a name. "Solonik?" Solonik was some sort of Russian underworld villain; Acton had worried he was involved in the last case—the one with raving-lunatic Owens, who had tried to put a period to the fair Doyle. In truth, her husband's misconception was her own fault; Owens had been obsessed with Acton, and was performing various and assorted murders as his own version of stalking, trying to catch Acton's attention. He had confessed as much to Doyle, but she could not bring herself to recite this particular motivation to her husband, being as he was a Section Seven, himself. So instead, she'd told Acton that Owens worked for Solonik, a name she'd heard in passing and a suitable scapegoat, being as he was a shadowy Russian kingpin and probably accustomed to having crimes laid at his door. Thinking of this, she paused for a moment, much struck. Acton had made no mention of Solonik in connection with this turf war, but it would only make sense that he'd have a hand in all this, as it appeared to be Russia versus Ireland.

Williams had glanced over at her in surprise when she mentioned the name. "Perhaps; but he's a very slippery character, and unlikely to get his fingerprints anywhere near a murder. More likely it's someone who is a local troublemaker; Solonik tends to keep to his own orbit." He paused. "Why— has Acton said something?"

He was worried, she could sense it, and so she quickly disabused him; she shouldn't be wildly mentioning names that gave Williams a case of the willies. "No; he's the only Russian kingpin that I know of, is all." She added, "And Drake said Solonik is not the type to show off—seems unlikely he'd be killin' everybody, left and right."

"Definitely not—he stays very much under the radar." Williams went back to his original line of thought. "If the factions are escalating the violence, the chances get better that they'll get sloppy, and the chief inspector believes we'll have an opportunity to nail some people that are up the chain of command—people who are usually more careful not to get caught."

Doyle decided to write this down later, as for now she was concentrating on the scenery. "You can still call him 'Holmes,' you know, Williams—I won't grass." She turned to smile at her companion, trying to shake him out of the dismals. He responded by smiling in return with some constraint. "Right, then."

There, better. But there was that residual emotion, simmering still. She'd best be careful; show him she was shipshape. "Are there any witnesses we'll be questionin' on the aqueduct murder today?"

He paused fractionally. "This one takes precedence."

Doyle hid her surprise. Witness statements should be taken as soon as possible, and they had already missed a day. If this one at Newmarket was indeed a tit-for-tat—a retribution murder for the aqueduct murder—then the two cases should be investigated in tandem; it would be easier to establish the players, the motive, and the timeline. She said nothing, though; she just didn't have the stamina to argue today and she wanted to be careful not to upset him further. Faith, she was miserable. It didn't seem fair that one didn't feel measurably better after one was forced to be sick at the side of the road.

They came to a frontage road near the racecourse and had to stop to ask for directions, as the directions given by the witness to the dispatcher were unclear and the GPS didn't have the address. They finally came to a dilapidated wooden structure just off Warren Hill that featured a crooked sign announcing, RACING SOUVENIRS—FORMS—TIP SHEETS, and the two of them sat for a moment in the parked car, he just as dismayed as she. "A wild-goose chase," she pronounced.

"Yes, unlikely that anything of import happened here."

"You never know," offered Doyle, trying to rally him. "The

last case, I gleaned a decent clue from a Jamaican cleanin'
woman who had the curious case of a dog that did not bark,
so to speak."

He turned to her, intrigued. "You did? How's that?"

Belatedly, she remembered that the woman had heard no
shots, meaning raving-lunatic Owens had used a silencer, but
Williams had presumably omitted this fact from the ballistics
report at the request of her husband, who was apparently a
shadowy kingpin in his own right. "Oh—she just helped set
time of death. Lovely woman—had earrings the size of knit-
tin' hoops. Shall we go in? The sooner we get this done, the
sooner I can get back to bein' carsick."

He gathered up his rucksack, indicating that she'd success-
fully dodged that dicey subject. "Right then; let's go."

Doyle followed her now-superior officer as he climbed the
creaking steps to enter a small one-room shop containing racing souvenirs and other paraphernalia that were displayed
rather haphazardly on various shelves. Much of it was visibly
dusty, as though the items had not been moved in quite some
time. Posters and photos on the wall proclaimed famous
horses from a bygone era, and Doyle waited until her eyes
had adjusted to the dim interior to survey these items with interest. She had always loved horses, although she'd never
been within hailing distance of one. A nearby shelf contained
replicas of Derby winners, and she tentatively touched one of
the small resin figures.

"Do you ride?" asked Williams, watching her.

"No; but it's in the blood. You?"

"We had horses while I was growing up. My parents still do."

Doyle reflected that their upbringings were probably not at
all similar. "That sounds grand."

The proprietor watched them with beady little eyes from
his perch behind the cash desk. He was a small man, wizened
and wiry, his face leathered from overexposure to the sun. A
former jockey, Doyle guessed, and thought of Dick Francis.

Williams showed his warrant card. "Mr. Thackeray? I believe we spoke on the phone. You thought you may have some information on the recent murder."

"Ye'll want t' know about t'spy," the little man said with relish. "Hah." He grinned and showed his teeth, which were better left out of sight.

Oh-oh, thought Doyle; nicked, and wanting some attention.

"Tell us about him," said Williams. Doyle could tell he was thinking the same thing.

"A spy," the man said contemptuously, and spit in his tobacco cup for emphasis. "Came here t'night of t'Barretson Cup." He seemed disinclined to elaborate.

After a pause whilst she carefully kept her eyes averted from the tobacco cup, Doyle controlled her rebellious stomach and asked, "And why are you thinkin' he was a spy, Mr. Thackeray?"

The man eyed Doyle with open hostility. "I'll have *no* truck with the Irish." He added darkly, "Not like some."

"Are the Irish a problem, then? Do any of these men look familiar?" Williams thought this a good opening to show the man photos of the known Sinn-split members, which he did, pulling them up on his tablet and scrolling through them.

Thackeray scrutinized the photos with a drawn brow. "Yar. They're about, all right." His calloused fingers indicated several. "Bloody Irish." He leaned forward to Williams, eying Doyle askance and lowering his voice. "Skimmin'."

"Which means . . ." invited Williams. Doyle was prudently keeping her Irish mouth shut.

"Settin' up t'races." He paused, and then added fairly, "Only oncet in a while, but enou'. On Irish horses," he added, giving Doyle another dark look.

"Has anything changed recently? Anyone different hanging around—foreigners, perhaps?"

The man scowled in disbelief at the absurdity of Williams's question. "Always furriners about; they come t' have a flutter."

"Have you heard any rumors of trouble?" Williams was asking out of form; it seemed unlikely that this fellow, with his struggling souvenir stand, would have his finger on the pulse of racecourse skullduggery.

The man considered this. "A lot more trailers, in 'n' out."

"What sort of trailers?"

This question was met with the apparent scorn it deserved. "Bah—wot sort a' *trailers?* Horse trailers, a'course."

"Did the spy have a horse trailer?"

"Gar," exclaimed Thackeray in disgust as he paused to spit again. "An' how would I know sech a thing?"

There was a pause. "Was the spy Irish?" asked Williams. Good one, thought Doyle—ask a misinformation question to see where this strange character may go.

"Naw," said the man, exasperated. "He were a spy, like I told ya." He regarded them and saw they did not understand. "Like James Bond—had a gun in his gullet." He indicated his armpit.

This seemed unlikely, as concealed-carry permits were as rare as hen's teeth in England; Doyle should know, the weapon in her ankle holster was not a legal one, and was courtesy of her protocol-skirting husband. "What did the man look like, Mr. Thackeray?" asked Doyle. It seemed to her the witness was sincere, but it could only be that he was sincerely nicked. "Like James Bond?"

The witness gave Doyle a malevolent look, being as she had forgotten she was supposed to stay silent. "No, no, no. A big 'un; drinks too much—and not martinis." He laughed at his own witticism. "No' much hair."

Williams persisted. "If we show you some photos, do you think you could recognize him?"

Thackeray spit into his cup, ruminating. "Don't see the point a' that," he said doubtfully.

"No?" asked Williams, trying to hide his exasperation.

"Got his snap—right here," said the witness. Doyle and Williams watched in wonder as he pulled out his mobile phone. "Took his snap to show me missus—no' often I sees a spy, I tells her."

Doyle didn't know which was more surprising; that Thackeray had a mobile and could take a snap with it or that he took secret snaps of his customers. The man scrolled through his archive with a casual thumb, then turned his mobile to them to display the photo. It showed a man reaching up to a shelf to examine a resin replica of Red Rum. His movement had exposed an armpit holster and a weapon contained therein.

"Holy Christ," breathed Williams.

"Who is it? Is it him?" asked Doyle in excitement.

"Solonik," Williams confirmed.

CHAPTER 1 2

"**A**CTON MUST THINK IT'S CHRISTMAS," SAID DOYLE, STILL exultant although it was nearly an hour later. "Who would have believed it?"

Williams smiled absently as he typed into his tablet. "Yes— up to that point I thought it was a wild-goose chase."

"Not a credible witness," agreed Doyle. "And unfairly prejudiced against my fair self, but the picture is worth a thousand ramblin' words." Forensics would enhance every detail in the photo and it was very likely they could identify the weapon, down to the serial number. That meant, if nothing else, they could pull the Russian in on an illegal weapons charge as a means to hold him while they investigated for other criminal conduct. His presence on the scene certainly seemed a strong indication that he was involved in the turf war murders; apparently the elusive Solonik had decided to get his hands dirty, and would now pay the price.

They were now finishing up their report in the unmarked—time was of the essence, in this situation, and they were sending e-mails and preliminary reports at a fast pace. Williams had confiscated Thackeray's mobile and then contacted Acton with the good news. The witness had to be coaxed into giving them a signed statement; he seemed disinclined to stay on topic, and especially disinclined to allow

Doyle to remain unwatched around the goods. She had willingly retreated outside to sit on the stoop and left Williams to it—in truth, she was happy to have the opportunity to sit her aching bones down. She could hear Williams trying to convince the man that he should speak of this to no one until his testimony was needed; the men they were dealing with were quite dangerous. Thackeray was loudly contemptuous of any potential danger, feeling he could handle himself against any paltry spy and give as good as he got. Williams finally hit upon the happy tack of telling him that his testimony in court was necessary to secure the kingdom. His patriotism thus invoked, the witness seemed more inclined to follow instructions. Presumably it would now be a simple matter to search Solonik's effects once he was in custody—something would turn up, and if nothing else, he was carrying an illegal weapon, which was a serious crime in England.

Williams finished up by making a note in his tablet, and rubbed his forehead, as though his head hurt. "I'll let Organized Crime know about the race-fixing."

Doyle had been thinking this over, and was skeptical. "D'you think that's truly the reason for the war? The Russians want to be takin' over the dopin' or fixin' operations? It seems unlikely—that's not what they do." Her research had shown no previous incursions into racecourse gambling by the Russians; they were usually involved in money laundering based on contraband and black market. Obviously, race fixing required a substantial expertise—no average blackleg right off the street would be able to pull it off with enough subtlety to slip unnoticed past the Racing Board.

"Something started it," Williams pointed out. "But whether there's a connection or not, Vice should nevertheless be taking a long look."

Doyle agreed with this and dropped the subject. Instead, she offered with some constraint, "I appreciate your not tellin' Acton about my troubles this morning, sir." When Williams had called in to report, she could tell there had been a question about her, and a neutral reassurance from Williams.

Her appreciation, however, seemed to irritate him, and he didn't look up from his task. "It's not my business—I'm not your keeper."

Doyle diplomatically did not respond, as she didn't want to give the impression she kept things from her husband. Williams, usually so even-keeled, seemed out of sorts today despite this exhilarating case-breaker that had made her even forget her own misery for an hour. He'd been ill, she remembered, and resolved not to cause him any more trouble. After dispatching the report, they drove over to the main stables with the object of showing around photos of the various Irish and Russian suspects—as well as the victims—to see if anyone could offer a lead. Solonik was only one-half of the war, after all; there should be another kingpin on the Irish side, literally calling the shots. Unfortunately, this was slated to be a long slog as there were many hands here at Newmarket, and many different stables.

Williams showed his warrant card at the gate, and as the guard waved them through, Doyle wondered aloud, "Why on earth would someone like Solonik be lookin' over souvenirs at a place like that?"

"Meeting someone? Or maybe he's just another foreigner, having a flutter."

She smiled at his ironic tone, but persisted, "It all seems so unexpected. Wouldn't Interpol be keepin' an eye on him?"

"Solonik didn't get to be where he is by making it easy for the good guys."

This seemed evident, and Doyle knit her brow. "And yet, here he is; I wonder why he came here." It was probably something she would soon know; Acton would no doubt want her to sit in on the interview, to listen to what the Russian had to say and sort out the true from the false.

As they walked into the graveled paddock area, Doyle

warned Williams of how their questioning might go. "We tried askin' some questions at Kempton Park when the trainer was murdered; no one wanted to give any information and everyone seemed frightened."

His gaze scanned the buildings, thinking about this. "Do you think these murders are connected to that case?"

"Perhaps—best to keep an open mind." Although the Kempton Park case was by all appearances closed because the erstwhile killer had been killed himself, she and Acton knew that Owens, Doyle's attacker, was the true murderer—but it was unclear why he had infiltrated the Kempton Park racecourse in the first place. Officially, no one knew why TDC Owens, a detective trainee, had not shown up for work one day and had not been heard from since; Acton knew how to dispose of a body with the best of them, which was a commendable trait in a husband.

As they began speaking to the various personnel, she hoped they weren't to be on their feet the whole afternoon—she continued unwell; her bones positively ached and she had a raging headache. The propagation of the species, she thought crossly, should not be anywhere near this hard on the propagator. Williams had made no further mention of her pregnancy, for which Doyle was grateful. On the other hand, she had little stamina; if he asked how she did, she decided she would request a short sit-down. He didn't, however, and so she stoically soldiered on. As they walked through the stable, she distracted herself by observing the horses they passed; the delicate animals were tall and slender, alertly watching their progress, ears pricked forward. "They seem so intelligent."

"The finest of the finest. It's in the breeding."

Doyle thought of Thackeray's dark comments. "Except when someone manipulates them; tryin' to take an unfair advantage."

Williams shrugged. "Money corrupts people. Newsflash."

"I still don't think that's the reason for all the killin' goin' on," Doyle mused. "Too chancy; too specialized."

"Perhaps we'll never know."

"Perhaps," she agreed. "At least we have Solonik; I suppose we shouldn't look a gift horse in the mouth." She glanced up at him, hoping he'd appreciate this very clever witticism. He smiled in acknowledgment, but she could tell he had to reach for it; for two detectives who had just broken a big case, they were a sorry pair.

Their inquiries proved unfruitful, but Doyle knew they were on to something because most of the people to whom they showed the photos were lying, at least with respect to the Sinn-split suspects. She would tell Acton when she saw him; she longed to go home and crawl into bed. For the first time, she considered the unthinkable possibility that she was too sick to keep on working. It was disappointing, but she must face facts; this kind of work demanded a sharp mind and long hours, and she honestly didn't think she could weather many more days like this. Acton would be that relieved; he had suggested she come in out of the field after her harrowing experience with Owens, and she knew he was hiding his concern even now. She sighed inwardly, reminded that she had a spanking new attitude. It was no longer possible to simply do whatever she wished anymore; she had a husband's wishes to consider—and soon a child's. But it was such a crackin' shame; she was good at this detecting business, and it just wouldn't be the same, sorting out who was telling the truth at the local PTA. This thought was so depressing that she turned her mind to other things.

It was after lunch time when they were finished with all the personnel on hand, and so before they headed back, they decided to eat at a local pub that was popular with the visitors to the racecourse. Doyle gratefully collapsed at a table and ordered ginger ale, taking a long and regretful look at the cappuccino machine behind the counter. No wonder you have a headache, she thought; it's a coffee addict, you are. She looked over the menu, but nothing sounded appealing and she didn't want to repeat the morning's experience with Williams; the poor man would swear off women.

Williams was apparently not very hungry himself, as he ordered only a pint of Guinness. It was theoretically against protocol to order alcohol while on duty, although some of the higher-ups skirted this taboo with the occasional beer. Williams, one would think, would be a stickler. He didn't seem to be doing well himself; he was a bit pale around the mouth and rather quiet. They drank, and Doyle tried to rally him by speaking of how exhilarating it was to stumble across a case-breaker, as they did today. His heart wasn't in it, though, and Doyle let the conversation lapse into silence.

Her companion ordered another pint, having disposed of the first one. Doyle hid her alarm; it would not do at all if she had to drive all the way back to the Met—perhaps Williams had forgotten she wasn't an experienced driver. She debated whether she should say something, but he seemed increasingly moody and she didn't want to point out to him, a DC to a newly promoted DS, that he shouldn't be drinking—he'd think she was being resentful. Instead, she'd be as subtle as a serpent.

"Are you feeling all right, sir?" she asked gently. He hadn't said anything to her in a considerable space of time, and he seemed lost in his own thoughts, beads of perspiration gathering across his brow.

"I wish you wouldn't call me 'sir,' " he said abruptly. "That's what you call Holmes."

Not anymore, thought Doyle, a bit taken aback. It appeared that her superior officer was drunk—and on two pints, no less.

"When we are alone, shall I call you Williams then, as I used to?" She pushed the pretzel mix that was on the table toward him, hoping he'd eat.

"I don't care." He rubbed the heels of his hands into his eyes. *"Christ."*

Unsure how best to handle the strange situation, she offered softly, "You mustn't blaspheme, Williams."

This triggered a hostile reaction, as he raised his head from his hands and stared at her in disbelief, his face flushed. "That's rich—coming from you. You're the one who got herself knocked up."

That this would be the obvious assumption of all and sundry when they heard of her pregnancy did not help to temper Doyle's reaction, which was immediate and heated. "That is *way* out of line, Williams."

But he had warmed to his theme and met her gaze, glare for glare, even though his eyes were unfocused. "How could you let him get you pregnant? Are you really that naïve?"

CHAPTER 13

Doyle was shocked, and struggled with her temper, torn between refusing to discuss this subject with him and setting the record straight. The record won. "Don't you *dare* be sayin' such a thing; I did not get pregnant until after we were married, and I resent the implication." The battle had been joined, though, and Doyle was reminded by his next words that Williams was a very good detective.

"You were not dating him—don't even pretend you were. You married on short notice, and now you are pregnant enough to be sick—it's obvious; you let him sleep with you and now look what's happened—you had to get married to someone you hardly knew."

Faith, here's a crackin' minefield, she thought, trying to control her temper so that she didn't say anything she oughtn't. "We'd been workin' together for months, Williams—Acton and me. I'm a good RC; I promise you we didn't have sex until after we were married." She realized suddenly that she was giving away state secrets, so to speak, and wished she didn't gabble when she was angry. With a mighty effort, she tried to calm down; he could think what he liked and it didn't matter to her. Although she did value his good opinion, and wished he thought better of her.

He seemed to have regretted his outburst also, and drew a

breath, looking down at his hands. His next words were a bit slurred, "I went by your building to see if you needed a ride one morning—I—I saw him coming out."

She could see that the memory was one that still stung. "Oh—oh; I see how it looked. But we were already married, Williams, believe me." And apparently Williams had seen himself in the role of a suitor; this was a revelation, and was excruciatingly embarrassing. For the love o' Mike, couldn't he have kept this to himself? It was water so far under the bridge it was out to the far isles, already.

"I apologize if I—if I offended . . . ," he started, then slumped over and fell to the floor, knocking his chair over with a clatter in the process.

Doyle leapt up, horrified, and went to him as others nearby offered to help. Amused glances were exchanged among the bystanders.

She felt for a pulse, and lifted an eyelid; he was out cold. "Williams!" she called imperatively, but there was no response.

Turning her head to address the other patrons, she announced, "I don't believe he's drunk—somethin' is wrong. We are police; please call for an ambulance." Doyle had seen Acton drink a half a bottle of scotch at a sitting; impossible that another big man like Williams could pass out on two pints. While a bystander began to dial for an ambulance, Doyle patted down his torso and then pulled Williams's wallet from his suit coat pocket. Yes—there was a medical alert card next to his identification, and she saw that he was a diabetic. This must be insulin shock; she closed her eyes briefly, trying to remember the first aid. "Orange juice with sugar," she demanded of the waiter. "Quickly."

She struggled to prop Williams up on her lap, which was no easy task as he was broad-shouldered and heavy. The waiter brought the orange juice, and she tried to get him to swallow, even though the smell of it made her own stomach heave. "Drink," she commanded sternly, and forced some between his teeth. Murmuring in protest, he swallowed and almost immediately his color was a bit better.

"I didn't want to press you." He opened his eyes briefly, then closed them again. "You seemed so shy."

"Whist, Williams," she said gently. "You mustn't say such things."

By the time the ambulance came, she had bullied him into drinking a goodly portion and he seemed to be recovering. The medical personnel had him swallow some sort of paste from a tube, and then loaded him into the ambulance. She sat with him on the way to the hospital, clasping his hand in hers while he lay quietly with his eyes closed. She took the opportunity to ring up Acton, and since she wasn't certain whether Williams was listening, she edited her comments accordingly.

"Kathleen."

"Acton, Williams had a little medical problem and we are on our way to the hospital." She didn't know if Acton knew he was a diabetic, and so didn't give particulars.

"Which hospital?"

Doyle realized she didn't know, so she asked the medical technician and relayed the information. "Can you notify his family, or whoever is supposed to know? I want to stay with him until they come." She thought about logistics. "Should I drive the unmarked back?"

"By no means," he said. "I will be there in about an hour."

At the hospital, the medical staff was efficient and reassuring. The doctor examined him, and then came out to speak with her, shaking his head. "Happens all the time—especially the younger ones; they think they needn't abide by the rules."

In a very short time, Williams was sitting up and seemed perfectly normal again, and the doctor told Doyle they would release him after an observation period. Thanks be to God, she thought; and now to try to smooth out this tangle patch. After entering his room, she pulled up a chair by the bed. "Hey."

He greeted her with his usual calm demeanor, even though she could feel waves of chagrin and embarrassment emanating from him. "Hey yourself. I am so sorry, Doyle—I know better. I shouldn't have given you such a scare."

"Well, my boyo, you did give me quite a turn," Doyle teased him. "You were clear out of your senses, and began professin' undyin' love for my fair self." She smiled, inviting him to share in the absurdity. "Best watch yourself, or you'll wind up married to some bystander who holds you to it, else."

He laughed ruefully. "Acton will kill me."

"Or bust you back down to DC." There; hopefully that was just the right touch and did the trick; he would think she hadn't believed him even though every word had been true. Mother a' mercy, she thought—more seething undercurrents. She remembered Munoz had once said that everything was usually about sex; Doyle was beginning to believe—rather to her dismay—that Munoz was right.

She sat and spoke with him about the case and what was needed, working very hard to restore their former tone even though she wanted nothing more than to find an empty hospital bed and pull the sterilized covers over her head. By the time his parents arrived, she believed she'd succeeded, and so retreated to the back of the room to lean against the wall whilst they reassured themselves that he was stable, scolded him, and then thanked Doyle for her actions. Williams's mother was a very refined and gracious woman—just the type to own horses, thought Doyle, who felt as though she was observing the Williams family from a different planet. The woman came over to speak to her after she was done with her son, and eyed her in a speculative and friendly way. "So—*you* are Kathleen."

Faith, what a mess, thought Doyle; mother clearly had not

been brought up to date. With a smile, she replied, "Yes, I am Kathleen Sinclair, Chief Inspector Acton's wife."

"Oh," mother answered with a blank look.

Doyle smoothly steered the conversation back to Williams's remarkable skills, which were instrumental in breaking a difficult case, and mother played along, still trying to sort it out.

CHAPTER 14

WHEN ACTON ARRIVED ON THE SCENE A SHORT TIME LATER, Doyle was ready to throw herself on his shoulder and weep with relief, but managed to refrain. She was still feeling wretched, although the headache had receded, and she was positively longing to lie down right here on the linoleum. He took a brief, assessing look at her and asked that she sit down and wait for him in the hallway; he would speak to Williams for a moment and then they would leave.

When Acton emerged from the hospital room, he was brusque to the point of rudeness with Williams's parents, and in no time Doyle was being escorted to the blessed Range Rover with its blessedly pre-heated leather seats.

"Have you been able to eat anything today?" he asked as he started the car.

"I will," she assured him. "Let's go home; I've had a crackin' foul day, and I have a million things to tell you." Leaning her head back against the headrest, she made an effort to put her thoughts in order. She was asleep before they hit the highway.

Sometime later, she awoke as the car slowed down to exit the highway. Acton had clasped one of her hands in his on her lap, his thumb brushing the back of her hand rhythmically—she was frettin' him to death again. "Michael," she murmured. "I am sorry for bein' so tiresome."

He looked at her for a moment. "Do me a favor."

"Anythin'."

"Don't apologize to me anymore about this. Ever."

He meant it. She replied with some heat, "It is all your *stupid* fault for bein' so virile."

He turned to watch the road again. "That's my girl."

"I won't go in to work tomorrow; I just want to stay in bed until the doctor's appointment. And I will eat when we get home—my promise, Michael."

He seemed reassured. "And I will stay with you tomorrow morning; I can work from home while we're waiting to hear whether Solonik's been brought in." Reminded, he added, "Starting tomorrow, we were to try out a new domestic—shall I cancel him?"

"It's a him, then? No, he can do for us, if he doesn't mind moppin' the floor around us while you lie atop me."

He smiled and lifted her hand to kiss its back. The compulsive rubbing, thankfully, had stopped. "That was good work today."

"It fell into our laps, more or less. Did you know that Solonik was lurkin' about?"

"No; but I am happy to discover that he is."

This was true, and was reassuring; she had thought it odd that Solonik's vaunted name had not come up in any of their conversations about these cases—although there hadn't been much in the way of conversations, truth to tell. She'd been worried that Acton was trying to hide something from her, but it was a false alarm, as it turned out. "I hope they can bring him in; Williams says he flies under the radar."

"It should not be too difficult; he'll assume we have no reason to arrest him, and so he will not have gone to ground."

Idly, she watched out the window as they neared their

building. "D'you think we'll be able to pin any of the murders on him?"

"We shall see; if we can, we can put him away for a long time."

She smiled at her reflection in the glass. "Wait until you see the witness, Michael; he's a gnome."

"As long as he can testify, I don't care if he's a leprechaun."

"Definitely not a leprechaun—he dislikes the entire Irish race, and could barely bring himself to be civil to me."

"Hard to imagine." He lifted her hand again to kiss it. "I missed you."

"And I you. Believe me."

They pulled into the gated garage, and took the lift up to their flat, Acton's arm carefully around her. She ventured, "I have two things to tell you that you may not like." May as well introduce the subject whilst he was being so solicitous.

"You alarm me." He switched on the lights and steered her into the kitchen, where she sat at the table, resisting the urge to lay her head down on the cool surface.

"Toast?" he asked, opening the pantry.

She thought about it. "Frosty flakes. It's the only thing that sounds good, but I confess I'm leery after what happened this mornin'."

He poured her a bowl and fetched the milk, then sat across from her. "Tell me."

"I was sick this mornin'; Williams had to pull the car over. It was *hideously* embarrassin'."

He leaned on his elbows, watching her. "Is that one of the two things?"

"No," she confessed. "I'm tryin' to stall."

"Let's hear it," he said firmly.

She recited to him her experience that morning with the newspaper reporter, and how her cab driver had helped her. He listened without comment, but she could feel that he was trying to suppress his extreme displeasure. "You are supposed to be using the driving service, Kathleen."

She sighed, and rubbed her face with her hands. "I know, Michael—I know. It just makes me feel as though I'm puttin' on airs, or somethin'. And my nice Rwandan man waits for me—he's very kind."

Acton leaned back and crossed his arms, considering. "I will call the editor about the reporter; I know the owner, and that should be enough to put a stop to it. Let me think about the driving service—you'd be safer with them, and we could count on them to be discreet."

Cautiously heartened by his mild reaction, she teased, "I could always make up a fanciful tale for the newspaper reporter. You could have rescued me from a shark attack, or somethin'."

"You don't swim," he replied mildly.

Faith, the man knew every detail about her—it was alarming, truly, although she was not alarmed at all, but was well-content. She ate the cereal, thinking that she did indeed feel a bit better.

"And the other thing?" he prompted.

She took a breath. "Michael, you know that I love you, and I always will."

He sat immobile, completely alert. "What has happened?"

Nothin' for it. "Williams has a crush on me, apparently." She paused, waiting for the reaction. He said nothing, but kept his dark gaze fixed on her, unreadable. As it did not appear that he was going to hunt Williams down and kill him, she continued cautiously, "When he was sufferin' from the insulin shock, he said a few things he shouldn't have."

But Acton was not outraged, or even surprised. "You knew this," she accused him in wonder.

He answered carefully, "I suspected."

She frowned at him, flummoxed. It made sense that he would be very sensitive to potential rivals, but his reaction, on the other hand, made no sense at all. She asked cautiously, "And you don't mind?"

"Do you?"

She said honestly, "It's a bit uncomfortable, to be sure. I'd rather not be spendin' the day alone with him again, I think. Although I played if off as a joke, and if I do avoid him now, he'll know I know, so I suppose I cannot, if you're followin' me."

Bending his head, he thought about it. "I doubt he will say or do anything to embarrass you again; this was an unusual situation. To the good, he will always put your interests above his own."

She was bewildered. "Are you not jealous?"

He met her eyes. "Should I be?"

"Not for a moment."

"Well, then."

They regarded each other. "You are a strange and wonderful man," she mused.

"If he steps over the line, let me know."

"I will do that," she agreed, privately hoping that day would never come. "Now that I'm done confessin', I don't know if I have the energy to take a shower, but I definitely need one— I smell of the stables."

"I'll help you," he offered.

She shook her head, smiling. "I don't know if I have the energy for your brand of helpin', either."

With a small smile, he cocked his head. "I promise I won't expend your energy."

"Michael, you knocker; you can't resist."

"Indeed I can. Try me."

She considered. "We can compromise; do you think there's enough room in the shower to lie on top of me?

"Definitely."

"Then let's to it, man."

CHAPTER 15

T HE NEXT MORNING DOYLE WOKE TO COMPLETE MISERY. HER joints were aching again, and her head was positively pounding. She was rarely ill, and the experience was horrifying to her; she wanted to groan aloud, and if Acton wasn't there, she would have. He was up and dressed and had made her some toast, which he offered to her in bed.

"Strawberry jam," he said, trying to tempt her, as it was her favorite.

She felt she could not possibly take a bite for love or money. "In a minute, please. Let me wake up."

He sat beside her on the bed, looking worried. "Your color is not good."

"Michael," she said crossly, "I am not good all the way down to my corpuscles, I assure you. I'll come around, just give me some time."

The concierge buzzed to announce the arrival of the new domestic, and Acton went to the door to allow him entry. He was a short, slight, very neat-looking man of perhaps fifty years who was introduced to Doyle as Reynolds. He bowed slightly in acknowledgment, and Doyle apologized; she did not feel she could yet rise from the bed. Acton said quietly, "My wife is expecting, and is doing poorly today, I'm afraid."

Reynolds said in a measured voice, "Perhaps a heating pad, madam."

Doyle thought this a good idea, and the servant called the concierge and acquired one in no time. Doyle pressed the pad to her aching joints gratefully whilst Reynolds retreated to the kitchen and began to assess what was needed. Doyle whispered to Acton, "He seems nice."

"We shall see," said Acton. "We have thirty days to decide."

At Acton's request, Reynolds prepared iced ginger tea, and Doyle tentatively took a sip, then lay back. Impossible. Hopefully, when she saw him today, the obstetrician would give her something to make life bearable. Privately, she was shocked that women were able to live through this and want to do it again and again; Mother of God, she felt wretched. Acton was fretting, but she honestly couldn't find the wherewithal to put up a brave front.

"I'm goin' to be sick, I'm afraid. Promise me you won't annul this short-lived marriage."

"Let me help you." He held her steady as she rose, and she swayed on her feet for a moment, but then with a monumental effort made for the bathroom for fear that she would disgrace herself in front of Reynolds, who certainly didn't need to clean up that kind of mess his first day. After shutting the door, she retched until she was spent, and then sat on the cool tile floor, too exhausted to rise again just yet. And I've started my period on top of everything else, she thought. Grand.

She then froze, remembering that she should not be having a period for many more months. No, she thought in horror; no, no, no, no. Fear made her spring to her feet, and the movement caused a gush of warm liquid between her legs. She grabbed a towel and applied pressure, then opened her mouth to call for Acton, but no sound came out. She tried again, and he was through the door in an instant, lifting her in his arms and bringing her back to the bed. As he set her down he called for Reynolds, and Doyle could see that the towel was soaked in blood. She lay back, stunned. "Merciful mother," she whispered.

Acton pulled out his mobile whilst Reynolds, without hesitation, replaced the bloody towel with a clean one and held it firmly between her legs. "Best not to look, madam," he cautioned. "Breathe deeply." He then held her eyes with his own and demonstrated. Doyle did as she was told, and felt her mouth trembling uncontrollably.

Acton said, "Timothy is in surgery; I will ring up Dr. Easton." Dr. Easton was the obstetrician she had not yet met. Doyle could hear Acton asking for the doctor, explaining it was an emergency.

Reynolds said to her, "May I call your mother, madam?"

"No," whispered Doyle. "My mother is . . ." she could not bring herself to say the word. Reynolds seemed to know, however, and asked gently, "Anyone else? Your priest, perhaps?"

"Nellie," whispered Doyle. Nellie was her good friend from church who had taken a motherly role in Doyle's life.

"It's in her mobile," said Acton. "On the table."

Reynolds said quietly to Acton, "The bleeding seems to have stopped, sir." Acton nodded, as he was in conversation with Dr. Easton. Acton then rang off and sat beside her, stroking her head and checking the towel occasionally. Doyle could hear Reynolds speaking in the background. "Nellie, we have not met, but I have an urgent request . . ."

The doctor arrived to examine her, sympathetic and efficient. Nellie also arrived, pale but composed, and Doyle realized she had not yet told her she was pregnant. She found she could not say anything, but apparently, nothing needed to be said; Nellie pulled up a chair and held Doyle's hand while in the other she held a rosary.

The doctor explained that a surgical procedure was necessary to ensure no material was left in the uterus. To preserve her privacy, it could be done at his offices. Nellie helped Doyle clean herself up, and they drove to the doctor's offices, Reynolds staying behind to mop up. Doyle had never been to a gynecologist and the experience was not a good one to serve as a first impression. After the procedure, she and Acton listened to the doctor explain how often this type of thing happened, and they were reassured that she appeared to have no other problems that would interfere with other potential pregnancies.

They returned home in the late afternoon. A thoroughly wicked day, thought Doyle; it's a fine test I've been given—in all things give thanks. She took her leave of Nellie with an embrace, and promised to ring her the next day. She then thanked Reynolds sincerely, and he offered to return in the morning. Acton closed the door, and she was finally alone with him.

"Michael," she said as he came to hold her close, "please let me say I'm sorry—just once."

"You've done it; that's enough." He pulled her onto his lap and they sat together, her head on his chest, staring out over the city as the light began to fade.

He asked gently, "Is it the wrong thing to say that there will be others—as many as you like?"

"Nothin' you say to me is ever the wrong thing, Michael," she answered softly. "Truly."

They sat very still as it grew dark, Acton stroking her head, again and again, while she breathed in the scent of him and tried not to think about the misery that seemed to have settled in the region of her chest. "I wonder," she finally ventured in a small voice, "if God is punishin' me because I didn't want my baby." There, the terrible words she had been thinking were out. She felt very bleak indeed.

His arms tightened around her. "I can't imagine that God would be so petty."

"No," she said. "I suppose not." She paused and then said

the other unthinkable thing she had been thinking. "Do you think the baby knew I didn't want it?"

"You were taken by surprise, is all," he said firmly. "You are an excellent mother."

She ran her thumb along his hand in imitation of his own habit.

"Besides," he added, "there was probably no baby; only a blastocyte that hadn't properly enfolded."

"Tell me what you are talkin' about, Michael. In plain terms."

He explained to her the process of early embryonic development and she listened, and felt better. "So perhaps it just didn't take?"

"Exactly."

"On the bright side, I have increased to three the number of men who have seen me completely naked."

"That's more than enough," he said dryly. "Are you hungry?"

"You'd think I would be, but I still feel crackin' awful."

"Let's take it easy, then. What shall we do tomorrow?"

"I would like to go to work tomorrow, Michael." When she sensed he would protest, she added, "My mother always said the best cure for sorrow is work. She was right."

"As long as you have a care."

"I should be back to normal; that's what the doctor said."

She went to shower, and hesitated for a terrible moment before crossing the bathroom floor. She felt numb, and drained, and so very, very sad. Time, she thought; this is going to take some time to recover from, which makes it all the harder to bear. Later they lay in bed, her back curled against his chest, and she found that the tears that she'd held back could be held back no longer. She tried to weep silently; Acton did not do well when she wept. He was awake, though, and cradled her closer, his forehead against the back of her head, his breath on her nape. Perhaps he wept also; she was too bereft to notice.

CHAPTER 16

He was happy to see her again; he had been worried for her, had told his wife that he was worried, although he didn't tell her the nice lady was mganga for fear his wife would chide him. Because of the new God, he no longer believed in the evil ones—the mashetani—and he hoped the nice lady did not believe in the mashetani either; they were not being kind to her.

THE NEXT MORNING, ACTON ACCOMPANIED DOYLE OUT TO the curb where the Rwandan cab driver leaned against his cab, waiting for her. He said something by which Doyle understood that he missed her yesterday, although she wasn't sure. Acton introduced himself as her husband and then began to speak to him in French, with the man responding in kind. Doyle stood and listened, bemused; she did not know Acton spoke French—faith, the man was a basketful of surprises. It appeared Acton thanked the other man for his chivalry the other day, and they agreed on something and shook hands, the Rwandan flashing his gleaming white smile. Acton then held the door for her before sliding into the cab himself.

"His name is Aiki, and he will be on call for you. Here is his card, please program your mobile, and I will pay him a retainer."

"That is excellent news, Michael; thank you." She was touched; Acton would much rather have used the thoroughly-vetted driving service. He did it to please her, and she was indeed pleased. That he was on pins and needles, worried about her, went without saying, and so she took his hand. "I'll be all right, Michael—truly. I'll be sad, and then I'll be myself again."

"I know. But I wish I didn't feel so helpless."

This was true, and not unexpected; he was one who was used to casually wielding power—even from birth, for heaven's sake; he wouldn't like this miserable feeling of having no recourse. She stilled for a moment, her scalp prickling as it did when her intuition was making a leap. What? She asked herself, when no leap was made. What is it? Acton doesn't like to feel helpless—news-flash, as Williams would say. Maybe if her head didn't ache so much she'd understand what she was supposed to be understanding, here. Shaking it off, she continued, "I'll mourn for a bit, but I'll come about—it can't be worse than when my mother died." She lifted her face to him. "Have you ever lost someone?" Obviously his father was dead, because Acton had inherited his honors.

The dark, unreadable gaze rested on hers. "No one I'd miss."

She nodded, trying not to be taken aback. "Oh—I see." He was not one to have a bundle of sentimental attachments—another news-flash. By contrast, not a day went by when she didn't miss her mother.

Apparently, Acton was done waxing non-sentimental. "I will be monitoring the Solonik situation, but do not hesitate to ring me up if you need anything."

"Can you run operational command from Candide's?" she teased. Candide's was a restaurant she favored.

He met her eyes, completely serious. "Let's go."

"Michael, you knocker, I'm teasin' you."

"After work, then."

"Done." Hopefully, she'd regain her appetite by then; it would be a crackin' shame to go to Candide's just for coffee. As they edged their way through the morning traffic that surrounded headquarters, she offered, "I was tellin' Williams that it seems unlikely that the Russians are tryin' to muscle in on the racefixin', or the numbers-runnin', because that takes a large dose of know-how. But Williams seemed reluctant to offer a workin' theory about what sparked this turf war."

He considered for a moment. "Do you have a theory?"

She watched out the window and sighed. "I am fresh out, my friend. But I do think it is somethin' new and different—and it must be lucrative, to attract the likes of the mighty Solonik." She turned to him. "Are you surprised he turned up?"

"No," said Acton, and it was the truth.

"I suppose I'm not either; now we only need to nick the Sinn-split kingpin, and we'll have ourselves a good day's work."

"Let's hope so." They arrived at work, and parted by the lift doors, Acton ducking his head. "You know what I want to say."

"I will be careful not to overdo it," she assured him. Many of the employees walking by glanced at them covertly, and she could feel the salacious curiosity, carefully concealed. I am never going to get used to being a freak at the circus, she thought. I'm not one who likes the limelight; but on the other hand, neither is Acton, and he is willing to brave it for me. Her scalp prickled again, and exasperated, she ignored it.

She made her way down to her cubicle and immediately fished around in her drawer for aspirin—she hadn't wanted Acton to see her take any. Faith, but she could not shake this miserable headache, which seemed wholly unfair. Hormones, she decided; my hormones are probably in an uproar. She sipped her latte, and it did seem to help her poor head. Feeling weak and nauseous, she settled into her desk, hoping some quiet research would take her mind off her ills. With any luck they'd bring in Solonik soon—it seemed to her that Acton had emanated confidence when they'd discussed it, just now. If Thackeray didn't break faith, the Russian could be held in custody on the weapons charge, and then perhaps they could pin the murder of Rourke on him—except that shadowy kingpins were not known for leaving incriminating evidence behind. After all, it was only the grossest good luck that they had twigged the photo that placed Solonik on the scene at Newmarket; without something more, it would not be enough to come within calling distance of a murder charge.

With a knit brow, she pulled up her prior research on her laptop. There had been seven killings altogether in this turf war, with Barayev and Rourke being numbers six and seven, over a space of four weeks. There may have been others that had gone undiscovered thus far; whether there would be more was anyone's guess.

Her chin resting on her hand, she remembered how Williams had said the aqueduct murder of Barayev was on the back burner, and how strange that seemed—any information gleaned on any of the seven murders could give them a lead on all the others, and with such a rapid succession of crimes, anything to staunch the bleeding would help.

After resting her eyes for a few moments, she drank more coffee and then pulled up the report on Barayev, including her own contribution. Why—that's strange, she thought, frowning at the screen. There was no firm timeline; only an estimated date of death due to the cool environment surrounding the body—but surely the insect people had come to their conclusion by now. She scrolled the report. There was no reference to an insect report, and the digital photos attached to the main report did not include any close-ups of the face as she had requested. Doyle sat for a moment, annoyed with the stupid SOCO photographer and annoyed on behalf of the late Mr. Barayev, who was apparently on everyone's back burner, poor man. She decided she would check the evidence box to see if there was a drive containing the photos; someone may have dropped the ball and forgotten to include them in the report.

Before she could gather up her bones to stand up, how-ever, Munoz called out, "Doyle, come here for a moment."

Getting up slowly so as not to worsen her headache, she went to see what Munoz wanted; judging by her tone it wasn't going to be girl talk, but then with Munoz, it never was.

The other girl was in a sullen mood, and looked up at Doyle from under beautifully knit brows. "They say you and Williams broke the Newmarket murder."

Faith, here we go. "We found a witness who handed us a snap of the suspect on a silver platter," Doyle confessed. "I al-most fell over. D'you know if they've brought him in yet?"

"Ask Williams, your new best friend," retorted Munoz, her eyes flashing. "I wouldn't know."

"There's no point in talkin' to you, Munoz, if you can't be civil."

Hunching her shoulders, Munoz complained, "I was work-ing on Drake's project when these murders started to break, and now I'm out of the loop."

"I predict," Doyle offered in a dry tone, "that there will be more murderin' in our fair city."

But Munoz would not be mollified, and drew her mouth down. "These are high profile; the kind that get you pro-moted."

"Not to worry; when I'm a DS, I'll be sure to put in a good word." That she would taunt Munoz in such a way was a mea-sure of the strength of her headache; Doyle was not one to es-calate a call to arms.

There was an ominous silence. "Out," ordered Munoz, glowering.

Only too happy to oblige, Doyle wondered if anyone would notice if she lay down on the industrial carpeting to take a nap under her desk. Faith, she was in a foul mood, and she shouldn't make everything worse by needling Munoz. Resolv-ing to do her work and keep her crabby mouth shut, she went back to her report, only to be interrupted by Habib, her supervisor, who came over to announce that there was a walk-in upstairs who wanted to speak to the Irish detective from the Newmarket racecourse.

A sound of extreme frustration could be heard from the adjoining cubicle.

Casting her resolution to the winds, Doyle threw over at her, "Sorry, Munoz; it's an ethnic war and you don't fit the bill."

Munoz's head appeared over the top of the partition to complain to Habib, her expression a cross between pathetic and sultry that Doyle could only envy. "It is *so* unfair, sir; I'll never get to work a decent murder."

Like a fish rising to the hook, Habib attempted to placate the unhappy beauty. "If you wish, Munoz, you may accompany Doyle."

"Grand," said Doyle crossly.

Her attitude much improved, Munoz appeared in the cubicle opening, smoothing back her hair. "Is it an ethnic war? I thought it was a turf war."

With poor grace, Doyle gathered up her occurrence book and resisted the urge to send a glare at Munoz behind Habib's back. "It's both, I suppose—the factions happen to be ethnic, but I think the theory is that somethin' has shifted, and the fight is over some fine new source of untraceable money."

Habib cocked his head, as though doubtful. "Perhaps. But I believe the escalation points to other factors."

Doyle paused to consider this; Habib was an odd duck, but he was a knowing one, and she respected his insight. "How so, sir?"

Habib crossed his arms and unbent enough to expand on his thought. "Businessmen do not overreact like this. Instead, here there are tribal loyalties which are very powerful when provoked. The resulting damage is excessive and uncontrollable."

This seemed a sound theory, and Doyle reflected that Habib, being Pakistani, knew of which he spoke. "So each side has lost its objectivity—all that's left is the desire for primal revenge."

"Yes." He gazed upon her with benign approval. "The war spirals out of control; there can be no coming to terms—as there would be if it were only about cutting into another's take."

Doyle recognized the truth of this; after all, many of the persistent problems in the world were based on this type of ethnic division and being Irish, she was well-familiar with the concept. The Russians and the Sinn-split were locked in mortal combat, and even the fact that the CID was racking up a body count and capturing the key players could not deter them; they were in it to the death. Doyle paused. This was important, for some reason, and if she didn't have such a headache she would realize why.

"Come along, Doyle," said Munoz in the brisk manner of someone already her commanding officer. "The walk-in may give us a lead."

Whilst Habib smiled his approval, Doyle shot her a glare behind his back.

CHAPTER 17

DOYLE WAS IN NO MOOD. "TWO THINGS, MUNOZ; I WILL NEED some more coffee, and this is not your case."

They were making their way to the interview rooms on the entry floor—not the ones where the suspects were interviewed, with their recording equipment and menacing bailiffs, but the smaller rooms for situations such as this, where a witness walks in off the street with nary a warning. Habib had directed them to Interview Room Two, where a white male would be waiting.

Munoz, having achieved her goal, was willing to be civil as they took a detour into the break room. "Give over, Doyle; you needn't be so touchy—it's not as though I'd be able to take a case away from Acton's new bride, even if I wanted to."

"That's not why I'm on the case," Doyle retorted, very sensitive to this assumption. "I am on it because it is related to the Kempton Park case." She paused in surprise as she carefully balanced her new cup of coffee and returned to the hallway. There was truly no reason to believe that the cases were related, and she wondered why the words had come out of her mouth. The Kempton Park case should be dead and buried, along with raving-lunatic Owens.

"Well, I worked the Kempton Park case, too."

This was true; Acton had enlisted Munoz when he had taken Doyle off the case, and it didn't help matters to be reminded of this. Munoz looked over at her, curious. "How are the two cases related?"

Having painted herself into a corner, Doyle reached for a plausible explanation. "The trainer who was killed was Irish and on the Watch List."

Munoz knit her brow as they approached the interview room. "So why was he killed? Is that what started the war?"

"Perhaps," Doyle offered vaguely. "The workin' theory is that everythin' since has been tit-for-tat."

Munoz shrugged so that her hair slid over her shoulder. "Good on them; makes our jobs easier."

Doyle was uneasy with such an attitude, and her conscience was stung with the reminder that the investigation would be multiple times more exigent if the victims were innocent citizens. "Murder is murder, Munoz."

"Not always, Doyle."

Further discussion was curtailed as they entered the interview room to behold a young man of perhaps thirty years, seated at the table and smoking, even though you weren't supposed to smoke in here. The walk-in was a bit reedy, and there was a tattoo on his neck, partially obscured by the collar of his shirt. He looked as though he did not ordinarily wear a collared shirt, and had cleaned up to make this visit, as his hair was still damp. Glancing up at them as they came into the room, he reached to stub out the cigarette.

Doyle checked her notes. "You are Gerry Lestrade?"

The man nodded. "That's me. You were the girl at the track, asking questions."

Doyle found two things particularly interesting; first, she knew she hadn't seen Lestrade at the track, and second, the man never took his eyes off her. Usually, when she was accompanied by Munoz, men did not even realize there was another female present. "Indeed I was; we were investigatin' the murder of a man named Rourke."

The witness nodded, and kept his thoughtful gaze upon

her. He is wary, she thought in surprise; wary and something else—confused, perhaps. She prompted, "Have you thought of somethin' that may help us in our investigation, Mr. Lestrade?"

He nodded. "I didn't want to say the other day, because I didn't want anyone to see me talking to you."

This was untrue, and Doyle waited, wondering if this witness was the sort who would tell a fish tale just to feel a part of the case—he didn't seem it; he was working-class, and rough around the edges, but then again, so was she. The tone of his voice was rather flat, and it was hard for her to judge his origins—south England, perhaps; she was not good with accents. "Do you work at the course, then?"

"Sometimes, the odd job or two—I'm a driver." This, to her surprise, was true, and she reassessed; she had already half-decided that he was an attention-seeker, since he was not one for telling the truth, was Mr. Lestrade. And although his outward demeanor was calm, he was wary and alert—almost as though he was afraid of her.

She took a sip of coffee, wishing she could go lie down. "And what would you like to tell me, then?"

He leaned forward, and tapped a forefinger on the table. "I saw that Russian man there—the one they think killed him. He was there that night." He paused, watching her. "It was early in the evening."

This was also untrue, and Doyle hid a flare of alarm; no one should know anything about Solonik, least of all this fellow, who seemed to be cadging his story. He is bluffing, she decided; trying to feel his way into a plausible tale that would put him in the witness books. He must have taken a look at the newspaper accounts, and guessed the suspect was Russian.

"Please describe him," said Munoz, who, like Doyle, knew better than to release a suspect's name.

The man looked at the other girl in feigned surprise and

lifted his hands from the table. "You know the one—the Russian."

Now convinced he was indeed feeling his way, Doyle poised her pen. "Description?"

The man looked at her, weighing his response for a moment, then offered, "About thirty-five; medium height, close-cropped blond hair; a narrow face with a broken nose."

Doyle jotted this down—it was the truth, but obviously he was guessing and had guessed wrong, which only cemented her conclusion that he was trumping up a false lead. Strange, he didn't seem the type. "I see. Did you get a license plate number, or anythin' that could help to identify him?"

"No." She caught a flash of amusement, which seemed a bit out of place.

"Did you hear him say anythin'? Are you certain he was Russian?"

She caught another flash of amusement but he answered, "Yes, I am sure he was Russian." It was not true.

Doyle hovered on the edge of allowing him to look at the suspect photos, but she had the strong feeling that it was he who was probing for information, and so she was reluctant to give him any.

"Your name's Doyle?" He indicated her security card, hanging around her neck.

"Yes, I am Detective Constable Doyle, and this is Detective Constable Munoz." She should have introduced herself when they entered the room, but she was annoyed that Munoz was there, and when she was annoyed she tended to forget the protocols.

The witness's gaze rested on Munoz briefly, but then returned like a lodestar to Doyle. Tilting his head with a self-conscious smile, he made a gesture toward her left hand, resting on the occurrence book. "You married?"

Doyle had to hide her own smile, as there were shock waves

of incredulity suddenly emanating from Munoz. "I am, indeed. Now, can you think of anythin' else that may help with our investigation?" If she was clever, like Williams, she's think of a misdirection question, but she wasn't feeling very clever at present, and mainly just wanted to bring the interview to an end.

The witness clasped his hands on the table, and met her eyes. "Everyone's nervous around the course—do the police have a motive for the murder, yet?"

"I'm afraid I'm not at liberty to discuss a pendin' investigation," Doyle responded automatically. She wasn't certain if he was fishing for information, or fishing for a date, but either way he had no real knowledge and was a waste of time. She rose, and instructed the witness to leave his information with the desk sergeant in the event they needed to contact him, then recited by rote, "Thank you for comin' in, Mr. Lestrade; oftentimes the public's help is instrumental."

The man paused, then nodded his head. "It has been a pleasure."

This was also untrue, which seemed a little strange if the man was angling to chat her up. Doyle didn't care, and as they retreated back to the basement she said crossly to Munoz, "I hope you felt that was worth turnin' Habib up sweet."

"Not really—he was obviously a bit nicked."

Quirking her mouth, Doyle observed, "Because he didn't fall at your feet."

"Not just that; he didn't even attempt to put together a story that was remotely interesting."

This was true; one would think he'd not want to be exposed as a faker at first blush, but he had very little to relate, and had seemed hesitant to give them even as much as he did.

"Did you see his watch?"

Doyle looked over at her companion. "No. Why?"

Munoz shrugged. "It was a Breguet—a very expensive French brand. Didn't really fit, unless he stole it."

But Doyle had lost interest. "They'll have run a check on him before lettin' him in the door; if he had a record, they'd know."

"Just saying."

Once in the elevator, Doyle leaned against the back wall and let out a breath as Munoz eyed her. "Why were you out yesterday—were you sick?"

Doyle firmly quashed the bleak misery that threatened to rise up again. "Yes, I was sick." Best not to mention it was the worst day of her life; or perhaps the second worst, after the death of her mother. Munoz wouldn't much care, anyway, and so she changed the subject. "How is your foreign beau?"

This, however, proved to be a sore point. "I don't know," Munoz replied, her brows drawing together. "He didn't call me yesterday, after he said he would."

"Then he doesn't deserve the likes of you." Doyle wanted to make up for her earlier unkindness, and Munoz had allowed Doyle to take the lead in the interview, which was appreciated.

"I don't know—he is just my type; rich and handsome." Munoz said this with a touch of defiance, which Doyle interpreted to mean that Acton wasn't the only fish in the rich and handsome sea.

"Then perhaps he had unexpected business, or somethin'," Doyle offered patiently, taking another tack. "What with the tariffs, and all."

Munoz looked a little conscious, suddenly. "Yes—that could be it. Are you hungry?"

Doyle could see that Munoz wanted to change the topic of conversation, and her antennae quivered; Munoz was feeling guilty about something—something apparently having to do with her boyfriend's business. Doyle hoped the other girl wasn't being foolish, but decided she couldn't issue any tacit warnings; Munoz was already fit to be tied due to the whole marrying-Acton-in-a-twinkle development.

"I suppose." Actually, Doyle was not hungry, but she had been secretly dismayed by the pale, thin face that had reflected back at her in the mirror this morning. No wonder Acton was worried; she needed to eat something if it killed her, even though she felt it might. Mentally girding her loins, she went to her cubicle to fetch her wallet and text Acton with this plan. Munoz needed cheering up, and Doyle didn't know if she could face Acton's carefully suppressed anxiety right now; it would do them both good to have a break from it—not to mention it would give him a chance to catch up on his caseload after playing nursemaid to her yesterday. Taking a deep, steadying breath, she marshaled her energy. She would eat, come back, and then report to Acton that she had eaten and felt better—surely it was past time to start recovering. With this resolution firmly in mind, she rejoined Munoz, who was signing off her mobile. "Williams and Samuels will join us."

Doyle's immediate reaction was dismay, but she quickly tamped it down; she had to face Williams again, and now was as good a time as any—she couldn't avoid him, or treat him any differently without giving away the fact that she knew he'd been in earnest when he'd said the things he had. Honestly, men; she thought with a touch of exasperation. Until she met Acton, she had lived a very undramatic life, although she supposed it wasn't Acton's fault that Williams was vying for her affections—although not in any way that she would notice. Recalling her husband's version of courtship with a fond smile, she thought, I'm afraid you lost this horse race, Williams; Acton left you at the gate.

CHAPTER 18

Doyle and Munoz picked up Samuels at his cubicle, and the three of them walked to the lobby to meet up with Williams, who now had a larger cubicle, courtesy of his recent promotion. Doyle noted that he seemed to be restored to health, and hoped he'd do as the doctor had cautioned and take better care of himself. He met her eyes briefly, and she received the unspoken message that she wasn't to discuss his brief hospitalization. She gave him a reassuring smile and thought, ancient history, my friend; that story's been well-trumped.

"Congratulations," said Munoz, smiling sweetly. She hadn't given up hope of securing Williams's interest, it seemed—particularly now that the foreign beau was not cooperating. "Your promotion was well-deserved."

"Who are you?" Williams teased as he held the door, "and what have you done with Munoz?"

They all laughed, including Munoz, and then walked outside to the local deli together. The weather was beginning to turn so that it was a bit brisk out, but the group decided it was not too cold to sit at the tables outside, and they settled into conversation between chips and sandwiches. Doyle breathed in the cool, fresh air and decided this was a good idea, to be outside; indeed, she seemed to be feeling better and better as the day went along.

"How is the rarefied air on the fifth floor?" Samuels asked Williams. Samuels was a fellow DC who worked on Drake's team, and Munoz had originally thrown him in Doyle's way as a potential beau. He was easygoing and unambitious—or at least compared to the rest of them, and Doyle privately thought he wouldn't stay in law enforcement long; he didn't have the thirst for it, and this was not an easy job, else.

Williams demurred with due modesty, "I'm finding my way; mainly I do whatever Acton tells me."

"Me, too," chirped Doyle, and they all laughed again. Grand, thought Doyle with relief; there appeared to be no constraint, and Williams was determined to behave as though the scene at the pub never happened. Acton was right; Williams would not embarrass her again.

As they ate, she and Williams entertained Samuels and Munoz with a description of their interview with Thackeray at the souvenir shop, which also evoked a great deal of laughter.

"The best part of the job," Samuels pronounced. "The interactions with the assorted citizenry."

"Some more assorted than others," Munoz agreed, taking a chip from Williams's plate.

Williams indicated Doyle with a nod of his head. "The witness wouldn't even speak to Doyle; she had to go outside to sit on the stoop."

Laughing, the others exclaimed at this gross injustice. "A misogynist?" asked Munoz.

Doyle smiled and shook her head. "No; the objection was to race, not gender."

Munoz tossed her long black hair. "If it had been me, he probably would have pulled a weapon."

Williams teased, "Sometimes I'm tempted to pull a weapon on you, myself."

Delighted that Williams was teasing her with such familiarity, Munoz bestowed a brilliant smile on him and made a tart response. Privately, Doyle wondered if he was trying to compensate for their little contretemps by politely flirting with Munoz; he'd best have a care or she'd be on him like a barnacle.

Apparently, the attention had put Munoz in a benign mood, because she was willing to reveal, "On the other hand, we had a walk-in today who was so enamored of Doyle that he asked if she was married. It was a shame she was already spoken for—he was just her type."

The men exclaimed and wanted to hear the story, and so Doyle recited it, admitting, "There are some men who like redheads—sometimes it's a curse."

"Followed her in from the racecourse like a puppy," Munoz continued. "It was touching, really."

"More like touched," said Samuels. They all laughed, but Doyle realized that the whole encounter was very strange, now that she thought about it. Lestrade wasn't touched—not really; and Doyle didn't have the feeling he was attracted to her. More like he was wary, which could be a sign he was involved in the turf war and was trying to find out what the authorities knew. She'd best follow up on him when she returned after lunch; if her brain had been working, this would have already occurred to her.

They began to discuss other cases while Doyle ate a small portion of her turkey sandwich. She could feel Williams's eyes upon her when she pushed the rest away, unable to eat any more. Oh, she thought suddenly; Williams.

She texted him on her mobile under the table, "Must speak 2 U."

His mobile buzzed and he read the message but did not look at her; she hoped he didn't think she was going to revisit that-which-should-not-be-spoken-of.

Samuels was entertaining them with the story of an arrest gone very awry when Munoz suddenly lit up like a candle. "Sergey!"

A man who had been heading toward headquarters turned toward her voice and came to greet her, hands outstretched. Doyle looked on with interest, as this was clearly the Belarus person; he was indeed handsome in an Eastern European sort of way, his dark hair slicked back into a small ponytail. He was dressed in the kind of suit that Acton would wear, which Doyle now knew meant it was ridiculously expensive.

"Isabel, I have come to ask you to lunch with me."

But Munoz was well-schooled in the art of romance, and shrugged with a casual smile, her glance indicating her male companions. "I have other plans, I'm afraid."

"Forgive me," he said, with an abundance of rueful charm. "I lost my cellular telephone and did not know how to contact you—I was going to ask at the desk."

This was deemed to be a plausible excuse by Munoz, who clearly forgave him. Doyle, who knew he was lying, was not so easily swayed. She did give him credit for easy charm, however—he could have been an Irishman, born and bred.

Munoz introduced him to the men; clearly enjoying what she hoped was their chagrin. "And this is Kathleen Acton."

Williams interrupted to explain to Munoz what Doyle had already attempted to explain several times; "Munoz, its either 'Kathleen Sinclair' or 'Lady Acton'; you don't mix them." Doyle, however, wasn't paying attention to them anymore; Sergey hid it almost immediately, but there was no mistaking that he was alarmed—alarmed and wary. Of her fair self.

The reaction was similar to that of Lestrade, only more pronounced; it was all very strange. The penny dropped, and she suddenly realized there was a likely explanation; Acton was miles more likely to strike fear into the breasts of others as opposed to her young and girlish self, therefore this must be all about her connection to him. Indeed, the Belarus banker may be a former suspect, and terrified that Munoz would discover this unfortunate fact. Doyle resolved to mention the encounter to Acton; it wouldn't be fair to stand by and allow Munoz to be duped by a charming rogue, however tempting the idea might be. As a consolation, perhaps she could be the one to break the sad news to her.

The aforesaid banker persuaded Munoz to accompany him elsewhere, and she agreed, her spirits buoyant again. Sergey assured the rest of them he was happy to make their acquaintance, but he didn't meet Doyle's eyes, and he could not leave fast enough. A blackleg, Doyle concluded, and wondered what his secret was.

Samuels rose to make a visit to the nearby bookshop, and Doyle and Williams were left together at the table. Neither made a move to get up, and he waited, saying nothing. She found she could not meet his eyes, and recited in a low voice, "I wanted to tell you that I had a miscarriage." She paused for a moment, controlling herself. "I would appreciate it if you didn't mention it to anyone."

This announcement was met with a silence that lasted so long that she glanced up to see if he had been listening. He was staring at her, white-faced. "Because of me."

"What?" she asked, completely at sea.

He ducked his head down, and she could see that his fingers were pressed hard against the surface of the table. "I behaved so badly; you were knackered and I didn't care—and then I was stupid and put myself in a coma."

She stared at him incredulously. "Williams, you tiresome knocker, I have no idea what you are talkin' about; I miscarried the next day and it had nothin' to do with you." Hopefully, this was the case; she hadn't thought about it before.

He bent his head back for a moment in acute remorse. "Acton thought I was an idiot; he blistered me for putting you through it."

She blinked. "Acton blistered you while you were in the hospital?"

He brought his head down and met her gaze. "I'm afraid so." He heard the hint of humor in her question, and a smile tugged at his mouth.

"Quite the bedside manner, in fact."

He smiled and she smiled—it truly was funny. Poor Williams; he could have been on his deathbed and Acton would have chided him for making her wait in the drafty hallway. Acton was a sad, sad case.

"I am so sorry," he said, and meant it.

She sighed. "As am I. Let's go back, then." They walked together in companionable silence, on a good footing once again, although it was different than their former good footing—better, as though they'd survived a battle together. Acton was right; Williams was not the sort to make things uncomfortable for her. It didn't change the fact, however, that she could still feel his longing and she wished she couldn't. Need to find him a nice girl, thought Doyle. An anti-Munoz.

CHAPTER 19

REYNOLDS WAS TO STAY; DOYLE AND ACTON HAD DISCUSSED IT and agreed that no further probation was needed. He had proved his mettle in the emergency and had just the right combination of aloofness, kindness and respect that was most pleasing. He had also realized that the most direct route to Acton's approval was to treat Doyle like a rare and precious treasure, which proved to Doyle that he was very shrewd indeed.

That evening they'd decided to tempt her appetite with Chinese food; Doyle had not eaten any recently because she realized Acton didn't care for it, although he would never admit to it, the knocker. So it was a measure of his concern that Acton had ordered in her favorite dishes, and they were now awaiting the order whilst Reynolds was preparing to leave. They had agreed the servant would come in three days per week, unless circumstances warranted. Doyle knew Reynolds was pleased with the terms, and she suspected Acton was overpaying him so that he wouldn't mind the part-time schedule. Doyle was content; although she couldn't feel comfortable with any sort of servant, she felt she owed Reynolds a debt she could never repay for his discreet support on that most miserable of days which must not be dwelt upon.

The intercom rang, and the concierge reported that their food order had arrived. Acton explained to Reynolds that the concierge service would then deliver the food; the security in the building did not allow a delivery person to come upstairs.

Reynolds seemed struck by this, and paused in putting on his coat. "I had a rather strange experience today, then—although I had not realized it was strange until now." He then explained that he had heard a key being inserted in the slot for the flat, but the door did not open and when the attempt was made again, the servant—thinking it was Doyle with her hands full—had opened the door.

"A woman stood on the threshold, very surprised to see me, if I may say so. She immediately turned and left; I assumed she was trying the wrong door."

Doyle and Acton looked at each other and came to the same conclusion. "Marta," said Doyle. "She didn't know you've changed the lock so that her key card no longer worked. They must have let her in at the desk; I wonder what she wanted—perhaps she left somethin' here."

"Then why not contact me?" Acton's brows drew together. "I don't like it; I will mention to the desk that she has been fired, and is not to be allowed through."

"Perhaps she is spyin' for your mother," suggested Doyle, who belatedly realized that this may not have been the most politic thing to say in front of Reynolds, who had assumed all the characteristics of a wooden post.

Nodding his dismissal of Reynolds, Acton then called to inform the concierge that neither Marta nor the dowager Lady Acton was to be allowed entrance, and that he was to be contacted immediately in the event of such an attempted visit. Excellent, thought Doyle as she listened; problem solved—although she imagined Reynolds would be more than a match for either of them.

She settled in beside her husband to watch the sunset and make an attempt at dinner, although she wasn't very enthusiastic and mainly entertained herself by using the chopsticks to pinch at Acton's fingers. In response, he used his chopsticks to feed her, as though he was coaxing a child, and she did manage to consume a small amount in this way—mainly because she liked the way his eyes watched her mouth. Her head still ached—although it had receded to a dull throb—and she still had the unholy aching in her joints. She didn't mention it to Acton, though; he would only overreact, and the very last thing she wanted was Dr. Easton pokin' about again.

Teasing, she used the chopsticks to pull at the dark hair on the back of his hand, and with a deft move, he turned his hand and caught the sticks to thwart her, setting them aside. "Until you've had a chance to recover, let's not set any new visits with Timothy and Caroline."

Doyle thought this a little strange coming from Acton, who presumably would like to have the good doctor checking in on her. "I truly don't mind, Michael; Caroline was much better behaved, last time."

With a tilt of his head, he reluctantly confessed, "Caroline has been talking to my mother. She claims she was trying to bring her to terms, but I have asked that she desist."

Ouch, thought Doyle—that's the second time in as many weeks that Acton has reprimanded Caroline, and she can't be likin' that. Placing a gentle hand on his arm, she pointed out, "We can't just drop them, Michael; they're your friends. Recall we were goin' to be patient, so that Caroline can grow accustomed to my alien self. Perhaps we can have a standin' date once a month, instead."

"Perhaps," said Acton with no real conviction. "Tell me about your day—you had a walk-in, I understand."

He'd know, of course—he kept a close eye on her, even from afar. "Yes; I had two encounters that seemed a little strange, and I wanted to tell you about them, in case you're at the root of them. The walk-in seemed to be nothing more than an attention-seeker—he had nothin' to offer, and spoke vaguely of evil Russians. He said he saw me with Williams at the racecourse, but he didn't; not truly."

Acton nodded, well-aware of her truth-detecting abilities. He rarely alluded to it directly, and in turn she rarely alluded to his obsessive condition—a mutual stand-off, so to speak.

"I got the impression he was wary, and I wondered if perhaps he'd had a run-in with you—he saw my last name on the badge and asked if I was married. No priors, though; I couldn't find anythin' amiss. He said he was a racecourse driver, which was true, but mainly he wanted to know what we knew."

"Can you send me a still taken from the CCTV? I'd like to have a look."

"Will do. And the other one was when we were havin' lunch today at the deli; are you familiar with a man named Sergey, a banker from Belarus?"

"No," he said immediately. He had very good recall.

"Well, he came by; he is datin' Munoz, but I got the distinct impression he was alarmed to have met me, but only after he heard my name."

Acton regarded her for a moment, his expression unreadable. "What does he look like?"

"Tall, dark, and handsome; a very fine suit. Lied to Munoz about losin' her number."

"Could be one of a hundred."

She laughed. "Good one; you have to love Munoz."

"How does she know him?"

"She met him comin' in at the entry desk—he was in the wrong building, and she offered directions."

"That is of interest." He rose and began packing up the leftovers, motioning for her to stay seated.

Willing to rest for a bit, she watched him for a moment, moving around the kitchen. "I've been stewin' like a barleycorn, tryin' to find a motive for this turf war—how the Russians fit in."

Acton's voice echoed from within the open fridge. "Perhaps the Russians hoped to simply preside over the rackets from the top, and leave the infrastructure intact."

This was a decent point; as was the case in many organized crime organizations, the fight for control was often at the very top while the foot soldiers that actually ran the rackets were left undisturbed—the only change being who would be given the take. She shook her head. "I don't see it—it's not just about who can wrestle control away; there are some racial overtones." She thought of Thackeray, who didn't even want her under his roof. "Some prejudices are very deep-seated."

Acton paused to rest his gaze upon her. "And how will motive be helpful?" Acton had long-ago taught her that motive was not as important as action and reaction; if no working theory could be put forth, it was best to process the evidence without the distraction of a theory.

She thought about it, tracing a finger on the table. "Just because it doesn't add up, I suppose. And if we could figure out what both sides are up to; we could be one step ahead— maybe stop the next retribution murder."

"Very sound," he agreed, but he was humoring her and she hated it when he humored her. It seemed clear that Acton was not going to tell her about his own theory on the cases or what he knew, and she found that she was not inclined to press him on it. She did not want to analyze why she wasn't inclined to press him, even though it was not in her nature to let it go. She also abandoned any thought of complaining about the missing insect report, courtesy of the stupid SOCO photographer. Now that her brain was functioning again, it was entertaining a niggling worry, and she didn't want to think about it just now—she was still recovering from the last crisis. With this in mind, she changed the subject, and spoke of other things.

CHAPTER 20

DOYLE WAITED WHILE ACTON PREPARED HIMSELF A SANDWICH, smiling to herself. Hates Chinese food, loves me—and sometimes beyond what is reasonable. She recalled Williams's story about Acton's visit to his bedside. "Please don't be too hard on poor Williams."

He brought his food over and sat next to her again. "Are you softening on that subject?"

"Indeed I am," she teased, looking thoughtful. "He's younger than you, and I am thinkin' of linin' him up as husband number two."

"By that time, you are welcome to him."

"Michael," she laughed. "When am I to see a show of jealousy? Some Section Seven you are." Remembering why she raised the subject, she went back on-topic. "After I was sick at the side of the road, he guessed I was pregnant, and so then I had to tell him about the miscarriage. He blamed himself, no thanks to you."

Acton looked as though he wanted to say something, but thought the better of it. She had a glimpse of deep unhappiness, and realized with some remorse that this was a subject she probably shouldn't have brought up—and they'd been doing so well, too. Reaching over, she placed her hand on his. "It was a malfunctionin' blastocyte," she reminded him. "It was no one's fault." Although she said it calmly, she found that her mouth began to tremble, and he immediately pulled her onto his lap and enfolded her in an embrace. "Change the subject, Michael. Please."

"Solonik is in custody," he said, and kissed her head.

This was a spectacular change in subject, and she lifted her head in surprise. "Truly? I hadn't heard."

"Just this evening; he's been booked and we'll soon have a warrant for DNA samples."

"D'you want me at the interrogation?" Together, they performed an excellent pantomime show whereby she sent him secret signals if the witness was not telling the truth.

He rested his chin on her head. "Not as yet—he'll hire some very good solicitors and we have to await them. We can hold him, though—the weapon was illegal." He squeezed her gently. "It was a good catch."

"Thanks to Mr. Thackeray, who is a James Bond fan."

"And to Solonik, who looks the part of a villain."

He began stroking her arms and hands, and it dawned on her that he was moving onto foreplay—which would definitely be a change in subject. He put his mouth on her shoulder only to hear her mobile vibrate on the table top. Lifting it, he checked the ID. "Caroline."

Doyle reached for the mobile. "I'd better take it; we don't want to hurt her feelin's."

Instead, Acton answered. "Caroline, this is Acton." He listened, and said, "She is sleeping, but I will give her the message." He rang off and resumed the movement of his hands. "She wants to meet you for lunch."

Doyle suppressed a groan—Caroline must have heard the sad news about the miscarriage from Timothy. She'd be full of platitudes, and Doyle doubted she could bear it without leaping up and overturning the lunch table. Correctly interpreting her silence, Acton said quietly, "I can tell her you will not be fit for company for a while."

Doyle weighed her options. She couldn't avoid Caroline forever, and the woman couldn't help being annoying, after all—she was one of those people who never realized how others perceived her. "I'll make time over the weekend—that would be easier, I think."

"Don't do it for me."

She placed a placating hand on his chest. "I'll call her tomorrow; I have to demonstrate to you how to be civil, husband."

"Civility is overrated."

Laughing, she shook her head. "That's easy for you to say, my friend—when you are rude everyone thinks you are brilliant and reclusive; if I did the same, I would be criticized as puttin' on airs."

"Why does it matter?"

He seemed genuinely curious, the blue-blooded aristocrat, and she had to smile. "I suppose that's the difference twixt you and me; that it matters."

He leaned in and murmured, his mouth on her neck, "There are other differences."

"Michael," she giggled, "d'ye think of *nothin'* else?"

"No," he admitted.

Leaning her head back, she kissed him. He responded immediately, deepening the kiss and cradling her jaw in his hand. She was almost surprised to realize she didn't much feel like it. Get along with you, Doyle, she told herself sternly; the poor man needs the reassurance of sex, and you can certainly go through the motions and be of comfort to him.

He must have sensed she was not eager, though, because he broke off the kiss and gently pulled her head against his chest again.

"Sorry," she whispered.

"Not at all. We will wait until you are fit for duty."

She lay curled on his lap whilst he resumed stroking her head, which he habitually did when he was worried about her, and a wave of sadness and guilt washed over her. Don't think about it, she commanded herself, and fiddled with the button on his cuff. "Did you ride horses, growin' up?"

"Yes, I did."

"D'you think I could try it sometime?" She had surprised herself with this new ambition whilst she was walking around the stables with Williams.

"Would you like a horse?"

She smiled into his chest. "No, Michael; I do not need a horse. I just wanted to try it, is all."

"Then you shall." He pulled on a strand of her hair and watched it fall to her shoulder. "Have you ever been to the seashore?"

"Never. Recall that I don't swim."

"Brighton was very pleasant; I thought you might like it."

"Are we to be tourin' like an old married couple, then?" she teased.

"I could teach you to swim."

"Oh, I don't know how much learnin' I would do, what wi' your fine torso on display." This pleased him, and she could feel him chuckle. Better, she thought; and I hope I am fit for duty soon—Acton was not one to enjoy abstinence. If only I could feel well again, instead of like a wraith in a witch's tale. On some level, she knew that they were making these idle plans to combat the grief and allay his anxiety about her health—whatever worked; they were not the kind of couple to make idle plans.

"I think you may have to visit Dr. Easton again."

She grimaced. "Give me a few days to recover, Michael. If I go back there I will relapse, I promise you."

He tightened his arms around her. "You couldn't afford to lose much weight to begin with; I feel as though I could break your bones if I squeeze too hard."

"I'm tryin' to eat—I did much better today."

"You are not doing well." He lifted her head with his hand

to meet her eyes seriously, his thumb brushing her cheek. "I'm afraid I must insist."

She sighed. "Aye, then." He was worried, and she shouldn't be such a baby. She was, in truth, a bit worried herself.

That night, the uncontrollable tears came again. Why is it, she thought, that everything that seems bearable during the daylight becomes unbearable in the darkness? She put her hand over her mouth, trying to smother the sobbing so as to not wake Acton, but his arms came around her and he pulled her against him, holding her close while she cried herself into an exhausted sleep.

CHAPTER 21

He convinced himself that he must have been mistaken,
and that the mganga was not in any danger from the
mashetani. Her husband was taking care of her, and was
taking care of him, too. He had enough money now so
that he did not have to work two shifts, and his wife was
so happy. In another month, they would send money to the
family in the old country, and tell them of his good
fortune. He would like to tell them about the red-haired
mganga; they would be astonished. If only he could be
easy, and if only he did not hear the beating of evil wings.

By sheer force of will, Doyle ate breakfast the next
morning and smiled brightly at Aiki when he opened his cab
door for her. She had awakened late that morning, and
Acton was already dressed and ready to leave when he leaned
over her in the bed and studied her as though she were on a
slide under a microscope. Frettin', she thought. She hadn't
slept much, as he well knew.

"I feel much better," she lied. "I'll be in shortly; please
don't worry, Michael." He had already suggested she stay
home and rest, but she was very resistant to the idea and explained to him that such a course of action would only make
her mopey. "I was not born to be a dosser," she explained. "I
would go mad."

He kissed her, and she could see that he wanted to say
something, but changed his mind. "Keep lunch free," was all

he said, and was gone; he had his hands full at work, what with an evil mastermind in custody.

For the love of Mike, she thought in disgust, as she propped up on an elbow; there is nothing physically wrong with you, ridiculous girl, so it must be mental; time to bite on the bit and fight. You don't want to lose Acton to some floozy in the bloom of health, after all—you know they're out there.

At work she took a double dose of aspirin to combat her unflagging headache and settled down with some reluctance to concentrate on the turf war project. She didn't want to address the niggling worry, for fear it would mushroom into a cataclysmic worry, and her poor head could not take a cataclysmic worry, just now.

"DC Doyle, have you seen DC Munoz yet this morning?" Habib asked diffidently from the opening in her cubicle.

Doyle blinked. She hadn't realized Munoz was not in yet. Unfortunately for Habib, he worshipped the beauty from afar, and this sad state of affairs could only end badly for him.

"No," Doyle admitted, and had the sudden certainty that the Belarus boyfriend had absconded with her. This irrational thought was immediately belied by the entrance of Munoz herself, apologizing for her tardiness. She was as cool and composed as usual, but Doyle could sense that she was unhappy.

With an attempt at sternness, Habib reprimanded, "You must report to me if you are coming in late, DC Munoz. Fortunately, there were no field assignments this morning."

Munoz gazed limpidly at him. "I'm so sorry, sir; female troubles."

Habib expressed his complete understanding and sympathy in the manner of the mortified single man, and Doyle shot Munoz a look that was met with a twinkle. Doyle did not approve of the use of feminine wiles to gain an advantage, but Munoz had no such qualms.

"Say, did we ever find out what happened to Owens?" Munoz asked Habib as she set down her rucksack.

Doyle schooled her countenance as she always did when the subject came up. Thankfully, it arose rarely.

"He did not report to work, and no one has heard from him." Habib disapproved of such undisciplined behavior, and did not want to give the mysteriously missing constable another thought.

"Why are you thinkin' of Owens?" asked Doyle against her better judgment. Munoz was not one to engage in idle speculation.

"No reason," said Munoz, as she checked her messages on her mobile. "I just was thinking about him."

This was untrue, and Doyle wondered what had triggered the question. Her own mobile vibrated, and the text said: "Front sidewalk; noon." Doyle smiled.

Observing this, Munoz asked, "What is it?"

"It's makin' a date, I am."

Munoz tossed her hair back and said mulishly, "I'm giving up on dating—an arranged marriage would be miles easier."

This pronouncement was met with much interest by Habib, who asked with forced heartiness, "What has happened Munoz? Surely no one has been unkind to you?"

Munoz hovered on the verge of speaking her mind, but thought better of it. "It's nothing; I'm just annoyed, is all."

"It may be just as well," ventured Doyle. "I was a bit worried about Sergey, what with all the Russian perps lyin' thick on the ground."

Munoz did not appreciate this aspersion being cast on her judgment, and lifted her lip in scorn. "Don't be ridiculous— you must try to control your prejudices, Doyle."

"It is my besettin' sin," agreed Doyle humbly. There; at least she had planted the idea, and Munoz was no fool.

Habib, however, could not conceal his confusion. "Never say you are romantically interested in a perpetrator, Munoz?"

"Report her to Professional Standards," Doyle suggested. "She's a menace."

"Doyle has a date with a superior officer," Munoz returned. "You should report *her*."

"Touché," Doyle acknowledged, rather proud that she had managed to use the word correctly. "You win this round."

Despite this reminder that he had no business angling after an underling, Habib offered, "If you need counseling, Munoz, as your supervisor, I am always available."

Doyle was half-afraid the girl would say something unkind, but instead she presented a sincere face to him. "I appreciate that, sir. I was wondering if you could put in a good word with Public Relations; I'd like to try my hand at it, and I think if I had an interest on the side I would not be so attracted to unsuitable men."

"Indeed," Habib agreed with alacrity. "I will see what I can do."

He hurried away, and Doyle watched him go, all admiration. "That was masterful."

With a self-satisfied smile, Munoz retreated to her cubicle. "Watch and learn, Doyle; watch and learn."

At noon, Doyle took more aspirin and made her way out to the front sidewalk, determined to show a cheerful face to her husband and *eat* something. He wasn't there as yet, but Doyle immediately recognized Father John from St. Michael's, standing near the entry door and holding a parcel. Doyle greeted him with surprise, "Why, hallo, Father; what brings you here?"

"Kathleen," he replied, taking her hand. "Your husband thought you might be needin' some quiet conversation."

Doyle nodded, too overcome to speak; it was exactly what she needed, and trust Acton to know. The priest gazed into her face for a moment, then squeezed her hand. "Shall we go over toward the river, then? Nellie packed us a lunch."

"That would be grand," Doyle whispered when she found her voice. She put her hand in his arm, and as they turned to walk away she lifted her face toward Acton's office, which faced the street—he would be watching. Thank you, she thought.

They settled on a bench, and the priest spoke of the divine plan which mortals perceived only through a glass darkly. Doyle wept, and Father John offered his handkerchief and assured her that her loss was heaven's gain. There was no attempt to speak of blastocytes; only the hard, hard reality of acceptance and faith. The priest held her hands in his while they prayed together, and Doyle felt immeasurably sad and immeasurably comforted at the same time.

After an hour, Doyle wiped her face with the handkerchief and told the priest that she should return to work, and that she appreciated the visit more than she could say. He seemed reluctant to rise, however.

"Kathleen," he began, and she could see that he was troubled. "I must ask that you answer some very delicate questions, and as honestly as you are able."

"Yes, Father." She knit her brow, puzzled by the change in his behavior.

He looked at her very seriously. "Do you trust that husband o' yours?"

She blinked. Whatever she had expected, it wasn't this. "Yes." Best not to mention Acton's other tendencies that were suspect—in the end, she did trust him.

The priest fixed her with his sharp eyes. "Truly?"

"Yes, truly."

He hesitated for a moment. "Could there be another woman, d'ye think?"

Doyle had to hide a smile; Acton had neither time nor energy for an affair—she kept him far too busy. "No, Father; I am certain."

The priest seemed to relax a little, although he frowned slightly. "Certainly, the man seems devoted to you," he mused aloud.

Understatement of the century, thought Doyle.

The other shot her another shrewd glance. "Is there any chance that he doesn't want to be married to you anymore?"

"None at all," answered Doyle honestly. "And what is this about, if I may be askin'?"

The priest leaned back, his brows drawn together, thinking. "Let me pray about it, I'll let you know."

Doyle returned to work, bemused. Now, what was that all about? Had the priest heard some salacious rumor? She was not alarmed; she was assured of Acton's full devotion, and then some. The conversation had invoked another train of thought, however; she was trying to avoid the niggling suspicion that refused to go away, but she knew, in the way that she knew things, that it was past time she took a hard look at these turf war murders in the proper context. Acton's a devoted man, all right, she thought a little grimly. That's the problem.

CHAPTER 22

U PON HER RETURN, DOYLE CHECKED IN WITH ACTON ON HIS
work line and was immediately sent to voice mail. Good; this
meant he had his hands full dealing with prosecutors and
Solonik's solicitors. He would be busy for a bit, which meant
there was no time like the present.

Walking lightly so as to spare her poor head, Doyle made
her way to the Evidence Locker, which held physical evidence
gleaned from pending cases. She pushed her ID card
through the slot to gain entrance, then signed the log while
her photo was checked by the attendant. After inquiry, she
was given the number and location for the cardboard box
that held the evidence from the aqueduct murder, and
walked through the rows of shelves until she came to the
right place. The Evidence Locker was air-conditioned to a
cool temperature which actually felt good to her, even though
she was ordinarily always cold. Resisting an impulse to sit down
and rest on the steel shelf, she opened the evidence box.

The personal effects of the victim, Yuri Barayev, were
stored in a large envelope. The next of kin were in Russia and
no one had come forward to claim them—she remembered
that he was a widower. Doyle looked through his wallet and
jotted down the names from several business cards that
Barayev had tucked therein, all English companies that

sounded financial in nature, but nothing that struck her as strange. One card was a Russian Orthodox icon of Saint Joseph, well-worn around the edges—a religious man, then. She checked the cash voucher, and saw that Barayev had carried an impressive amount of cash, all British denominations. She paused, frowning, because so far there was nothing that leapt out at her as important, but she knew—she knew the items arrayed before her were indeed important, somehow.

A paper copy of the ERU forensics report was included in the plastic sleeve that contained the computer drive, and Doyle pulled it out and read it carefully. There was no time of death, only a twelve-hour estimate. The aqueduct was not the kill site; the murder had taken place elsewhere and the body had been dumped there. There was no insect report, and no indication one had even been requested. The victim's hands had been processed and revealed nothing. There were no wounds or other signs of a defensive struggle before the victim had been shot in the face. There were no stray epithelials or trace fibers, although presumably he had been transported to the aqueduct in a car, and car fibers were notorious for clinging to corpses.

Clean, thought Doyle; cleaner than any normal person walking down the street would be.

The photographs of the victim were included, as well as photographs of the area. Doyle remembered her search with Williams, and was now struck by the fact that the shrubbery on either side of the cement aqueduct was undisturbed. There were no signs that the victim had been thrown or dropped from the bridge—there would have been post-mortem injuries sustained in the fall. So how did the body get there? Doyle paused again, leaning against the shelves and thinking about it. Someone could have carried him up the cement aqueduct for a distance—but one would think there would be evidence of this since there had been no water, this time of year, to wash it away.

Coming to a decision, she straightened up; nothin' for it—she needed to view the scene again. Last time she was there she had been distracted, busy confessing to Acton she was pregnant. The memory evoked a stab of sadness, but it didn't seem as overwhelming, this time. Remember what Father said, she thought; world without end.

With careful, methodic fingers, she reviewed the other evidence, looking for she knew not what, and then reviewed the photographs of miscellaneous items found in the area that may or may not have any connection to the murder. Going through them, she suddenly froze, her scalp prickling, as she realized that she had been half-expecting this. A silver tiepin had been found on the bridge, and Doyle was certain it was Acton's.

She took a deep breath and ignored her headache—which was suddenly much worse—and thumbed through the envelopes until she found the appropriate one, opening it to look within. Yes; there it was. He hadn't been wearing the tiepin the day of the investigation—she was certain; she'd noticed he held his tie back with his hand. She was with him the whole time before he left for Newmarket, and he was never on the bridge that day. Acton, Acton, she thought; what am I to do with you?

Slowly, she shelved the box again as she pondered her next move. The tiepin wasn't engraved; there was nothing to connect it to Acton and even if someone did, they would presume he lost it during the investigation and not when he brought the body there. Suddenly overwhelmed, she pressed her pounding forehead against one of the cold metal brackets that supported the shelves. What was it Habib had said? The two sides in the turf war had lost all objectivity, and were locked in mortal combat. It was as though a raging bonfire had been ignited between the warring tribes, and the CID was conveniently picking up the collateral damage. A bonfire had been ignited.

Her head still pressed against the bracket, she checked the time on her mobile. She needed to view the scene and now was a good time, whilst Acton was dealing with the wily Solonik—not so wily, it turned out; he had come to England, sporting his illegal weapon, even though apparently it was very unlike him—he tended to stay close to home. Here was a puzzle; how had Acton lured him here, to land in the middle of this messy turf war?

She straightened up. No point in wasting time speculating; she needed to review the crime scene whilst Acton was still busy and it was still daylight. There was a problem, though— she needed someone to drive her, and that person should be Williams, as he was her lead on the case. Williams, however, was apparently a loyal foot soldier to the renowned chief in- spector, and he had been remarkably uninterested in solving the aqueduct case, which was not his style at all. And on top of these worries—which were many and sundry—she was also reluctant to spend time alone with him again. After viewing the problem from all angles, she decided there was nothin' for it; it would be very odd indeed if she went to the scene without Williams knowing about it. Not to mention it would be a nightmare for her to get to the aqueduct using public transportation—she didn't dare drive a car such a distance on the highway. She really needed to practice her driving; mental note. After leaving the Evidence Locker, she scrolled up Williams on her mobile, and he promptly answered.

"Hey."

"Hey yourself. Any chance you are free to be visitin' the aqueduct scene this afternoon?"

He didn't miss a beat. "Certainly, if you'd like."

"I just wanted to figure out how the body was deposited on the site. It might lead to some clues."

"Good idea," he said, although he truly thought it wasn't. "Meet me at the garage?"

"Grand." After ringing off, she mentally sighed as she made

her way to the utility garage. Faith, she didn't want to be alone with Williams and forced to fend off the drama—she'd much rather be home with Acton and creating a little drama of her own, preferably beating him with a rolling pin.

When she arrived at the garage, Williams was already unlocking an unmarked. She slid into the car and said, "I appreciate it, on such short notice. I was lookin' at the evidence and I couldn't figure out how the body was dumped."

"Let's take a look," he said easily. There was a pause while they drove for a bit. "How are you feeling?"

Here we go, thought Doyle. "Horrible," she said shortly. That should discourage any further discussion. She immediately repented, feeling childish. "And you?"

"Slightly less than horrible."

Doyle couldn't suppress a smile. "We're a pair, aren't we?" She realized belatedly that she probably shouldn't put it in those terms—honestly, she had to watch her tongue. "Do you take insulin?"

"Yes," he replied in a tone that discouraged any further questions.

She sighed. "There's nothin' worse than havin' your private weaknesses made public, is there?"

He thought about it. "It would be worse if there was no one to tell; no one to help you."

She turned to consider him. "Don't you be goin' all wise on me, Williams; I'm intent on sulkin'."

He smiled as he drove. "Be my guest."

After a few more minutes of silence, he ventured, "At the risk of being snubbed again, I want to point out that you don't look well enough to be at work."

She found she didn't have the wherewithal to snub him. "I feel hideous. I am seein' the doctor tomorrow."

His concern was palpable, and he glanced over at her. "Should we call it a day, then? Can I drive you home?"

"After we take a look, you may." Good try, she thought, although he was sincerely worried about her; she could feel it. Every man jack I meet wants to wrap me in cotton wool, she thought; little do they know that I am on to them and their wily ways. Reminded, she texted her symbol to Acton, checking in with him as she did every hour. She had considered leaving her mobile behind so that Acton couldn't keep track of her through the GPS, but there was no shame in investigating the aqueduct murder scene. She gazed out the window and decided that if it made her wayward husband a little uneasy, that was not necessarily a bad thing.

CHAPTER 23

DOYLE AND WILLIAMS ARRIVED AT THE AQUEDUCT SCENE AND parked. After emerging from the car, Williams removed his suit coat and then opened the boot of the car to grab a field kit. Doyle thought to lighten the mood, being as this field trip must be a sticky wicket for DS Williams, who in his own way was as loyal to Acton as she was. "Do you note that I'm not callin' you 'sir'?"

He slung the field kit over his shoulder. "I appreciate it."

"Habib would skin me."

He glanced at her and slammed the boot shut. "No, he wouldn't; Habib is afraid of you."

This was of interest, as she had not gained that impression. "Afraid of me? Because of Acton?"

"No." Williams hesitated. "Because you know things."

Indeed, she did—and sometimes better late than never. With a shrug, she tried to joke it off. "He thinks I'm the Hindu equivalent of a witch, then?"

"Something like that."

"Good to know." She relapsed into silence—the last thing she wanted was to discuss her intuitive abilities with this particular superior officer.

They began walking the gravel road that led to the aqueduct, and after a moment she ventured, "Takin' my own chances of bein' snubbed again, I hope you are bein' more careful with your health."

"I am. I've learned my lesson."

"And a frightenin' lesson it was, my hand on my heart. Has somethin' like that happened before?"

She could see he was trying to decide whether to discuss it—touchy about his condition, he was. "Nothing that bad. I was not taking care of myself."

Oh-oh, she thought; we are wandering back into Doyle-broke-my-heart territory. "If we are to be workin' together," she said in a brisk tone, "I should be kept informed. As it was, I had to rifle your wallet."

"I *am* missing some money," he teased, glancing down at her.

"I had to pay for your Guinness," she teased back. "And the orange juice, to boot."

They smiled at each other. Better, she thought as their footsteps crunched in the gravel; I believe all that crackin' awkwardness is nearly gone. She rather hoped they could be friends—as a result of knowing the things she knew, Doyle did not have any close friends. It was no easy thing, to be aware of the insincerity of others, or when they were trying to pull a fast one, with DS Williams being an excellent case in point.

"My mother enjoyed meeting you, even though the circumstances were not the best."

"Your mother is a very nice person." Best not to mention she mistook Doyle for a potential daughter-in-law.

He gave her a hand as they stepped over the rocky edging that separated the road from the aqueduct. "Does your mother still live in Dublin?"

"No; my mother died over a year ago." Doyle thought she delivered this information in a neutral tone, but Williams put his hand on her arm, contrite.

"I am so sorry; I seem to be saying the wrong thing repeatedly today."

She looked at him and mustered a half-smile. "Whist, don't be sorry—I am in a crackin' foul mood, is all." With good reason, she added mentally. As well you know, my friend.

"Do you want to stop and rest? We can sit on a rock for a minute."

She teased him. "Faith, Williams; do I truly look that bad?"

He smiled. "Yes." He was not embarrassed this time. "You look completely knackered, and I have half a mind to put you on my back and carry you."

"Please refrain." Although he did have a very fine body, did DS Williams. She glanced at him sidelong, and wondered if she would have fancied Williams if Acton hadn't gotten to her first. Perhaps, but it would have been slow going; Williams would never have wrestled her to the altar as Acton had.

They came to the footbridge over the aqueduct, and Doyle leaned on the railing, pausing to catch her breath. She then walked halfway across—where the tiepin had been—to consider the scene below for a few long moments, Williams standing beside her. Aloud, she reflected, "I was thinkin' that someone may have carried the victim up the floor of the aqueduct for a distance to stick him in the conduit, but it seems unlikely, lookin' at it. There is no access road for a half mile, and there would have been evidence—footprints, or tamped down leaves along the way."

"I see what you mean," he agreed. "And the shrubbery wasn't disturbed on either side, so there must have been another means of access."

Doyle took the bull by the horns, her intuition tuned on Williams like a laser beam. "Actually, I'm thinkin' the body was lowered from this bridge by some sort of sling—somethin' that didn't leave rope marks. It's the only way that makes sense, the evidence bein' what it is."

Williams nodded, but she could feel he was suddenly very wary, which told her she was on the right track. Doyle leaned out to inspect the underside of the railing, even though the movement worsened her headache. "There is some slight scratchin'," she observed, indicating with a finger. "Not somethin' that could be easily explained, in such a place—it is not as though the railin' is used for anythin'."

Williams dutifully leaned over to observe. "Yes—some friction has definitely been applied."

She glanced at him. "A lot of trouble to take, one would think."

"Yes," he agreed. He offered nothing further.

Doyle scrutinized the cement floor of the aqueduct, fifteen feet beneath them. "And not a convenient dump site; I think it was deliberately chosen to obscure the time of death. A very careful killer, also; the body was completely clean."

"So it would seem."

Enough, thought Doyle; I know what I need to know—except for one more thing. "I am wonderin' if there is a connection between the victim and our Mr. Solonik."

Williams did not respond for a moment, and Doyle almost felt sorry for him, but then remembered that obstruction of justice was a felony, and she shouldn't be feeling sorry for him at all. Of course, she couldn't grass on Williams without grassing on her exasperating husband, but still and all, it was a matter of principle. With some impatience, she chided, "Thomas Williams; recall that I am knackered, and if you make me spend an hour researchin' this, I am likely to keel over in my cubicle. Tell the truth and shame the devil."

Williams related with no emotion, "He was Solonik's brother-in-law; he was married to Solonik's sister, before she died."

She blinked in surprise; that this very significant fact was nowhere to be found in the notes spoke of a thorough scrubbing of the files. She rested her gaze on the cement below them, unwilling to force Williams to reveal anything further, and in truth, it was hardly necessary. Acton had instituted this turf war—probably by murdering the first two victims and then standing back so as to allow nature to take its course. Then he'd lured Solonik—the main target of this retribution plot—to England by murdering his brother-in-law. Perhaps it was the only bait that could have lured him; the two Russian men must have been close. This was why Barayev was shot in the face—to send a brutal message of vengeance. And presumably, now that Solonik was in custody, some of his DNA or other trace evidence would find its way into that cardboard evidence box, so that the Russian would be framed for his brother-in-law's murder—icing on the vengeance cake. Only Acton had the stick by the wrong end—thanks to her—and this was exactly why the nuns taught you that even little lies have big consequences. He was taking a vengeance because she had lied to him; on that never-to-be-forgotten night, she'd told him that raving-lunatic Owens was working for Solonik because she didn't want to tell him the real reason— and now look what she'd done. There was nothin' for it; she must make a clean breast of it to her husband, and remedy the situation as best she could, although unfortunately the situation seemed without remedy. I tried to outfox Acton, she thought; I should have known that I was not up to the task.

Williams's voice cut into her somber thoughts. "He may have been keeping a clean profile, Doyle, but Barayev was a bad actor. He was directly responsible for a lot of misery in the world."

This was little consolation. "Murder is murder, Williams."

"Not always," he replied, and meant it.

She looked up at him and quirked her mouth. "Careful— that's what the fair Munoz said, too."

But it was no time for humor, apparently, and Williams did not smile. "Come on, I'll take you back."

They drove back to London as the light was fading—in a strange way, she was relieved not to have the niggling worry anymore, but her thoroughly Catholic soul was troubled by the current dilemma. Vigilantism was not to be condoned, no matter the ultimate good; if the rule of law was not respected, then only those with power would prevail, and the powerless would ultimately suffer. Law enforcement officers always walked a fine line to begin with; it was so tempting to arrange matters—or to intimidate others—so that the perceived correct result would be achieved, and again, to hold such power was dangerous, regardless of the purity of the motive. She could not be easy with what Acton had wrought, here; retribution was best left to God, whose motives were never suspect.

She and Williams did not speak on the way home. He knows that I know, she thought, and neither one of us dares to discuss it. She gave an inward sigh; it was so tiresome to guard what one said—and indeed, that is what got her into this mess to begin with.

Williams dropped her off at her building and watched as she went through the revolving door to the lobby. What are the odds he's calling Acton right now, she thought; I wouldn't take a bet on it.

She was exhausted and emotionally drained as she rode up the lift. She knew that Acton was already there; he wanted her to have an early night. Frettin', she thought; I'll fret him one, I will.

CHAPTER 24

WHEN DOYLE ENTERED THE FLAT, HOWEVER, IT WAS TO DIS-
cover that Acton was to be given a reprieve in the form of a
visitor. Father John and Acton were seated before the fire,
drinking scotch, and Acton rose to greet her, approaching to
kiss her cheek. He paused. "What is it?"

"It can wait," she replied, and hoped this was true—although surely, as long as he was here with her he was not ar-
ranging to murder people, left and right. Or one would
think.

"I thought we were to go to Candide's," he chided her gently as he helped her remove her coat.

"I completely forgot; I was too busy sleuthin'. Has Williams
reported?"

"No."

It was the truth. Interesting, she thought—Williams is
going to stay well out of it. Perhaps he has divided loyalties;
after all, his mother likes me. "Is it instruction night?" Occasionally Father John and Acton met at the flat for Acton's instruction; more often they met at the church.

"No; he wanted to come speak to both of us."

Reminded of the probing questions the priest had asked at
the end of lunch, Doyle found this to be ominous—faith, it
never rained but it poured—and indeed, it seemed the cler-

gyman was not his usual self as he rose to meet her. "Kathleen; I'm sorry to be disturbin' you at home."

"Not at all, Father; I'm that glad to see you again."

"Come sit down," suggested Acton, and Doyle could only sink gratefully into the sofa next to her husband, resisting an urge to put her head in his lap like a child, and sleep away every unsolvable problem.

The priest hesitated, and Doyle could see that he was deeply troubled. "I am not certain how to go about broachin' the subject."

Oh-oh, thought Doyle, and remembered his questions about Acton's fidelity. Merciful God, she pleaded; no more bad news, please—a body can only bear so much. She sat up straighter and sidled closer to Acton. No matter what, she thought as she firmly took his hand in both of hers, I'm his wife and I love him.

Acton glanced at her in surprise before addressing the clergyman with his best interrogation technique. "Why don't we start with explaining what you were doing, and then we can explore what it was you saw and heard."

"Oh," said the priest, startled. "It's not that I'm a witness, or anythin'. Well, not in a manner of speakin', anyway."

Doyle reminded herself that she should not be impatient with a man of the cloth, even if he was taking forever to get to the point and it was something very bad—she could feel it. She clung to Acton's hand and closed her eyes to ward it off, whatever it was.

"I hope you're not thinkin' I'm a foolish old man," Father John continued, apologetic. "I read a lot of mysteries and it puts ideas in my head, sometimes."

"What is it, then?" prompted Doyle, who had opened her eyes because she was thinking rather optimistically that this didn't much sound like an adultery speech, thanks be to God.

"I'm wonderin'," said the priest, "if Kathleen is bein' poisoned." There was a profound silence for a moment, whilst

Doyle stared at the priest in astonished silence. "Look at her nail beds," the clergyman urged Acton.

Acton snatched up her hands and walked over to the floor lamp, Doyle necessarily following. He studied them under the bright light. *"Christ,"* he breathed.

"You mustn't blaspheme, Michael." And in front of a priest, no less. She tried to look around her husband at her nails, which were bitten embarrassingly short.

Acton pulled her around without ceremony and held her face to the light, turning up her eyelids one at a time whilst she winced from the brightness. He then held her head in both his hands; closed his eyes and pressed his forehead to hers. Rattled, he was, and he was not one who was easily rattled. Gently she placed her hands on his arms and squeezed them. "It's all right, Michael; it's a hardy banner I am, and I'm goin' to be fine." I hope, she added silently. She was shaken herself, but had to put on a brave front for her husband, who had a tendency—apparently—to overreact when something went badly for her.

Father John stood at a small distance, bewildered. "Who would be wantin' to do such a thing?"

Acton pulled back to look at her, carefully shuttering his reaction. She knew they both harbored the same thought; the dowager Lady Acton had been at the flat, unsupervised. He replied, "I don't know. We should isolate the source and perhaps that will be indicative—it may be the result of a mistake." He didn't believe this, and neither did she.

"I haven't been eatin' much lately." She thought about it. "Mainly the lattes at work, the ginger tea, and the cereal."

"Any of which I don't eat," Acton pointed out. "It must be one or a combination of them. We will have them tested."

"Will you be callin' the police?" asked Father John, equal parts horrified and fascinated.

They both looked at him in silence. "We *are* the police," Doyle pointed out gently.

"Of course, of course—forgot for a moment," said the priest in flustered apology. "All the excitement."

Excitement is not what we need, thought Doyle. "Father, it may be best to say nothin' of this until we know a bit more."

"Kathleen is right," Acton agreed. "We may need to set up a trap and seizure, if someone is attempting murder. We shouldn't let him know we are on to him."

Father John completely understood this strategy, as it was a common ploy in murder mysteries. "Not a word," he agreed, nodding.

Doyle assured him, "As soon as we know somethin', I will bring you up to speed." Hopefully there would be no need to bear false witness to a priest, which must be some sort of double sin.

Acton explained they needed to seek immediate medical attention, and Father John took his cue to leave. They saw him out the door, Doyle embracing him as Acton thanked him for his sharp work.

"Thank yourself," said the priest practically. "If you hadn't called me I wouldn't have had the chance to notice." He paused and put a hand on Doyle's arm. "I'll be prayin', lass."

"Go raibh maith agat, Athair."

As soon as he shut the door, Acton pulled Doyle into his arms, holding her so hard it was difficult to breathe. She cautioned, "Don't forget that you can break my bones."

He loosened his grip, but she had a quick impression of fury, white-hot and frightening in its intensity. The last time she'd seen such a glimpse, the ensuing wreckage saw the demise of half the criminals in greater London. "I'm goin' to be fine, Michael. Truly."

He buried his mouth in the side of her neck and murmured against it, "How did I miss this?"

"We assumed it was the pregnancy makin' me sick," she said soothingly, stroking his back and hoping he'd ease up a bit, or her fingernails would be even bluer. "You'd have noticed, sooner or later." She could only imagine his chagrin; he studied her constantly, and he must feel that he had failed her.

"What now?" she asked, trying to sound matter-of-fact. No need to point out that the next step needed careful consideration.

He was thinking, and had thankfully loosened his grip. "First, we need to assess the damage; you may need treatment."

She nodded. "Do we keep it private, or go to the hospital?" She had a feeling that she already knew the answer.

"We'll ask Timothy."

She made a sound of acute embarrassment. "He'll think you married a walkin' disaster, Michael."

But Acton had already pulled his mobile. "We need to keep it quiet, but you must be examined immediately."

This was unarguable, and she bowed to the inevitable. "All right, then; ask him if we can get some sort of discount."

Acton met her eyes, but she could see that he didn't appreciate this attempt at gallows humor. Don't be flippant, she cautioned herself; he's hiding it now, but he's still simmering on the edge of an eruption, and if he does erupt, Katy bar the door. To soothe him, she began gently stroking his arm, in a manner similar to his own as he waited for Timothy to pick up.

"Tim, can you come over at your earliest convenience?" Acton glanced at Doyle when listening to the response. "No; no need for the surgery kit this time."

Doyle suppressed an inappropriate urge to giggle; God only knew what Timothy thought was going on over here at the House of Acton.

"He'll be over." Acton lifted her hand from his arm and kissed it. "Come into the kitchen, I imagine that milk is a good idea."

"Unless it's poisoned," Doyle cautioned. "I put milk in my cereal, and you don't drink it a'tall."

This gave him pause. "Water, then; and plenty of it."

He sat across from her whilst she obediently drank a large glass of water without protest; she was shaken by the discovery but was trying to bear up so that Acton didn't run amok. He watched her, his dark brows drawn together. "I wish I knew how long."

"Not long, Michael," she assured him. "My symptoms changed; I started gettin' a splittin' headache, and my bones would ache." She thought about it. "Less than a week, I think."

There was a small pause while he regarded her with an unreadable expression. "You didn't tell me this."

"No." She found that she didn't want to explain why she hadn't wanted to tell him; he hated any sort of discussion about his condition, and the last thing she wanted, just now, was a discussion about his condition since she may be forced to confess about Solonik and she *truly* wasn't up to it. Not yet.

He regarded her for a silent moment, and she had the lowering conviction that he knew exactly what she was thinking. You are a coward, she chastised herself—you are married to this man, and you mustn't tiptoe around him.

"A week," he repeated, breaking the silence, and she knew neither of them wanted to say what was uppermost in their minds—the wicked dowager had visited about a week ago. Doyle pointed out, "Marta would know the items that only I would be eatin' and Marta didn't like me much."

"So Marta may or may not have acted alone."

Doyle thought the same thing and was silent. She wondered what Acton would do if it could be shown unequivocally that his mother had tried to murder her.

"And Marta tried to get back in yesterday."

She had forgotten about this. "Holy Mother," breathed Doyle. "Another dose, d'ye think?"

"Or an attempt to remove the evidence; we will soon know. I intend to visit Marta tomorrow to seek some answers."

There was no question he was fit to murder—which was not

a good thing, as apparently he was well-practiced. "Then I should come also, Michael, so we know if she's lyin'."

He looked like he might protest, but finally had to agree with the wisdom of this plan. "Right. I have her address—assuming she still lives with her cousin and has not yet returned to Trestles. We can go in the morning."

They conferred, and decided to tell Timothy that Doyle had shown symptoms but they weren't certain of the source. Acton said he would take samples into the forensics lab early tomorrow and when she looked up in alarm, he assured her that he had someone at the lab that would do the testing off the record for him. So, she thought with interest as she examined her bitten-and-blue fingernails; there were other loyal foot soldiers—aside from Williams—scattered about the Met. And small wonder he wanted to keep it off the record; it was entirely possible that his mother was poisoning his wife. Faith, thought Doyle; like a Greek play, it was.

CHAPTER 25

TIMOTHY APPEARED IN SHORT ORDER, LOOKING CALM AND GENIAL, and as though being called to address yet another home-bred emergency at Oakham Mount Mansions was completely routine. He became quite serious, however, when the situation was explained. "Poison?" He stared at Acton, incredulous, but Acton only nodded.

"She has the symptoms, and has been doing poorly."

Timothy immediately regained his composure. "I see. Well then; let's have a look." He walked briskly to the kitchen to wash his hands, and Doyle was reminded that he handled all manner of strange cases at his free clinic; it probably took a lot to shock him.

"Am I back on the sofa?" she asked nervously. She hated doctors, but did not hate Timothy, so she harbored mixed emotions.

"Please sit here right here, Kathleen—under the light."

Pulling up a chair, he examined her, gently probing along her throat with his fingers and taking a look under her eyelids as Acton had.

"Have you had any secretions from your nose?"

"No—not to speak of."

He reached in his bag for one of those things with the light bulb to look down her throat. Thus far, he had given no indication that he was going to give her a shot, and she was cautiously optimistic that no needles were slated to make an appearance.

"Have you felt confused, or unable to concentrate?"

"No more than my usual," she teased, and he smiled in response, but she could tell he was alarmed beneath his kindly manner.

He applied to Acton. "Have you noticed any problem with her mental faculties?"

"Not at all."

The doctor sat back in his chair, regarding her. "That's good news; it does not appear to be anything that attacks the nervous system. Arsenic, maybe; or an organophosphate pesticide. It could be the devil to figure out how you got it."

Doyle and Acton carefully did not look at each other.

"I'll take some blood and hair follicles for testing, just to verify, but you are right, she does have the symptoms." The doctor glanced at Acton. "A blind test; no names."

"No need," said Acton. "I will make the arrangements for testing."

"Timothy," Doyle ventured in a small voice. "Is the blood test truly necessary?"

"Perhaps not," said Acton immediately.

But Timothy took her hand in his. "I should do a multiple screen, Kathleen; I must rule out liver damage, and check for other indicators."

"Oh." For the first time, she felt the prickling of tears. Don't cry, you knocker, she chastised herself; you've been poisoned, for heaven's sake.

"Don't watch." Acton gathered her up into his arms and she ducked her head into his chest, gritting her teeth while the tourniquet was deftly twisted around her arm. I am such a baby about this, she thought; and rubbed her face back and forth on Acton's shirt when the needle pinched. I think it comes of feeling that I am a fortress, or something, and I don't much like being breached. Unless it is Acton, doing the breaching in bed, of course. This seemed such a profound thought that she almost forgot her present misery.

"Almost finished," said Timothy.

I tend to stay very much within myself, she realized, because of the—of the gift, or the sight, or whatever it is; but Acton scaled my walls and planted his flag despite this, and I am very happy he did. We are alike, in that way; he stays within himself too—even with me—but he is in turn very happy I breached his walls. We will sort this marriage business out, between us; we are not your ordinary mister and missus, after all.

"Well done; do you need to lie down?"

"I am fine, Timothy. Truly."

She disentangled from Acton while the good doctor rooted around in his bag. "Good—I have some charcoal tablets in my kit—rarely see the need for them, of course. Take them—it can't hurt—and it will also help to eat sulfur products; eggs and such." He paused. "Best not to eat any of the food on hand; I imagine something is tainted and until we know, don't take any risks."

Acton nodded. "I will take care of it, Tim."

The doctor reached to take Doyle's hand again. "Please don't be alarmed; as long as there is no damage to the organs—and I don't believe there is—this type of thing will clear up in no time."

Mustering up a smile, she assured him that he relieved her no end.

He had not made any reference to her miscarriage, but now offered, "I haven't had a chance to offer my sympathy for your sad loss, Kathleen; I'm so sorry."

"Thank you," she said softly. "So am I."

Acton swiftly interceded to engage the doctor in a conversation about a his caseload, and Doyle thought with relief that she would hear sympathy from only one person more, and then she could be done with it. With a stab of guilt, she offered, "I must call Caroline—I have neglected her."

"Don't worry about Caroline," Timothy assured her. "She's a brick."

Yes, Caroline was a brick and they were lucky that they have each other, thought Doyle. She wondered why neither had married, as they were about Acton's age, in their late thirties. Caroline could be a little trying, but some men liked that type of officious, managing woman, and as for Timothy, not only was he a kind man, he was a doctor, to boot. Of course, Timothy had little chance for romance, with Caroline constantly about, but if any of the four friends had wanted to make a push to get married, presumably it would have happened. Yet again, she tried to imagine a young Acton, attending classes at university and becoming the man he was today, but fell short in this exercise. Perhaps it was because he never spoke of his past, his family, or even his estate, and she respected his fortress in the same way he respected hers. She knew instinctively that she made him vulnerable, and so was very reluctant to press him; to use her power to control him. On the other hand, murder was murder—despite what everyone else seemed to think—and she should make a push to curb some of his more bloodthirsty tendencies.

They thanked the doctor and saw him out; then Doyle made ready for bed while Acton gathered samples from the food in the pantry to be tested tomorrow, his movements quick and efficient as he worked in silence. He wanted to be busy, she could sense, and although his manner was carefully controlled, beneath it all simmered the white-hot rage. She waited for him, thinking she'd have to tell him about raving-lunatic Owens soon, but not just yet; tomorrow was soon enough. They had already wrestled with a basketful of drama tonight, and mainly she wanted to soothe him; he was in a state, was her husband.

As Doyle watched him from the bed, she realized that she felt relieved in a strange way. There was a good reason for her recent misery; it wasn't just her body showing an exasperating frailty. And God had not broken faith with her; an evildoer had interceded. Doyle may not understand God's mysterious purpose, but she could well-and-away understand murder; it was her job, after all. She fell asleep before Acton came to bed, and for the first time in a week, slept the night through.

CHAPTER 26

He remembered how his grandmother was mganga, and his father did not allow her to live in the house with them because of it. Then, when the Hutu came, she was one of the ones killed, because she was alone and there was no one to defend her. He was very young at the time, and he learned you should not speak of mganga, or else no one would defend you.

THE NEXT MORNING DOYLE WOKE EARLY TO FIND ACTON LEANing over her, dressed and ready. She remembered their plan to call upon the traitorous Marta, and said sleepily, "I'll be ready in two shakes, Michael."

"No, you have time yet. I wanted to tell you I'm delivering the samples to the lab and then I'll be back—I wanted to get her started on the testing before the other personnel came in."

So; his operative in the lab is female, like Fiona, thought Doyle. I hope she doesn't think she'll fulfill the same role in his personal life; not on my watch, she won't.

He continued, "I researched the poisons that Timothy mentioned; as long as it's caught early enough, you should have a complete recovery. The liver scan will give us an indication, and he'll let us know as soon as he can review the results."

Sitting up so that the sheet fell away, she pulled his head toward hers to kiss him. "I'll be fine, Michael." He was still in a state, and in an attempt to distract him she held his head in her hands for a moment in invitation, but for once the sight of her naked form did not ignite a heated reaction, and he gently removed her hands, kissing her palms one at a time before he left. She watched him go and worried; she'd best hang on to his coat tails for awhile until he calmed down.

Doyle showered and dressed, feeling remarkably better already. Her appetite continued absent, which was just as well because everything in the kitchen was now under quarantine. A respectful knock at the door reminded her of another complication; Reynolds had arrived. Best consult with Acton. She opened the door to the domestic with a bright smile. "Good mornin' Reynolds; please don't go into the kitchen until I've had a chance to ring up Acton."

"Very good, madam," said Reynolds with a slight bow, as if this were an ordinary request. A very fine sort of servant, Doyle thought, and not for the first time.

She phoned Acton and he answered immediately, as he usually did when she called his private line, unless he was doing something uninterruptable. "Michael, Reynolds is here."

There was a pause while he thought about it. "Do you think he can be trusted?"

She thought about it in turn; she hadn't entertained any qualms about Reynolds thus far, and her instinct was usually very accurate. "I do."

"Then tell him as little as you can; we'll need new food and he should be made aware. Warn him of Marta."

"Right then; shall I meet you downstairs?"

"Yes, twenty minutes."

She rang off and walked over to where Reynolds was organizing cleaning supplies. "Reynolds," she began, "We believe somethin' in the kitchen is poisonous, and Acton is havin' the food tested to see what it is."

He straightened up and looked at her, then folded his hands across the front of his apron. "I am very sorry to hear of it, madam."

"I would appreciate it if you would dispose of all the food and replace it; Acton has already taken samples."

"Very good, madam."

She added as an afterthought, "Best wear gloves. Don't eat anything."

"No," he agreed with a little nod of his head.

Trying to appear matter-of-fact, she continued, "We believe the woman you saw at the door may be responsible, and since you saw her here, you may be in danger. If you see her again be very careful; don't allow her to be alone with you." She could easily picture Marta braining him with a frying pan when his back was turned; Marta was a wily one.

The servant continued unperturbed. "Thank you for the warning, madam. I will be careful."

Doyle went downstairs to meet Acton out front. Aiki was leaning against his cab, waiting for her, and he smiled his flashing smile. "Not today, Aiki," she explained. "My husband is comin'." She should learn how to say a few phrases in French; it would be a friendly gesture to this nice man who was always so nice to her. She had made great strides with her English vocabulary since she met Acton; no reason to stop there.

Acton pulled up to the curb and Aiki hurried over to open the door for Doyle, saluting Acton with a gesture. She smiled her thanks and said to Acton as she slid into the car, "Perhaps you could teach me a few things in French to be sayin' to him."

"Better he improved his English."

"I don't think he understands my English very well, though."

"Better you improved your English."

She punched his arm lightly as he drove away. "There is nothin' wrong with my English, my friend. It is everyone else who has a very strange accent."

He nodded but said nothing. Not good, she thought, and redoubled her efforts. "Fine, don't help; but then all I will be able to say to him is *beaux yeux*."

This managed to inspire a half-smile. "I would appreciate it if you didn't encourage your cab driver to proposition you."

She laughed, in part because it was rather funny and in part because she wanted him not to feel like a volcano about to erupt. "He's got a wife and baby—I've interpreted that much. And I get the feelin'—" here she frowned, trying to decide what she was trying to say, "I get the feelin' he is a little afraid of me; or afraid *for* me, or somethin'."

Alert, Acton looked over. "Do you think he's a danger to you?"

"Oh, no," she said with certainty, then shook her head. "I don't know what I'm thinkin', Michael, but I like him very much. I feel that we are both strangers in a strange land, together, if that makes any sense."

"Have a care, is all."

"I will, Michael. I am feelin' much better." She had the distinct impression, as a matter of fact, that she was feeling much better than he.

He took an assessing look at her, but the planes of his face did not soften as they usually did when he looked at her. "Yes, I think you are recovering already."

"I am; I think a lot of it is mental—knowin' it's all over." After a small pause, she put her hand on his arm. "It's over, Michael."

"No," he said in an implacable tone. "It is not over."

"We may not like where this leads, my friend."

He glanced at her, and she saw that he was carefully hiding his emotions. "I can assure you that whoever is responsible will not like where this leads, either."

Faith, she thought; there's going to be no one left in London, if this keeps up. "I think we need to speak about what's to be done, and come to an agreement together."

"No," he said, and meant it.

"It won't be a discussion," she promised. "We'll just decide together."

"I'm afraid this is not a subject that is open for a non-discussion, Kathleen."

Trying to tease him, she insisted, "I'm the one who was poisoned, and forgiveness is a virtue."

"I will take that under advisement."

Simmering, she thought in dismay; almost to a boil, he was. "Michael, I'm thinkin' of myself here; if you wind up in prison, the conjugal visits will be few and far between."

"I will keep that to mind, also," he answered evenly.

She lapsed into silence, and wished she knew how to handle this—she very much feared he was descending into another black mood, as he had done when Fiona was murdered. It was a chilling and fearsome thing, and she'd felt helpless against it—all the more because she felt it so acutely. I should try to stay with him, she thought; he does better when I am present, I think.

They drove to the middle-class residential area where Marta's cousin lived, and found the address. A woman answered the door, took one look at Acton, and was immediately defensive. Can't blame her, thought Doyle; he'd scare the cows out of milk, he would. Acton showed his warrant card, and asked to speak to Marta.

"She is not here."

Doyle brushed her hair back, which was her signal to Acton that the woman was not telling the truth. He paused, debating. They were not here in an official capacity and had to be careful; they dared not behave in a way that could draw a complaint to the CID. He pulled his card from his wallet and handed it to the woman, who was clearly reluctant to accept it. "It is important that I speak with her as soon as possible. Please have her contact me at her earliest convenience."

They drove to work in silence. His mobile rang, and he checked the ID and took the call. "Acton," he said, and listened. He rang off, and then said quietly. "It was the cereal."

Acutely dismayed, Doyle breathed, "Holy Mother of God." Although she had guessed as much, it was a shock to have it confirmed and it also made it clear the poison was administered by someone who knew that Doyle loved frosty flakes and Acton never touched them; aside from the two of them, only Marta would know this. Doyle suddenly found she sympathized with Acton's foul mood—it was a despicable act, for the love o' Mike. And Acton was right; it seemed unlikely that Marta would have decided to do it alone; if she hated Doyle that much she would have simply quit and gone back to Trestles. Unless she was nicked, amended Doyle; there was plenty of that going around, too.

Once at the Met, they came to the lifts in the lobby, Acton still distracted and Doyle worried about his state of mind. "Can I work from your office, perhaps? Or can we meet for lunch in a couple of hours?" She bestowed upon him her most beguiling smile.

Unfortunately, it didn't have much of an effect. "Solonik is to be interrogated; I will text you if I am free."

This was of interest. "Do you want me in the gallery, to listen in?" The gallery had a one-way mirror that allowed someone to listen in, unseen.

"Not necessary at this point; but I will text you if you are needed."

But now she knew that the summons would never come; he'd keep her well away from it, because he didn't want her to know that Solonik's protestations of innocence were, in fact, true.

"Be certain to eat," he reminded her, and watched her step into the lift.

CHAPTER 27

DOYLE WAS ACTUALLY FEELING A BIT PECKISH, AND DECIDED TO take the current while it served and visit the canteen before descending to her cubicle. After wandering in, she looked over the offerings and for some reason the prepackaged fruit pies looked delicious, even though she'd never had one before. Making up for lost calories, she thought. She bought a cherry pie and was tucking into it when her mobile rang, the ID showing it was home. "Hallo?" she answered, licking her fingers—faith, these things were *crackin'* good.

"Madam," said Reynolds. "I am very sorry to disturb you at work."

"Not at all, Reynolds," she replied. "What's afoot?"

"The concierge desk has phoned to say there is a plant left for you downstairs by florist's delivery."

She remembered her warning to him. "Do you think it is suspicious, then? Who is it from?"

"It is from the dowager Lady Acton, madam."

Doyle froze, the pie forgotten. Reynolds obviously remembered her comment and didn't think the dowager would be delivering floral tributes to Doyle. Neither did Doyle.

"Don't go get it, Reynolds. Stay where you are until further notice, please, and don't let anyone in."

"Yes, madam. Please let me know if I can be of further assistance."

Saints and *holy* angels, thought Doyle as she rang off. Their building ran all incoming packages through a screener—which was an unfortunate but routine reality in this day and age—but this was a seemingly harmless plant, and wouldn't receive that treatment. Unlikely it was a bomb, anyway; poison was the weapon of choice.

She looked at the time; no doubt Acton was hip deep in Solonik's interrogation. She debated, then rang him on his work line, but he did not answer. She pondered texting him on his private line; they had an emergency symbol and he would respond to that in an instant. She remembered his volatile state, however, and decided this did not qualify as an emergency—she would call for reinforcements instead. She rang Williams.

"Hey." He was wary, and rightly so, with all his cross-allegiances going on.

"Hey yourself. Are you busy? I need some help on a suspicious package."

"Bomb squad?" He was obviously wondering why she was enlisting him.

"No, not a bomb." I hope, she added mentally. "A plant has been delivered to my flat's concierge and there is reason to believe it may be dangerous." She wondered how much to tell him, and then decided to err on the side of discretion. "It may contain some sort of harmful chemical, I'm thinkin'."

There was a pause. He thinks I'm mad, she thought.

"I'll get some latex bags and gloves. Meet me at the utility garage." Williams, bless him, understood without her having to say it aloud that this was not to be handled through regular channels. Doyle took several more big bites of the pie and then regretfully threw the remainder away. Brushing off her hands, she made her way to the garage, where Williams was waiting at the lift door when it opened.

"Thank you again—for an inferior officer, I'm pullin' you hither and yon, lately."

"It is my pleasure," he said, and meant it.

They walked over to the unmarked. "I'm afraid I can't tell you what's afoot; it's awkward, but there it is."

"Understood." After yesterday, he was well-aware that they may necessarily have secrets from each other. It was all very complicated, but apparently Acton trusted him and so she would also.

As they stopped at the vehicle he paused and indicated her face with a gesture. "You have some sugar or something—there."

Presumably from the pie, which she had devoured like a starving pilgrim. Embarrassed, she brushed at her cheek.

"It's there still—here, let me get it." He stepped forward to brush his thumb near the corner of her mouth, then met her eyes and went very still. She stepped away and could feel herself blush to the roots of her hair. He opened the door for her and she slid in, refusing to look at him. He walked around to the driver's side, and they drove in silence for a few minutes.

"How do you want to handle this?" he asked, very much himself again.

She had already been pondering this dilemma. "Not as official business. I think we just go in and get it. They'll recognize me."

He looked doubtful. "You shouldn't touch it."

"They won't release it to you, Williams—they'll think you're some sort of plant thief. I'll put gloves on."

"You'll come in with me and we'll say you're allergic."

She looked over at him with approval. "Good one, DS Williams. Make sure you wear gloves—I'll not have you keelin' over again."

He looked grim. "Let's not speak of it."

"Whist, Williams. We bonded in our mutual misery."

She could see he was trying not to laugh. "Did we?"

"Indeed we did. Never doubt it."

He couldn't help himself and started to laugh, and she joined in. Williams, Williams, she thought; what am I going to do with you?

When they entered the lobby, they approached the concierge and explained the alleged allergy situation, which the concierge seemed to accept without a blink. The plant was placed on the mahogany counter, and had a plain brown paper wrapped around it, beneath which was a sheathing of cellophane, all tied up with a satin bow. Under normal circumstances, the brown wrapping would have been removed by Reynolds, and thank all available saints she had given him warning. Doyle stood back, trying her best to appear allergic, whilst Williams carefully took the plant with gloved hands and double-bagged it. Doyle was certain he saw the card indicating the tribute was from the dowager, but there was nothin' for it; he would get no explanation from her. Doyle smiled her thanks at the man behind the desk and they left before anyone would wonder why they hadn't simply been asked to keep it, or give it away to someone else.

Williams carefully placed the bagged plant in the boot of the unmarked. "Now what?"

"That's for Acton to say." She phoned him again on his work line and this time he answered. She could hear people speaking in the background, in the echoing, muted tones of the interrogation room. He was busy, so she said without preamble, "There was a suspicious plant delivered to me at our building. Williams and I have it and it will need some testin', I believe."

He didn't miss a beat. "Put Williams on." She handed her mobile over, and Williams listened without expression. "Right." He rang off. "I'm to take it to the lab."

"Who's his person at the lab?"

He glanced at her, quickly. "That's for Acton to say, I'm afraid."

"Understood," she replied philosophically—she'd find out, one way or the other; she was a very fine detective, when people weren't trying to poison her. "Please see to it the card is removed, but be careful; it may be tainted also."

"Yes, ma'am," he teased, as though she were his superior officer.

They arrived back at headquarters, and as they parked in the garage Williams said rather apologetically, "He wanted me to see that you had lunch—he'll be tied up for a time."

"Thanks, but I'm meetin' Munoz." She would try to avoid being alone with Williams; she knew that if she hadn't moved away when they were in the garage earlier he would have kissed her, and Acton would then have to be told. Men, she thought in exasperation; *honestly.*

CHAPTER 28

LUCKILY, DOYLE'S EXCUSE TO AVOID WILLIAMS WAS PLAUSIBLE as Munoz was indeed available for lunch. As the other girl reached for her mobile, Doyle suggested they keep it just the two of them. "But I'll treat. Where to, the deli? It's our last chance before the rain comes."

"Not off-premises," said Munoz. "I'm trying to avoid Sergey, and he may be watching for me."

They made their way upstairs to the canteen, and Doyle eyed her. "The prince fell short?"

Munoz's jaw was rigid, and waves of chagrin were emanating. "I checked his background; I think he's a poseur."

"That's a shame," said Doyle neutrally, hoping she'd hear more; she knew that Acton had found this romance of extreme interest—although he didn't want to let on—so something was up, and in light of recent events she wanted to keep abreast if she was to talk her volatile husband down from the precipice.

"He just kept asking a lot of questions—too many questions." The other girl looked mulish, and said defensively, "I didn't tell him anything, of course."

"Of course," agreed Doyle. "Was he the one askin' about Owens?"

Munoz scowled in annoyance. "Isn't that strange? As if I would know or care what happened to Owens."

Doyle decided there could not be a surer indication that Sergey was up to no good, and she'd best mention it to Acton—if he didn't know what was afoot already, that was. It was past time that she was brought up to speed; she may be needed to save Acton from himself.

They arrived at the canteen, and Doyle surveyed the waxed-paper fruit pies yet again. Another one certainly wouldn't hurt—she didn't get to finish the last one, after all—and there were so *many* delightful flavors. "What made you decide to check the prince's background? Did somethin' give you pause?"

"I wanted to see if he was a potential husband." With an annoyed gesture, the other girl slid her credit card through the payment machine. "I have to start looking around."

Doyle blinked, as this was the first time she had ever heard Munoz speak of marriage. On reflection, however, it seemed likely that her own abrupt entry into matrimony had prompted this newfound desire—Munoz was fiercely competitive. Faith, Munoz was fierce, period.

They sat down, and Munoz watched Doyle eat the fruit pie for a moment with thinly-veiled disgust; Munoz had chosen an arugula salad. "Does Acton have any eligible friends?"

Doyle hid her alarm; she wouldn't willingly pair anyone she cared about with Munoz. Therefore, she equivocated, "They'd be older men, you know."

The girl tossed her head. "Doesn't matter; if they have money and would like to spoil a younger girl, I could live with it."

The only friend of Acton's Doyle had met—thus far—was Timothy, and Munoz would eat Timothy for breakfast. "I'll ask Acton," she temporized, and then ventured against her better judgment, "Habib is single."

Munoz gave her a withering look and didn't deign to respond as she addressed her salad. I tried, Habib, Doyle thought; believe me, you're better off. "Drake?" she suggested next. Doyle was not certain of the exact relationship between Munoz and the other team's DCI.

"Too much like me," Munoz replied, and Doyle thought this was very perceptive of her. "Does Williams ever speak of me?"

Another flippin' minefield. "I don't think he's lookin', just now. He seems a slave to work, anyway."

Munoz drew her mouth down into a sulk. "It's not fair."

"Give it some time. You don't want to rush into it," suggested Doyle.

This earned a flare of anger in response. "Why not? You did."

This was inarguably true, and Doyle retorted with her own heat, "I'm tryin', Munoz, but you're not makin' it easy."

"I'm the one who should be working the turf war cases; you've been sick."

"I'm not sick anymore, and they're *my* cases."

Before they could come to blows, their mobiles rang almost simultaneously. It was Habib, asking them to report to Detention; an attempt had been made on Solonik, and all available hands were needed to process the scene—Inspector Chiu would take the lead, and they were to report to her.

Annoyed that Munoz was to get her wish, Doyle accompanied the other girl at a brisk pace to Detention, where suspects were held for the brief period allowed by law until the prosecutors decided whether they would be charged with a crime or set free.

By the time they arrived, the solicitor's briefing room in Detention had already been taped off, and SOCOs were donning their bunny suits, preparing to enter. Samuels was there also, waiting with Inspector Chiu, and once they were assembled the DI informed them that a man posing as Solonik's solicitor had managed to smuggle a bladed instrument through security. Fortunately, the weapon was necessarily small and Solonik knew how to defend himself; the wound was superficial, but by the time the alarm had been raised, the suspect had fled.

They all listened in surprised silence; such a turn of events was almost unthinkable, here at the Met. Doyle asked, "Is Solonik conscious, ma'am? Was he familiar with the attacker?"

"Yes; he was conscious throughout, but he claims ignorance," Chiu replied. "They are reviewing CCTV as we speak, and the local PCs have set up a perimeter."

Doyle did not know Chiu very well, but she felt she should point out what to her seemed rather obvious. "If the suspect wasn't truly his solicitor, Solonik would have known immediately. Yet he didn't raise an alarm when the man was shown into the briefin' room by the guard."

Munoz brought up another good point, "And all it would have taken was a shout when the attack was attempted; it's not as though it's easy to make a quick exit from this place. Solonik must have allowed him time to escape."

They considered this in silence. "Honor among thieves?" suggested Samuels.

"I don't know," said Munoz, dubious. "He tried to kill him; I would think all bets were off."

This was true, and they all paused, trying to come up with a working theory. The DI, however, must have gone to the school of Acton because she said briskly, "We will gather the evidence and see where it leads. You two; oversee the processing of the scene," she indicated Doyle and Samuels. "Munoz, oversee what is happening in CCTV and get witness statements—everyone who saw the suspect is already being held in the family waiting room. I'll have another go at Solonik at the infirmary."

"Is DCI Acton about?" asked Doyle. Last she was aware, he was here, interrogating Solonik, and no doubt making the man's future look very bleak. She imagined Acton would like to be the one grilling the Russian at the infirmary, and was rather surprised he wasn't on the scene.

"No, he is in the field." The woman gave her a quick, assessing glance. "Carry on, Constable."

Doyle tried not to be annoyed that the DI thought she was not worthy of Acton—perhaps the woman could compare notes with the SOCO photographer—and stood with Samuels by the briefing room door while they donned paper booties and gloves. "What would you like to take?"

"Bloodstains, I suppose," said Samuels.

Doyle wished she hadn't asked, as she liked bloodstains, herself. "Don't forget to check for inert drops; if the suspect was wounded, we can get a DNA profile." Knife fights were notoriously messy; oftentimes the attacker cut himself because the blood would make the weapon's handle slippery. Blood from a standing attacker tended to land in round, inert drops, as opposed to the spray of the victim's blood.

"Will do," Samuels agreed, and she could see he was a little annoyed that she thought he needed this obvious instruction. Samuels was not the best detective, though, and the case was too important, so she didn't care if she offended him.

Whilst Samuels carefully inspected the bloodstains in the room, she helped direct the SOCO team to test the table and chairs for fingerprints, fibers, or other trace evidence. It would be a thankless slog, though; a lot of different people came through the unhappy confines of the solicitor's briefing room at Detention, and it would be like trying to find a needle in a haystack.

Whilst she was carefully surveying the area under the table, Doyle's mobile vibrated; it was Acton, and she picked up. "I am knee-deep in Mr. Solonik's bloodstains."

"I am at Marta's residence. She has taken an overdose, and killed herself."

Doyle leaned back on her heels, stunned. But truly, when you thought about it, not completely unexpected. Turning her head so as to speak quietly, she said as much to Acton. "When she heard you were at the door, she must have known it was over—she would have no chance in court." England was still England, and no one would look kindly upon a domestic attempting to poison a peeress.

There was only silence in response, and Doyle knew he was profoundly angry; he had been thwarted of whatever action he had wanted to take, which may well be to the good. However, he also was deprived of the chance to find out whether his mother was involved.

"I don't know if I can come right now," Doyle cautioned. "I'm processin' the scene. You've heard?"

"Yes," he said, his tone clipped. "Stay—I have a lot of work to do."

She didn't like the way he sounded. "When will you be home?" she persisted.

"Late—you need your rest; don't wait up."

She rang off thoughtfully. He was in a state, and it was perplexing that he was at Marta's house even though he knew Solonik had been attacked. Perhaps he didn't much care that someone tried to murder Solonik; no doubt Acton had efficiently framed the man for murder already. She froze for a moment, and considered the possibility that Acton had murdered Marta. Acton had disposed of Owens without benefit of authority so that no unwanted attention would be directed at her, and this was a similar situation. He may have wanted to ensure Marta did not implicate his mother, or that the fair Doyle's testimony would not be required in an attempted murder trial. No, she concluded almost immediately; he didn't kill Marta—she could sense that he was very unhappy the wretched woman was dead, and that he was without the answers he sought.

"What is it?" asked Samuels, watching her return her mobile to her belt.

"Nothing," Doyle replied, "I was woolgatherin' is all." Samuels was a likeable fellow, but it was a little odd he was a detective—he didn't have that driving curiosity; indeed, he'd shown little interest in the puzzling circumstances of this attack on Solonik.

After the scene had been thoroughly processed, they returned to their workstations late in the afternoon and began writing up their reports. Hopefully, ERU would come up with *something;* it seemed likely the suspect's DNA—whoever he was—would be on file because such a bold attack on a kingpin was not your ordinary crime. Munoz had said there was an image on surveillance video, but the suspect had been well-aware of the location of the cameras and a clear shot of his face was never caught; he'd strategically held a folder to obscure his image. He was a bit taller than average, average weight and dark hair—not very helpful. Because he was disguised as a solicitor, security had given him short shrift, and thus he had been able to smuggle in the blade. A very daring attack by someone very desperate, one would think.

Munoz packed up to leave as evening fell; Doyle packed up with her but decided a visit to her errant husband was in order, and they parted at the lobby lifts. Doyle made her way across the walkway, aware that she was tired and not quite recovered from the ordeal of the past week, but also aware that she mustn't be a baby and keep putting it off—it was her own fault, after all. After contemplating the best way to broach the subjects she needed to broach with Acton, she finally decided she would play it by ear; if he was in one of his black moods, she would proceed cautiously.

His floor was nearly deserted as she approached his office, but his assistant was still at her desk and his door was closed. Doyle had met his assistant only once; at work they moved in different orbits. As she approached, the woman looked up and said quietly, "He has asked not to be disturbed."

Doyle paused in surprise, thinking that the woman must know that such a stricture shouldn't be applied to the DCI's better half. No point in pulling that card, however; his assistant was only doing her job, and loyalty was a virtue. "I'll check, then," she replied in a mild tone.

She texted Acton, "I M outside your door."

Almost immediately, the lock clicked. Doyle couldn't resist smiling kindly at the assistant as she went in, and intercepted a poorly-concealed flash of envy and resentment. Put that in your pipe, Miss Can't-Be-Disturbed.

CHAPTER 29

ACTON HAD BEEN DRINKING, AND SHE HID HER SURPRISE THAT he would drink this much at work. Occasionally he would drink rather heavily at the flat and sit quietly for a time, watching her. During these occasions, she respected the mood and left him alone. She didn't drink herself, but didn't mind when he did; she was Irish, after all. Since her pregnancy, however, these sessions had been few and far between.

She shut the door behind her. Doyle had rarely been in his office, as Acton was constantly busy and was more likely to visit her when time permitted. They also tried to keep their relationship at work on a professional level, so as not to invoke any resentment, and a DC wouldn't be dropping in to visit a DCI.

He walked away from her and went over to stand by the window, looking out. He was in a crackin' foul mood, she saw, and didn't want her to see that he was swilkin' drunk. This would take some careful handling and so she waited, trying to gauge him.

"I used to watch you come into work," he said. "I still do."

"Michael," she said gently, setting down her rucksack beside his desk, "what is troublin' you and how can I help?"

He paused, and she thought for a moment he would not answer her, but then he replied a bit abruptly, "You were declining. I had begun to entertain the possibility that you might die."

"We caught it, though, and I have been eating fruit pies all afternoon. I am well, Michael; my hand on my heart."

"I wanted to kill her," he said conversationally.

"I thought perhaps you had," she admitted.

Surprised, he glanced at her. "No." It was the truth, but she had already come to this realization.

This was the right tack, she could sense it—to be matter-of-fact and even; he was responding to her, but she wasn't certain if now was the time to make her confession about Solonik. She wished she knew how best to handle this—unlikely there was a chapter in a marriage manual on the subject. Perhaps she should start with broad generalizations. "You can't just go about killin' people, Michael."

He turned to look out the window again, and she worried that the generalization was perhaps not broad enough. He mused, "I know you are very clever. I don't know why I underestimate you."

She realized he was speaking of the aqueduct murder. He knew that she knew, then. "You lost your tiepin, my friend."

He glanced at her over his shoulder. "Indeed?"

"Indeed," she replied, imitating him. When he was drunk, he became more aristocratic than his usual—which meant that he tried to tone it down otherwise, so that she wouldn't feel so much like an unworthy Cinderella in this unorthodox fairy tale. I used to feel that way—like an unworthy Cinderella—she admitted to herself; but not so much anymore. This man and I are very well-matched, but I cannot help but think his wayward ways will come a cropper, sooner or later, and if I can use my influence to prevent such an outcome, I will. Someone like Acton would not do well in prison—there were too many inmates who were already there, courtesy of him. "You must leave retribution to God, Michael."

He shook his head, and leaned against the windowsill so

that she wouldn't see that he was unsteady on his feet. "No. Not if someone tries to kill you."

"If you believe that this world is only temporary, and the next one is eternal, then you are servin' the short-term but sacrificin' the long-term." She paused, trying to decide if she had explained it clearly. "It's a matter of perspective."

He said nothing, but turned his gaze to the carpeted floor. Faith, he was in a mood. Reaction, probably—the crisis had passed and he had been thwarted of revenge, unless he was going after his mother, and that did not bear thinking about. Tired of standing—she'd had a long day—she moved over to sit at his desk, maintaining her matter-of-fact air and trying to read him despite his best efforts to block her out. Displayed on his laptop screen was a still photograph from the building's surveillance tape; Sergey meeting her outside at the deli, his face clearly visible. She looked up in surprise. "Do you know him?"

"No."

She knit her brow, confused. "I wonder why he was so spooked of me, then." She glanced up. "Munoz says he is a fake."

"Munoz is right."

In mock-annoyance, she chided, "Now, there's a phrase I'd rather not be hearin' again from you, if you don't mind."

But he would not be teased, and lifted his gaze to her. "You must go home and rest. Call the driving service."

It was said in the form of a command, but she stood her ground. "I'd rather stay with you."

"I am not good company, Kathleen."

"Nonsense; you are very appealin' when you are three sheets to the wind—I have no idea what's next." Then an idea dawned on her; why, I know exactly what's next, she thought. Standing so as to begin unbuttoning her blouse, she issued her own command. "Come over here, husband."

He was alarmed, and glanced at the exposed windows. "No," he said firmly.

"No, yourself." She stepped out of her trousers and laid them over the back of the chair before unhooking her bra. "Either you're comin' over here, or I'm goin' over there and puttin' on a show for whoever is workin' late across the way."

They had not had sex in a week and Acton—being as he was—was ripe for exploitation. "I'm afraid I am drunk."

"Then I will go door-to-door until I find someone who can perform." She was down to her knickers, and she could see he was no match for her scantily-clad self; as though mesmerized, he stood upright and approached the desk. Meeting him halfway, she slowly ran her palms up his chest but he was in no mood for foreplay, and caught her hands, pinioning her arms roughly behind her and bringing his mouth down on hers. He was none too gentle and tasted of scotch.

Deciding that she would give as good as she got, she bit his lip, gently, and if it was possible, he pressed her more tightly against him and began to move his hands over her body with some urgency. Ordinarily, he was careful not to escalate his lovemaking until she was ready for him, but he was not possessed of patience at this point and so with little preamble, he hoisted her up against him and lifted her onto his desk.

It was fortunate, she thought as she shifted to accommodate his weight, that he was OCD and the desk was not cluttered. After laying her back, he began kissing her roughly, sliding a hand between them to unfasten his trousers. The heat ignited between them—as always—and she gasped into his mouth with the intensity of it. She could hear him rip her lace knickers aside and then they were joined in their own familiar rhythm; she clinging to him, arms and legs, and panting into his neck.

When the storm was over, she rested her head back on the desktop, his face buried between her neck and shoulder. Staring at the ceiling in satisfaction, she shifted slightly so that his pen set was not poking her. "My favorite knickers," she lamented.

"I'll replace them."

"There's no point, really."

She could feel him chuckle in his chest. Good. She said softly into his ear, "Let's go home and do this properly."

A bit groggy, he lifted his head and kissed her ear. "I'm afraid I have more work to do."

"I was thinkin' I would drive you home."

"I'm not that drunk," he protested. She lifted her hand to brush her hair off her forehead, and she could feel the chuckle again as he rested his head against her. Good one, Doyle; you have discovered the cure for the black mood. It is very similar to the cure for morning sickness, only much more vigorous.

Acton suddenly said into her ear, "Promise me something."

"Anythin'," she murmured, and meant it.

"If there is a chance I might lose you, you must give me warning."

"There is no chance, Michael," she replied with complete sincerity. "I just worry, sometimes."

He kissed her throat, and said nothing.

No time like the present, she thought. "I have to confess somethin' to you, and beg your pardon on both knees."

His fingers stilled on her skin, and she could sense he was struggling to pay attention, aware this was important. "What is it, then?"

She swallowed. "The real reason Owens wanted to kill me was because he wanted you for himself. He didn't work for Solonik—it was strictly personal. He even apologized." She could feel the gooseflesh rise on her arms, remembering. "He realized I was a rival, and wanted to eliminate me so that he could take my place."

Acton lay very still and said nothing. She continued, "I didn't want to tell you; I was afraid—I was afraid it cut a little too close. And I didn't think it would matter."

But it had; Acton had instigated this crackin' bloodbath and for his final vengeance, had framed Solonik for the murder of his own brother-in-law. Each of the warring tribes would be left in ruins and at least one kingpin would go to prison; it was a brilliant strategy and it had Acton's fingerprints all over it—not that anyone knew but her. And Williams, apparently. No wonder Williams had been so swiftly promoted; he was Acton's man, and Acton needed him to rise through the ranks so that he could be of use. She wondered for a moment why someone like Williams would be ripe for such an unorthodox alliance; it did not seem in keeping.

Acton's voice, resonating next to her head, interrupted her thoughts. "You could not tell me the truth."

"I am so sorry, Michael. I should have."

"Not at all; it was my fault, after all, that you couldn't speak the truth."

This was unexpected, but very much in keeping with the whole Section Seven thing; she could do no wrong. "No, you knocker—I should have made a clean breast."

"I will seek therapy; you should not have to guard what you say to me."

"I'm not leavin'." She knew instinctively this was why he was making such an effort to be a normal couple; to relinquish his intense privacy. He didn't want her to abandon ship.

"You should not have to guard what you say to me," he repeated, his diction very public-school.

"We will see," she temporized, mainly because she could not be easy about such a plan. It did not seem that this particular secret should be shared with anyone, except maybe a stout-hearted priest.

There was a silence for a few moments, and he evidenced no desire to lift himself off her squashed but compliant body. Smiling to herself, she gently kissed his throat, but it seemed he was not marshaling his energy for another go, but was instead thinking about what she had revealed. "Did you discover why Owens was at the Kempton Park course in the first place? He was a professional—there must have been a reason."

Leave it to Acton to think of this; she had not considered this particular loose end, what with being shot and then hiding the truth from her husband. She knit her brow, trying to remember what the raving lunatic had said even though she never wanted to think about it again. "He made some comment about infiltratin' the course for some reason—he was pursuin' a relationship with the dead trainer for business."

There was a pause. "Did he mention Savoie?"

"No. What is Sav-waa?" She was not good with words, and this was a strange one.

There was a small pause, and she knew he was in the process of deciding he was too drunk to discuss whatever it was with her, so she threw his own words back at him. "Michael, you shouldn't have to guard what you say to me."

"Savoie is a person; a Frenchman."

This was little enough to go on, but it was enough, and her scalp prickled. "Is this Savoie character a bit reedy, and does he have a tattoo on his neck?"

"Most certainly not. Why?" This was apparently interesting enough to inspire him to rise up on his elbows and look down at her.

"The walk-in—the driver from the course. Munoz said he was wearin' a fine French watch even though he was a bit rough around the edges. I had the impression he was wary, and he asked if I was married."

"That is of interest."

Mother a' mercy, she thought; were we dealing with the wrong kingpin, all along? Small wonder Lestrade was wary and confused, if Acton was laying waste to the wrong tribe.

Her vengeful-but-mistaken husband had lapsed into silence, and she decided he could do his thinking at home where there was no danger his assistant could walk in at any moment. She helped him to straighten up, kissing him repeatedly, and coaxed him down to the premium garage where the Range Rover was parked. He was a bit unsteady on his feet, and she wondered how much scotch was needed to make him so. Without a protest, he allowed her to seat him in the passenger seat, and then she slid behind the wheel, hoping she wouldn't crash his fine car between here and home. After adjusting the seat so that she could reach the pedals, she unsuccessfully tried to put the gearshift into reverse. He leaned over and showed her that the device had to be pulled to one side to achieve reverse; she tried and it stalled. Unable to help it, she started to giggle.

"Dosser," he accused, imitating her accent.

Laughing, she pulled his head to hers to kiss him, openmouthed, and then they were havin' at it once again, even though there was little enough room in the passenger seat. Thank God the windows are tinted, thought Doyle; the video surveillance people at the Met were not known for their discretion.

CHAPTER 30

He was happy, and the nice lady was happy, too, he told
himself as he tried to ignore the mashetani, who hovered
so close that he could hear the beating of their wings. Her
husband would take care of her—he was a strong man, a
shujaa. There was little he could do, after all—and they
had fled from the old country so that he would not to be
forced to fight. The new God said be not afraid, but it was
easier to flee.

At Doyle's request the next morning, Acton accompanied her to the corner store so that she could purchase a sup-
ply of the prepackaged fruit pies. When he saw the product in
question, however, he was quick to express his general disbelief and horror that she would be inclined to eat such a thing.

"Isn't it strange?" she agreed. "But for some reason they're
very appealin', Michael, and I suppose I should be makin' up
for lost time." She glanced at him sidelong. "It's burnin' up
the calories at an alarmin' rate, I am." After the lovemaking
session in the car, there had been an additional session in the
middle of the night that seemed to be over before she fully
woke up for it. The cure had worked, and now he seemed
himself again, thank the saints and holy martyrs who may not
have wholly approved of the remedy administered. "But I
have to have a care; if I don't limit myself to a daily ration of
these things, I'll be enormously fat and you'll be unable to lift
me onto your desk, if the need arises."

He smiled, but was preoccupied, as he had been since the revelations of the night before. By contrast, she was in high spirits; she had made her confession, Acton's dejection had passed, she was no longer miserably sick, and the despicable poisoner had conveniently relieved them of the time and trouble of bringing her to justice—although Doyle could not approve of suicide. The only cloud on the horizon—and it was a crackin' great big black one—was his mother. If she was involved in Marta's attempt, she could very well try again—although perhaps the failure of the plan had discouraged her from such a course; by nature, a poisoner was not a bold creature. Another discussion about what was to be done was needful, but she eyed Acton and equivocated; she didn't want to set him off again—they were out of scotch.

It was the weekend, and since Reynolds did not work on the weekends, Doyle had phoned him that morning to tell him of Marta's death so that he was aware the threat had passed and no further attempts would be made. Reynolds, as unperturbed as ever, expressed his satisfaction with this turn of events, and further expressed to Doyle, in measured terms, that he owed her his life.

"Reynolds," she reminded him, "if it wasn't for me you would never have been in danger in the first place."

"Nevertheless, I am grateful, madam." The brown paper wrapping around the plant had contained a mercuric alkaloid; he would have been dead within minutes. Acton had traced the plant's purchase and discovered it was paid for in cash and there was no CCTV tape—a dead end. This information, however, only added to the conviction that Marta had not acted alone; it was hard to imagine the woman going to such sophisticated lengths as to poison the paper wrapper on a plant.

Upon returning to the flat, Doyle happily sat at the kitchen table to eat one of the pies, noting that Acton had to avert his eyes from such an appalling sight. "I should mix it in a bowl with Chinese food," she teased him. "You'd never be comin' near me again."

To belie this accusation, he came over and kissed her full on the mouth, his hands cradling her head, and she experienced a jolt of blissful happiness—although it may have been only in comparison to how wretched she had been recently. Acton's kiss made her consider postponing her lunch date with Caroline, but she decided she'd rather just have it done with. She had agreed to meet for lunch today, mainly because she couldn't come up with a plausible excuse quickly enough—for a detective, she wasn't always very fast on her feet.

"After an hour and a half," she instructed Acton, "you must phone me and insist that I come home. I just don't want it to turn into an entire afternoon."

"I will set my watch," he agreed.

Caroline texted to say she was downstairs, and when Doyle came into the lobby, the other woman greeted her by kissing her cheek. Doyle returned the favor as warmly as she was able; she wasn't a casual kisser, herself. As the weather was turning, Doyle had worn her heavy coat and Caroline expressed her admiration as they walked outside. "Cashmere," she said, brushing it with an appreciative hand. "Acton chose it, I imagine."

Doyle overlooked what may have been an aspersion on her own taste and agreed. "He did indeed—he told me I needed a proper coat." It was black, three-quarter length with a fur-lined hood; it was entirely unlike anything Doyle had ever owned, and truth to tell, she felt a bit ambivalent about walking about in such an expensive thing. She wore it because Acton liked it, and said it went well with her hair.

"He is very generous with you, I think."

Again, Doyle sensed an underlying unkindness that had not been evident when last they met. She had the impression Caroline was amusing herself, thinking Doyle was not clever enough to recognize the implied insults. Honestly; if the woman was only being nice to her in front of Acton, then why set up this lunch date? Doyle would much rather be with Acton, trading sexual innuendos. With this in mind, Doyle was able to answer mildly, "He is a giver, that man." Three times last evening, in fact. Behave, she warned herself.

They were to walk to the fashionable café Caroline had selected, and although Doyle had made up her mind to be friendly, her resolution was tested almost immediately. Aiki was in front of the building, leaning against his cab and reading a newspaper, which Doyle noted was in English. Good one, Aiki, she thought, and said, *"Bonjour,"* having practiced it with Acton.

Aiki dropped the paper and smiled his white smile. *"Bonjour,"* he replied with delight. He then added something in rapid French which Doyle didn't understand, and so she spread her hands helplessly whilst he laughed.

"Come along," said Caroline, taking Doyle's arm. "You must remember your station, Kathleen."

This was uncalled-for, and Doyle gently rebuked her companion. "Aiki drives me to work, Caroline; Acton put him on a retainer so that he's always here if I need him. We are friends."

Caroline glanced at her in acute surprise, her disapproval palpable. "Kathleen, you are Lady Acton, now. You mustn't encourage people like that—who are only trying to make up to you. It reflects poorly on Acton."

Doyle was speechless, as this stricture was wrong on so many levels she didn't know which to address first. Instead, on reflection, she said nothing; best not to lose her temper before they'd gone fifty paces.

Caroline interpreted her silence for acquiescence and pulled Doyle's arm through hers approvingly. "You will learn how to go on—it's only a matter of becoming accustomed. Isn't it lovely, to be out and about, just the two of us? And I have something for you." She pulled a security card from her purse and presented it to Doyle. "Here is my key; I hope you will not stand on ceremony, and will drop over anytime you like—just us girls."

It was falsely hearty but true, and Doyle gave her points for trying to make the usurper feel welcome. "Thank you, Caroline; I appreciate it."

"I thought perhaps you could come over from time to time and I could give you lessons in comportment—discreetly, of course; no one need know. You wouldn't feel as lost."

Then again, perhaps the points had been awarded too hastily. Rather than refuse outright, Doyle said only, "You are very kind, Caroline."

They arrived at the café for lunch, and Caroline ordered wine for both of them before Doyle demurred, saying she would have water, instead, as she did not drink alcohol. Caroline apologized; she had assumed Doyle hadn't been drinking due to her condition. This naturally led to an expression of sorrow about the miscarriage which Doyle took in good part. The other woman then lowered her voice. "If you need any advice of a medical nature, you may always ask me. It may be too embarrassing to ask a male doctor."

Doyle expressed her appreciation for the offer, having no idea what was meant. If she is going to start giving me advice about sex, Doyle thought, I am going to fall out of my chair.

Watching her reaction, Caroline hid her frustration and was more explicit. "Are you using birth control?"

Deciding this was none of her business, Doyle simply replied, "Yes," meaning if they were going to rely on Acton's controlling himself, the births would be many and plentiful.

"Good," said the other woman, leaning back in satisfaction as she reviewed the menu. "Acton must have been taken by surprise last time; I know he doesn't want children."

Doyle hid her reaction by studying her own menu. It was

possible Acton had expressed such a view in the past, but things had definitely changed; he had said it was wonderful news that she was pregnant, and it had been the pure truth. He wanted to father a child on her—perhaps as part of his need to bind her irrevocably to him. In any event, it was time to change the subject. "Tell me, Caroline; what it was like—the four of you such friends at university together?"

This was the correct tack, as it allowed Caroline to recite their history and make it clear that Doyle was merely a looker-in. "I was two years behind the others, but I met Acton through Tim. They shared some classes—music, I believe, and biology. Tim became Acton's good friend, and Fiona was in Tim's study group." She smiled at the memory. "It was a challenging time—except for Acton, who was always so brilliant. We spent a great deal of time together, and we were very close-knit."

She thinks this is true, thought Doyle as she listened politely, even though I know Acton is nowhere near as fond of her as he is of Timothy, and no one is close to Acton—not even me, although I believe I am as close as he will allow. And I think Caroline is one of those people whose own unhappiness makes them want to take jabs at others. If I pointed out to her that she speaks in a way that is unkind, or does not show me to advantage, she would be aghast and apologetic; then she would keep doing it.

"Of course, Acton and Fiona were extremely close; her death was a terrible blow." Caroline carefully kept her gaze on her wineglass; the words said in a way to make it clear there was more to be said, but that she was refraining.

Annoyed, Doyle offered up her own little jab. "I hadn't realized you were aware they had an affair."

Caroline lifted her gaze in surprise. "Acton told you?"

How else would I know? thought Doyle, but instead answered mildly, "Yes, of course." She regretted the comment;

she should better control her wretched tongue. There was no point in retaliating with this kind of person; it would only result in escalating the covert hostility.

But before Caroline could marshal a pointed response, they were unexpectedly joined by Timothy and Acton himself. Her husband met her eyes, and Doyle nearly laughed aloud. He has come to rescue me, she thought. Good one.

CHAPTER 3 1

"A CTON," CAROLINE LAUGHED. "YOU ARE AFRAID YOUR WIFE is revealing all your secrets, I see. How did you know we were here?"

The GPS in my mobile, thought Doyle, and waited with interest to hear what he would say.

"Educated guess," he replied easily, and indicated to the waitress that more place settings would be needed.

"Yes, we would be delighted if you would join us."

Interesting, Doyle thought; she is not at all happy about this development—she must have wanted to prime me for information, not that I would have given her any. I suppose I could have told her that Acton beats me, which probably would have been welcome news.

"Have you ordered?" Timothy looked over the menu while Doyle leaned over to help him decide what he would like, and the next hour was spent more pleasurably than she could have hoped. Acton, as always, spent more time listening than speaking, and Timothy entertained them with tales of yesterday's cases at the charity clinic.

"Goiters, and pertussis—diseases I've only seen in medical school books. And there is such ignorance and superstition; it is very difficult to convince the new mothers to inoculate their children because they believe we mean to harm them."

"How do you manage it?" Doyle was secretly sympathetic, feeling as she did about needles.

The doctor sighed. "It's slow going. One evening as we were cleaning up, there was a knock at the back door. It was one of the young mothers, and she wanted to inoculate her infant. She would only do it under cover of darkness and anonymously, so that none of her friends would know. It is so frustrating; if she would tell the others they would see no harm was done, and they would be encouraged."

"Who funds the clinic?" asked Doyle.

"Holy Trinity Church, mostly; along with other donors. We never charge for treatment, but the patients will nonetheless try to pay me. Oftentimes it is some inedible offering that I must pretend to enjoy."

They laughed; Timothy liked plain food, plainly served. Such a nice man, thought Doyle, and with a good heart—even though he had a lucrative practice, he spent two days a month at the clinic. She should be volunteering somewhere, herself; she didn't have a talent to share, but surely an extra hand would be appreciated.

"Who does your cooking, now?" asked Caroline of Acton; the question made it clear she had dismissed Doyle as incapable.

"We have a new domestic named Reynolds," Doyle volunteered, just to show she was up to speed.

"Is that so? And is he satisfactory?"

Acton made no response, and so Doyle replied, "Yes, we're very pleased with him."

Timothy asked, "Is Marta back at Trestles, then?"

There was a pause. Saints, thought Doyle; this will not sound good.

"Marta is dead," Acton announced in his abrupt way.

Timothy and Caroline stared in silence. Acton seemed disinclined to elaborate, so Doyle disclosed, "Unfortunately, she's killed herself."

"A shame," said Timothy. "When was this?"

"A day ago." Grand, thought Doyle—it sounds as though I threw her out and drove her to suicide.

"I can't imagine taking my own life," Timothy mused, rather shocked. "There is too much to hope for."

"It would show a lack of faith," agreed Doyle.

"I don't know," said Caroline. "I think you can never know what another person's life is like—perhaps it became unbearable."

To Timothy and me, it would be unthinkable, thought Doyle. Acton and Caroline, on the other hand, are another story—she had little doubt that Acton was capable of taking his own life. Not that such a thing would happen now; he wouldn't leave her under any circumstances. Struck by this, she explored the thought. I do keep him happy, and it's not just the fixation—the man delights in me, he does. She found his gaze resting on her, and so she smiled at him.

"It is clear you two are newlyweds," teased Caroline in mock-chagrin. "And here I hoped to have Kathleen to myself."

As if on cue, Acton glanced at his watch. "I'm afraid I must spirit her away."

"I won't have it, Acton," Caroline protested with a smile. "I was going to take her shopping and help her put together some outfits to impress you."

Again, an implied insult, thought Doyle. But I won't let it bother me; Acton is at his most impressed when I am not wearing anything, anyway.

"I'm afraid its work-related, Caroline. We are going to interrogate a suspect who has been hospitalized."

This was true, and Doyle hid her surprise. They must be going to see Solonik, and Acton needed a truth-detector, after all.

"Another time, then. I will have your promise, Kathleen."

"Of course," Doyle agreed, thinking it unlikely. She had

gained the distinct impression that Acton was unhappy, and didn't want her to converse privately with Caroline. On board with that, she thought.

They rose and said their good-byes, and then she and Acton walked back toward the flat while the McGonigals departed in the other direction. Doyle waited a few moments, but Acton walked in silence, and seemed deep in thought. "Thank you," she said finally. "I was havin' uncharitable thoughts, I was."

"I think you should avoid her. She does not mean well by you."

This was true, and Doyle gazed at him thoughtfully, but he did not elaborate. He would not say it unless he meant it. It didn't matter; she had already come to the same conclusion and she was tired of talking about Caroline. She put her hand through his arm. "I'm to visit the wounded Mr. Solonik, then?"

"If you would. I would like to ask a few questions."

Again, the maddening man wouldn't elaborate, and so Doyle ventured, "The attack on him made little sense. I was wonderin' if perhaps it was preplanned so that he could more easily escape from the infirmary. That would explain why he didn't raise an alarm, and instead let the attacker take a bunk."

"I don't know what I think." After a moment, he continued, "He is a very dangerous man, and I would appreciate it if you would stand quietly and say as little as possible, please."

She teased, "That's askin' a lot of me, Michael."

But he met her gaze with his own serious one. "Not a laughing matter, I'm afraid."

"Sorry—I will be silent as the grave."

He nearly recoiled, and she mentally chastised herself for her poor choice of words. Still touchy, he was.

CHAPTER 32

Doyle and Acton showed their identification at the infirmary's security suite, and went through a rigorous security check; after the episode with the fake solicitor, no chances were being taken. They arrived at the room, and were asked to show identification once again to the guard who was posted outside the door, although the man had immediately risen when he recognized Acton. On occasion, Doyle had been inside a prison to question a witness or a suspect, and she heartily disliked the experience, being one who was so attuned to undercurrents and atmosphere. Unimaginable, to have to reside day after day in so bleak a place—having no hope of being free to wander about for the foreseeable future. It went against her nature completely, and she was well-aware that Acton had arranged just this kind of future for the man he thought had masterminded the attack on her. Glancing at her husband, she wondered if he had any regrets, and then decided it was unlikely; Acton was not one to dwell on past mistakes. Instead, he would think the world well-rid of a criminal, and move on to the next case.

She entered the fortified, windowless room after Acton, and saw that Solonik was lying in the hospital bed, bound with restraints and hooked to an IV from which she averted her eyes. The bandaged corner of a dressing was exposed at the neck of his hospital gown, near his throat. The attacker had meant to slash his throat, then, which was probably the most lethal option when the blade was a small one. Solonik looked like the image in Thackeray's photograph, and he watched them enter with interest, his dark eyes focused on his visitors. Acton said nothing to him and did not introduce Doyle, so she stood against the wall in her best imitation of a DC poised to take notes. She didn't lift her gaze, but could feel Solonik's eyes resting upon her.

"*Rizhaya,*" he said. "That is what we call hair that color. Like a beautiful sunset."

Doyle made no response and Acton ignored him, instead pulling up a photograph on his tablet. He approached Solonik and showed it to him. "Do you recognize this man?"

Solonik looked at it carefully. Doyle had the impression he recognized him immediately, but was wary. "Perhaps," he equivocated.

"Is he Russian?" asked Acton.

Solonik is surprised by the question, thought Doyle, and is trying to hide his surprise. "I do not know every *rooskiy* in England, Chief Inspector."

Acton referred to the photograph. "Is this the man who attacked you?"

Solonik pretended to study the photograph, but continued wary. "It is possible. I did not get a close look at him." This was untrue, and Doyle brushed her hair back.

"Did he say anything to you?"

"No." This was true.

"Do you think his intent was to kill you?"

Solonik looked amused. "It would seem so, certainly." True again.

Acton leaned forward. "Who is he?"

Solonik tilted his head to the side and hunched his shoulders, but then winced because it hurt. "I know not."

Doyle paused to brush her hair off her forehead with the hand that held her pen.

"Shall I call for your solicitor? I would like to know why you are protecting this man."

Solonik was surprised and dismayed, but he stared at Acton without evidencing this. "Why do you think I am protecting him? I do not know him, and he tried to kill me. You make no sense, Chief Inspector."

Acton regarded him for a long moment, and then with a resigned gesture, closed the photograph. "If you will not co-operate, I cannot give you assurances."

The other man was suddenly alert, and seemed to be re-assessing. He asked slowly, "What kind of assurances?"

Acton stood before him, implacable. "The evidence shows you murdered Barayev. Your solicitors are putting up a brave front, but you and I both know you are going to prison. You are a dangerous man—who knows, perhaps there are even more murders which would implicate you under the Anti-Terrorism Act. If this is the case, you could wind up in a Category A prison—Maghaberry, perhaps." Acton paused, to let the man picture his future in a maximum-security Irish prison. "I imagine you would be a marked man."

Solonik sat very still, never taking his eyes off Acton. Despite his unreadable expression, he was emanating waves of hatred and frustrated rage, the intensity of which made Doyle drop her gaze.

There was a small silence, and then Acton continued, "Or, perhaps you will not be implicated in any others, in which case you would no doubt be placed in a Category B—Wexton is a possibility." Doyle listened in surprise; the reference was to a moderate-security prison on the outskirts of greater London, currently in the director-general's black book because the guards had been caught taking bribes.

Solonik's gaze traveled to Doyle, who had not betrayed by

the flicker of an eyelash her realization that the law enforcement officer was threatening a suspect with trumped-up murder charges. "Why should I trust you?"

"Perhaps you shouldn't, but I will have some answers from
you, or all bets are off. Did you arrange for anyone to make a
delivery to my flat?"

Doyle almost gaped, and had to resist the urge to look up
in surprise. This must be why Acton had brought her in on
this unorthodox interview—even though up to now he'd
been keeping her well away from it; he needed to know if
Solonik was behind the attack against her. It was a valid theory, she supposed; Solonik could have enlisted Marta to take
his own vengeance for Acton's unexplained war on him. And
such a turn of events would only illustrate exactly why you
stayed out of the vengeance business—it never ends.

The other man said slowly, "I do not understand."

Acton did not yield. "Answer the question—did you arrange
to deliver anything to my flat?"

Doyle glanced up, to see the other man watching Acton, a
speculative look in his eye. "No." It was the truth. "I have
heard that you have taken a young wife, Chief Inspector. Perhaps she has taken a lover, and it is he who sends her gifts."

But this insinuation did not rattle her husband, who returned, "I have heard you have a young son in St. Petersburg.
It is a simple thing to replace a wife; it is not so simple, when
a man is in prison, to replace a son."

Saints, thought Doyle, trying to decide where to look; little
chance of finding this particular interrogation technique in
any police manual.

His unreadable gaze on the other man, Acton continued,
"We understand each other?"

Solonik nodded. "Yes. Speak to the solicitor."

Acton tapped his tablet with an emphatic forefinger. "Who
is in the photo?"

"I do not know," the other reiterated, and Doyle brushed her hair back.

Acton watched the other man thoughtfully for a moment, then indicated to Doyle that they would leave. As she walked out, Solonik called to her, "Wexton prison is not far, *rizhaya*. You must visit me, yes?"

Doyle did not respond, and she and Acton walked out to the car in silence. Once they were out of earshot, Doyle reported in a low tone: "He did not arrange to have anything delivered, and was genuinely surprised by the question. He knew the man in the photo immediately. He was surprised about the Russian question; perhaps the man is not Russian. It was not a staged attack; the other indeed wished to kill him."

"Then why protect him?" Acton was deep in thought, and Doyle didn't interrupt him—she was a bit on end, and trying to regain her equilibrium. A very bad actor was to be put away, but Acton's behind-the-scenes staging had led to his arrest, and Acton had no problem threatening more behind-the-scenes staging to elicit the information he wanted. Solonik would cooperate because Acton made a thinly-veiled threat in response to Solonik's thinly-veiled threat. It was all like a knife fight with no rules; a bit shocking to a young constable, steeped in protocol and training. Did the ends justify the means? Acton obviously thought so. She thought about how Solonik had flirted with her, and wondered if he would ever discover she was, in fact, Acton's wife.

Turning her mind to the present investigation, she took an educated guess, based mainly on the fact Acton had been careful not to show her the photograph. "Do you think the attacker was Munoz's Sergey?"

Acton glanced at her but hesitated in responding. Annoyed because he was still trying to leave her out of it, she persisted, "You might want to talk to Munoz; maybe she can tell you somethin'."

"I have talked to Munoz."

"Oh," said Doyle crossly. "You are bein' *so* tiresome, Michael."

He was unapologetic. "I don't want you involved. These are bad characters."

Without responding, she looked out her window in the car to let him know she was annoyed. It was a continuing problem; he would rather she spent her time knitting at home, except he would probably put a flippin' cork on the flippin' needles so that she wouldn't flippin' prick herself. Her job was dangerous, and they had agreed that he could control her assignments to suit his anxiety level, which unfortunately appeared to allow only for a parking ticket detail. She chafed at it, even as she acknowledged he had a valid concern; they had been married less than two months and thus far she had been both shot and poisoned. Still and all, it was a shame he hadn't fixated on a woman who would love to be pampered and treated like a flippin' princess in a flippin' tower.

She took a long breath and withdrew the thought immediately; it's not a shame, she amended. I want him and I wouldn't trade him for anyone, nicked or not. She just needed to face facts and quit being such a baby; there was no shame to being an obscure DC, working behind the scenes—it was not as though she craved fame. "Home?" she asked, to show him that she was done sulking.

He took her hand. "Office. Before prosecution can cut a deal with the solicitor, I need to speak to the DCS and see what I have. I will drop you off."

"I'd rather stay with you."

He looked at her, amused. "I do need to work."

She assured him, "I will be as prim as a nun, Michael; and remain fully clothed."

CHAPTER 33

DOYLE DIDN'T WANT TO GO FETCH HER OWN LAPTOP, SO SHE looked through some of the manuals Acton kept on his shelves whilst he participated in a conference call with the prosecutor and Solonik's solicitor. It sounded as though the solicitor was surprised by Solonik's sudden capitulation—the poor man was a step behind, it seemed—but they were rapidly coming to terms. There was some discussion about the security measures needed at the prison; apparently Acton would keep his word, and see to it that Solonik was protected from the wrath of other prisoners. Perhaps he'd need a favor someday with his guns-running operation—she was fast coming to the realization that her husband tended to hedge his bets.

Acton rang off and she glanced up, hopeful, but then he rang up someone else, deep in thought. She wondered how much longer he'd be, but did not want to interrupt and so she opened a bloodstains binder and thumbed through it, listening to the negotiations with half an ear. By the tenor of the conversations, she guessed he was speaking to the detective chief superintendent.

"He'll plead to twenty years and has agreed to tell us what he knows; we may be able to bring in some others."

He listened for a moment. "I wouldn't recommend letting the Home Secretary's people put a finger in; Solonik's very good at manipulation. Next thing we know he'll be playing them against us and he'll have them giving him immunity just to spite us."

The DCS was apparently in agreement. "Good," said Acton. "And stay alert for any unexplained reluctance to prosecute over there; Solonik is an expert at digging up blackmail."

So is Acton, thought Doyle; and Acton apparently held the trump card, because Solonik capitulated immediately. After all—as Acton had pointed out—a mere wife is replaceable.

Acton was disagreeing about something. "No; I would keep it as quiet as possible. We wouldn't want someone getting to him before he gives us what he knows."

He listened and was apparently asked to give a prediction as to how helpful Solonik would, in fact, be. "I am skeptical, frankly. He may give us enough to keep us interested, but he may purposefully give misinformation to serve his own ends."

The DCS must have expressed some dismay over this, because Acton reassured him, "No—to some extent he must play it straight; he will have reason, believe me."

Whether he gives good information or not, at least he's off the streets for twenty years, thought Doyle, which is to the good. If he survives in prison, that is; he'd already been attacked in custody. She realized that Sergey must have been poking about the Met for the express purpose of planning the attack on Solonik—no wonder Munoz was out of sorts; if Acton had questioned her about Sergey, she must have felt like a fool. I tried to warn her, thought Doyle, with a twinge of self-righteous satisfaction, but she didn't want to hear it.

Doyle realized that the manual she was holding was the one that Owens, the raving lunatic, had put together as a project for Acton, before he tried to kill her. Owens had expressed an interest in the science of bloodstains, and Acton had asked him to put together demonstrative photographs. The project had been a ploy, though; Acton suspicioned that Owens was the killer, and wanted to keep the man close to hand.

Doyle looked through the photographs, repulsed and fascinated at the same time. One of the photographs portrayed a victim Owens had killed himself. Sick, she thought; how he must have enjoyed putting this together—proud of his handiwork, he was.

The photograph was of a woman who had been shot in the face. Giselle, thought Doyle, although she was unrecognizable. Doyle and Acton had interviewed the woman at the Laughing Cat pub, and the next day she had been murdered as a result. They'd been gathering information about the Kempton Park racecourse murder, and Owens must have been afraid she would talk. She wasn't Irish, but she had doings with the Sinn-split people, who were thick on the ground at the Laughing Cat.

Doyle suddenly remembered where she had heard the name Rourke. The victim from Newmarket was named Rourke, and the owner of the Laughing Cat pub was also named Rourke. It was a common enough name, but Acton often said he didn't believe in coincidences.

Acton was still on the phone with the DCS as Doyle approached and silently indicated she wanted to use his laptop. He nodded, and she shifted it toward her and pulled up the file on the Newmarket murder. A photo of the victim was found; Todd Rourke. She minimized it and pulled up the list of witnesses from the Kempton Park investigation. The Laughing Cat owner, Robert Rourke, was on the list. Doyle pulled up his photo and compared the two Rourkes side by side. Not the same person.

Acton put his hand over his phone and quietly said to her, "Brothers." She nodded.

She pondered the photos for a moment, and then felt her scalp prickling as it did when her intuition was making a connection. She pulled up Acton's surveillance photo of the Belarus man—Sergey—taken the day they had lunch at the deli.

She displayed it on the screen next to the photo of Robert Rourke, the Irish pub owner. It was the same person.

Acton abruptly told the DCS he needed to call back and rang off. He looked at the screen, then at Doyle. "Well done," he said.

CHAPTER 34

ACTON IMMEDIATELY MADE A CALL TO WILLIAMS, EXPLAINING Doyle's discovery and asking Williams to accompany him to the Laughing Cat to question Robert Rourke.

He then called forensics and asked them to expedite their analysis with the aim of linking any trace evidence at the Detention Center to Rourke; it would alleviate the need to rely on Solonik's equivocal identification of his attacker.

Doyle had been thinking over this latest surprising development, but if anything, it only added to the general confusion. Solonik was apparently trying to protect Rourke, a member of the rival Sinn-split and the man who had tried to kill him—not to mention Solonik's people had presumably murdered the man's brother. Why would Solonik try to protect Rourke, even in the face of Acton's many threats? The two should be bitter enemies. It made little sense, although Doyle now knew why Sergey had been afraid of her; he wanted to stay well away from someone who could expose his deception.

They were to meet Williams in the premium parking garage, as Acton wanted Williams to accompany him to the pub. Hopefully, Rourke would betray himself during questioning somehow. They could always bring him in for a short hold, but unless they could link him to the attack on Solonik, they had little on which to hold him—it was no crime to impersonate a Russian to impress a girl.

As they waited for Williams, Doyle asked in as neutral a tone as she was able, "Am I to come along with the both of you?"

Acton's own tone was even, and she knew he'd been anticipating the question. "I'd prefer that you wait in the car. It was a mistake to put you in the same room as Solonik."

He said nothing further, and Doyle struggled mightily to control her resentful self. It seemed so unfair—it was her catch, after all, and besides, she would know if the man was lying. She tried to remember her new attitude, and her resolution to accept the situation; Acton was as he was and he was not going to place her in danger. The personal was more important than the professional. Grow up, Doyle; don't be bitter. Her self-scolding didn't help much, and when Williams arrived at the scene—all bright-eyed and ready to break the case, he was—she had a hard time controlling the sulks.

Acton realized he'd forgotten to bring his tablet with the surveillance photograph, and so he went back to his office to retrieve it, leaving Doyle and Williams standing by the lift to wait for him. After a moment of silence, Williams asked, "Is everything all right?"

"No, it is not," she replied shortly. She refused to look at him, but could feel him watching her.

In a serious tone he said quietly, "If you ever are in need of help, I will help you, you know. You need only ask."

This caught her attention, and she stared at him a little blankly. She could see that Williams was genuinely concerned about her, and she was suddenly reminded that she shouldn't be alone with him. In her present mood, if he was going to think about kissing her again she would belt him one, she would. She could take him—as long as he didn't fight back.

Williams hesitated, and then added, "He was in a bad way, last night. Not himself."

"That he was," she agreed, wondering how Williams knew.

Then the light dawned. "Williams," Doyle said with some heat, "Acton doesn't beat me."

He was acutely embarrassed. "I only meant—"

"I don't need you to be protectin' me from my own husband."

"Kath—," he said, trying to defend himself.

"And don't call me Kath," she retorted through her teeth, furious with him for taking her place on the case and for even *thinking* that Acton could mistreat her. "I'll be takin' no advice nor help from the likes o' you; I can very ably handle meself."

"I didn't mean to suggest—"

"Oh, yes you did; you are hopin' for a chance to pick up the pieces and don't be denyin' it."

But this was an accusation too far, and Williams was now angry in turn. "You needn't be so sharp; I had every reason to be concerned—Acton was not himself last night."

Enraged, she retorted, "He certainly seemed like himself when we had sex on the desk—"

"Stop," he demanded, white with fury.

"No—*you* stop," she hissed. "Enough, Williams."

The doors for the lift slid open, and Acton stepped out into what was obviously a heated argument between them. He was surprised, and looked from one to the other.

"I lost my temper with Williams," Doyle confessed immediately. She faced the other man, saying with constraint, "I was unforgivably rude, Williams; I am wretchedly sorry."

Williams had also brought himself under control and replied stiffly, "No; the fault was entirely mine."

There was a small silence. Doyle refused to look at either of them.

"Then let's go," said Acton.

They got into Acton's car, Doyle and Williams each insisting that the other take the front seat. As they made their way to the Laughing Cat, Acton and Williams discussed possible strategies in questioning Rourke while Doyle listened and made an occasional subdued suggestion. I am a trial to my poor husband, she thought.

As it turned out, Rourke was not at the pub and when they asked at his residence, he was not there, either. The personnel at each location were a little vague about where he was or when he was expected. Acton concluded they had little choice but to await the lab results; hopefully an arrest warrant could be issued if the missing man could be linked to the attack; if nothing else, they could say they were investigating the very real possibility that the Irishman was illegally running numbers from the pub.

After concluding this unfruitful exercise, they returned to the Met, and Williams was dropped at his car. He and Doyle had been scrupulously polite to one another, but they hadn't made eye contact. As she drove away with Acton, Doyle looked out her window and bitterly regretted her flippin' temper. I never learn my lesson; I never stop to think about the consequences, she chastised herself with shame. Someday it's going to catch up with me, it is.

After a moment, Acton offered in a conversational tone, "If you don't tell me, I am afraid I may presume the worst."

"It was so *stupid*, Michael. He said somethin' and I took offense." She felt an absurd desire to cry. "I am too ashamed to tell you."

"Should I speak to him?"

Doyle was not sure how much he guessed. "No; least said, soonest mended, my mother would say. It will blow over." She managed a smile. "My flippin' temper."

Acton said quietly, "Remember your promise—I am to get a warning."

"*Michael*," she said in exasperation, pressing her palms to her eyes. "Don't be an *idiot*."

By the time they arrived back at the flat and had ordered some food, Doyle had found her feet again and miserably repented of her outburst with Williams—she had no idea how she was going to face him again, after what she'd said.

Acton was at his desk, working on his laptop, and to take her mind off her misery, Doyle walked over to see what he was researching. She needn't have bothered; Acton was viewing the garage's CCTV footage of her argument with Williams. Thankfully, there was no sound recording.

"Oh," she said. "How humiliatin'."

"You are very attractive when you are angry," he said mildly. "Not the best strategy to take, perhaps."

She said fairly, "He has never crossed the line, Michael." Best not to mention that he wanted to. "It will sort itself out, I promise; I was spoilin' for a fight."

"Speaking of which," said Acton, "I received a letter from my mother in the post today."

Saints, she thought in surprise; all it needed was this. "And?"

"Read it." He gave it to her.

The letter was on heavy vellum, with the Acton coat of arms imprinted at the top in its understated splendor. *My dear son,* it said. *Your wife may have informed you that I had a visit with her the other day. While I cannot endorse your choice, I found her not wholly lacking in redeeming qualities. Perhaps you will bring her to Trestles in the near future. There may have been a misunderstanding which offended; please convey my apologies if this is indeed the case.*

Doyle couldn't help laughing. "I threw her out, Michael, bag and baggage."

"Good one," he replied, imitating her.

"What do you suppose she wants?" Doyle asked tentatively. They still hadn't discussed the very real possibility that his mother wanted to kill her, as it was not an easy topic to bring up in everyday conversation. The fact that the woman was trying to lure her to her lair did not bode well.

"I do not know what she wants, but you will not be subjected to her."

"Thank you—she's terrifyin'; I'd rather face Solonik."

But this was apparently the wrong thing to say. "You will never face Solonik again."

She ventured to tease him. "I don't know, Michael—he is fond of redheads and he probably wouldn't quarrel with me like Williams does. Is he very rich?"

"Not funny." But she could see he was amused as he looked at the time. "Are you hungry yet?"

"Time for another fruit pie," she announced, and wandered into the kitchen.

CHAPTER 35

He closed his eyes, and thought of his home country and the bright, bright sky there—not like here. In his mind, he could see the white clouds against the blue sky—so peaceful. In the end, he could not stand by, could not leave the mganga to face the mashetani with no one to defend her. He thought of his home country, and could hear his grandmother's voice.

In the morning, Acton made ready to leave for his final conference with the prosecutor and Solonik's solicitor; they would go to court to enter the plea deal on the record and formally transfer the Russian into custody. Acton seemed a bit preoccupied, and so she respected his mood and stayed quiet until he departed.

"I have to do some fieldwork," he informed her as he shrugged into his coat. "But be certain to check in."

"I will, Michael."

It was not a day for Reynolds, and so Doyle had the flat to herself as she made ready for work. She enjoyed the solitude—she missed it sometimes, having been on her own for so long before she met Acton. The place was silent; Acton did not use the television unless he was monitoring the news for a case, and he never listened to music, not even in the car. Not very Holmesian, she thought. She remembered that Caroline had said that Acton and Timothy had studied music together, and thought it odd that he would take such a class if he had no interest.

Unable to resist, she took the opportunity to pull out a package she had hidden away in her drawer. It was a black knit dress; she had seen it displayed in a window several weeks before and had made the purchase on impulse. Pulling it over her head, she regarded herself in the mirror; the last time she had worn a dress was her confirmation, many years ago. It was pretty; Acton would like it, she knew, which was why she bought it in the first place. It had simple lines and he told her she looked well in black. She had no idea when she would wear it, but the comment Caroline had made about her wardrobe stung because it was true; Doyle made little effort. Acton didn't care, but her appearance did reflect on him and she should at least make an attempt to look the part—perhaps their monumental mismatch wouldn't be as obvious. The shopgirl had been very kind; not letting on that she thought Doyle was the next thing to a barbarian, so perhaps she could enlist the girl's aid in the future. A little guidance was needful, but it would have to be someone other than Caroline, who would only set her teeth on edge.

She turned around and reviewed herself critically over her shoulder. Yes, it was nice. She would buy shoes with heels, perhaps, just to see if she could manage it. And a purse, to put her gun in—couldn't accessorize an ankle holster, really. After smiling at her reflection, she pulled the dress off again and carefully folded it away.

The morning was a fine one, crisp and a little cool; the sunlight beginning to slant as it did this time of year. Doyle walked out in front of the building and looked for Aiki, but he was not leaning against his cab waiting for her. Instead, she saw him parked in the taxi queue and seated inside—praying, perhaps; she had the impression he was a spiritual man. She did not want to interrupt him, and so did not approach for a few moments, instead hovering on the sidewalk. He didn't move, however, and his posture seemed strange—perhaps he was unwell. Tentatively, she walked up the sidewalk to the passenger-side door and leaned down to peer in the window. "Aiki?"

His only response was to moan softly. Alarmed, she opened the door and slid onto the seat, reaching over to touch him. "Aiki," she repeated, "are you all right?" He fell sideways toward her and she could see a smear of blood on the seat behind him, and blood pooling on the seat itself. Quashing her horror, she went into police mode, pulling out her mobile as she propped him back up against the seat. "I need an ambulance for a wounded cab driver." After giving the address, she shouted out the window for the doorman to help. He ran over, and together they pulled Aiki out and laid him carefully on the sidewalk while Doyle wadded up her windbreaker and pressed it against the wound in his back. The concierge came running with a first aid kit, and Doyle replaced her bloody jacket with a bundle of gauze—the blood was only oozing, but Doyle knew he had lost a substantial amount already. Hearing a siren in the distance, she felt his pulse; it was thready and weak. Passersby were beginning to stop and gawk.

"Aiki," she commanded in a loud voice, "listen to me; try to stay awake." His eyelids fluttered open and he mumbled something in what sounded like French. Doyle said to the assemblage, "Does anyone speak French?"

No one volunteered. Doyle bent over Aiki, holding his hand tightly, her face close to his. "Help is comin' Aiki—you are goin' to be all right."

Aiki mumbled again. The wound was in the back, so he may not have seen his attacker. "Who did this, Aiki? Do you know?"

No response. He did not look well, and his eyes were beginning to appear glazed—Doyle had seen that look before, and shied away from the unbidden memory of her dying mother. A small silver crucifix hung around his neck on a chain, exposed where his shirt had been unbuttoned. Doyle stared at it for a moment, then made the sign of the cross and leaned in so that she was inches from his ear. "May the Lord who saves you from sin, save you and raise you up, Aiki."

She could see a tiny spark of awareness in his eyes as they opened to meet hers, and she felt a jolt of something—something strange and powerful, that seemed familiar, somehow. She recited what she could remember of the last rites as his eyes closed and, almost imperceptibly, he squeezed her hand. Then he was gone.

The ambulance came a moment later, but Doyle was already calling for a police unit and wiping away angry tears with the back of her hand. "It's a homicide investigation now," she explained to the medical personnel. She showed her ID card. "Thanks, anyway."

Pulling herself together, she asked the concierge and the doorman if they had seen anything, anyone arguing with Aiki. They hadn't noticed anything unusual or suspicious, and at this time in the morning there were many passersby; if he had brought a fare, the doorman did not remember opening the door for the cab.

Doyle looked up to gauge where the security cameras were, but the cab was not close enough to the entrance to be in the frame. To calm herself, she pulled out her occurrence book and began making notes. The doorman fetched a blanket and respectfully asked if he could cover Aiki; Doyle gave permission but asked that he not touch anything.

The police unit pulled up and two uniformed PCs alighted; Doyle did not recognize either, as they were from the local station. She introduced herself as a DC, and requested that they call for a SOCO team.

One of the constables, a world-weary-looking woman, surveyed the scene and offered very practically, "Do you think that's a good idea? It's unlikely we'll be able to isolate anything of interest."

Doyle turned on her and said with icy calm, "I am Lady

Acton, the chief inspector's wife, and I would like every possible avenue pursued, if you would not mind."

"Yes, ma'am," the woman said immediately, and was on her mobile, enlisting a SOCO team.

Doyle's mobile vibrated, it was Acton. She took the call; he would be wondering why she had not moved from the front of the building. "Michael, Aiki's been stabbed."

"Are you injured?" he asked immediately.

"No, it happened perhaps a half hour ago." It was so *flippin'* unfair. Poor Aiki.

"Has he been hospitalized?"

"No," she replied. "It was too late."

"Do you need me?"

"No, I'm gettin' a SOCO team, although it seems hopeless—there'll be all kinds of prints and trace everywhere."

"I'm so sorry, Kathleen."

She paused and took a breath. "I'm afraid I invoked the power of your name."

"You're entitled," he replied gently. "It's your name, too."

She rang off, and put her mind to directing the SOCO team.

CHAPTER 36

DOYLE MADE HER APPEARANCE AT WORK JUST AFTER LUNCH, having endured a thoroughly miserable morning. Forensics had duly dusted the cab, inside and out, but Doyle didn't need to see the glances the team exchanged between them to know it was hopeless; even if they could isolate a suspect's DNA, any solicitor worth his salt would argue there was nothing to prove that the suspect was a killer as opposed to a mere passenger. The coroner's people reported that the stab wound was a slim blade, and Doyle immediately thought of the blade that had attacked Solonik, but discarded the thought just as quickly. There could not be a link; she just had stabbings on the brain.

She then took on the grim task of informing Aiki's family. After contacting the cab company to verify that the dead man had a wife and child, she explained the situation and was given the address. The cab company spokesman wondered how soon they could have the cab returned from forensics, and Doyle didn't trust herself to speak for a moment.

Aiki's little flat was located in a crowded housing project, and Doyle gently informed the stricken woman that she was now a widow. Wiping away tears, she recited her profound sorrow and described how kind Aiki had been to her. The widow listened and nodded but did not weep, her eyes dry and wide. The weeping comes later, thought Doyle; I remember it all too well. She contacted their parish priest, and waited with the woman until his arrival.

Acton texted to ask if she was available for lunch, and she felt an almost overwhelming desire to be next to him; such a sad day, truly. "Please," she texted. She met him in the lobby at headquarters and kissed him, not caring who saw. "I love you," she said. "I love, love, love you and I don't tell you near enough. Don't die."

"You are beginning to sound like me," he replied, and took her arm in a comforting gesture. They walked to a local restaurant and went in; it was too cold to sit outside. She told him of the stabbing, and of her actions afterward while he listened sympathetically. "I was that angry, Michael; it seemed so unfair. He was such a nice man."

He warned her, "It is unlikely something like this will ever be solved."

"I know, I know, believe me. And the robber was a crackin' idiot; why rob a cab driver in the mornin' when he hasn't made any money yet?"

"Perhaps money was not the motive. That is not an area where random crime usually occurs."

"Then what would it be?" asked Doyle, who'd traced this logic herself. "Did he overhear one of his fares say somethin', or did he witness somethin'? Even if that was the case, we'll never find out."

"I am sorry, Kathleen, I know you will miss him."

"Yes." She rested her head in her hands for a moment. "I'm overreactin', I know—we see this kind of thing every day. But I felt like we were kindred spirits, or somethin'." She lifted her head and confessed, "I'm afraid I got carried away, and mentioned to his widow that there was a pension payout comin'."

"Ah," said Acton.

Contrite, she reached to take his hand. "I know I should have asked you first, but they were *so* poor, Michael. I thought perhaps some of the fungible assets could be used; we don't need them now."

"We soon may."

She couldn't suppress a pleased smile—they hadn't discussed having another baby, being as he didn't like discussions, but now that she'd suffered the loss she felt an unexpected yearning, burgeoning within her breast. "Yes, I suppose we can't let your vile cousin be inheritin' your estate."

"Perish the thought." He said it mildly, but she caught a flash of extreme dislike, and wondered if she would ever hear the backstory to yet another Acton family rift. He continued, "A pension would be too difficult to put into place with the cab company; instead the widow will be informed there was a third party administrator, and I will arrange for a trust that can come through Layton."

"Thank you, Michael." She squeezed his hand in gratitude, thinking that now Aiki's wife and child would at least have a chance to break away from their scratching existence—some good would come from his death. "The widow said she trained as a nurse assistant, but she's had trouble landin' a job. Timothy's charity clinic is near there; perhaps he can hire her." Doyle had a burning need to help, to erase the powerlessness she had felt all morning.

They telephoned Timothy, and found that he was taking his own lunch at home with Caroline. Acton explained the situation, and gave Timothy the widow's address. "I will stand the salary, as a donation," he added. There was a pause while Acton listened, and he then said, "No, I'm afraid we can't make plans; Kathleen and I are going to Brighton this weekend." His eyes rested on her, and Doyle mustered up a grateful smile. Cheering her up, he was. It would be too cold for swimming; so presumably he planned on strictly indoor activities. The thought of a holiday was immensely appealing; there had been a lot of trouble lately, both in their personal lives and at work, but now that the turf war was winding up and she was back on her feet, they could take a break for a few days. She would wear her dress and surprise him—although it was unlikely she would be wearing it for very long. When the mood hit him, it was every lass for herself.

After he rang off, she said, "That sounds grand, Michael."

They smiled at each other for a moment. Faith, thought Doyle—maybe we truly are an ordinary mister and missus; next we'll be wearing matching shirts and taking photos together on the boardwalk.

"Good news; Timothy says your liver scan shows no damage."

This was indeed good news. "I feel like my old self, I do."

He reached to touch her cheek with a finger. "Your face is beginning to fill in a bit."

"It should be; I've been eatin' like a horse."

"I love you," he said softly. "I don't say it near enough, either."

Doyle returned to work in a far better frame of mind. She went to look up Habib, and as she approached down the hall, she could hear him arguing with Munoz—not really arguing, she amended; just being firm with her for a change.

"It's not fair," Munoz complained, and Doyle would not have been surprised if the girl had stamped her foot; she was in a temper.

"What's not fair?" asked Doyle.

Munoz whirled on her, and accused, "You went on the Solonik interview because you're married to Acton. I am passed over, *every* time."

Habib offered fairly, "Doyle has very good interrogation skills."

He's probably making the sign against the evil eye as we speak, thought Doyle, remembering what Williams had said.

"It was no big deal, Munoz, and I was handy." Not to mention that Acton would not have allowed anyone else to hear the verbal knife fight between the two men—he was regretting he'd allowed Doyle to hear it.

But Munoz would not be mollified and turned back to Habib. "Doyle has an unfair advantage; I should file a complaint."

As Habib was caught between his two loves—his job and the fair Munoz—Doyle stepped in to give an assist. "The interview wasn't helpful; Solonik claimed he knew nothin' about the attack and Acton did all the talkin', believe me." She wondered if Solonik would have told Munoz her hair was beautiful in his insinuating way; it was probably his usual procedure. To divert Munoz's rage, she added, "And I wanted to ask the both of you for ideas; Solonik's attacker was an Irishman posin' as a Russian." She carefully didn't look at Munoz—no point in letting Habib know about her foolishness. "He was actually one of the Sinn-split people—a pub owner named Rourke—but Solonik is protectin' him and let him get away. Why would that be?"

This puzzle did work to divert Munoz, who had firsthand knowledge of the hoax, and the three of them thought about it for a moment. "Solonik's motivation may not be to protect Rourke," offered Habib in his precise voice. "Solonik may be unwilling to identify him because it is in Solonik's best interests."

"I don't understand why Rourke tried to kill him in the first place," added Munoz.

Doyle looked at her, not following, and Munoz impatiently explained, "Solonik will be going to a maximum-security prison for years—he'll be out of the picture. Why take such a chance to try to kill him? There's really no point."

"Was it just a wild attempt at revenge, then?" Doyle glanced at Habib, thinking of their earlier conversation about tribal warfare. "Rourke not carin' about anythin' other than gettin' retribution for his brother's murder?"

"If it was just that—an attempt at retribution—Solonik would not hesitate to identify him," Habib pointed out logically. "Something else is at stake. Perhaps it was a business decision, not to identify Rourke. Solonik is acting as a businessman in this instance, not a member of a rival tribe."

Doyle paused, her instinct telling her that this was important, and tested this idea aloud, saying slowly, "For some reason, Solonik cannot afford to grass on Rourke—it would hurt him more than the satisfaction he would get in turnin' him in to the police."

"Yes," agreed Habib with a quick nod. "But as Munoz pointed out, why is this? There is nothing left for Solonik but prison, and indeed, any information he could offer against Rourke may help him in a plea deal."

It was a puzzle, and they traded ideas for the next few minutes, but could not come up with a plausible theory. Nevertheless, Doyle went back to her desk feeling they were on to something. She wrote Acton an e-mail, suggesting that they consider this angle; if it wasn't a revenge attack, why would Rourke want Solonik dead, rather than locked away in prison? And how were Solonik's interests served by protecting Rourke, who had tried to kill him? She looked over the message, and then sent it. Acton may have some good insight; in truth, sometimes she had the uneasy feeling that his thought processes aligned with the perpetrators'.

She saw she had a message from Williams, asking if she could meet for coffee. She didn't respond; there would be more apologies and stifled feelings, and she just didn't feel up to it. It was too soon to face him again after her tantrum, and she had certainly put paid to any chivalric feelings he may have entertained toward her. She couldn't avoid him forever, though; if he was Acton's man and she was Acton's wife they'd be thrown together regularly and she must not make her husband's work more difficult. There were difficulties enough; hopefully he'd not be sharing a cell with Solonik anytime in the near future—that would be the wrong kind of matching shirts.

CHAPTER 37

THE NEXT MORNING, DOYLE AWOKE TO ACTON'S MOUTH, IN-sistent upon hers. "Reynolds," she murmured to remind him.

"He will have to wait his turn."

She smiled while he kissed her throat, moving southward. "Michael," she said, looking at the clock. "He'll be here any minute."

"This won't take long," he said, and it didn't.

When Reynolds arrived, Doyle was in her robe and heaping strawberry jam on toast, her face as rosy as the jam. She found she couldn't bring herself to eat frosty flakes anymore, which was a crackin' shame, but there it was.

Reynolds brushed off his coat, as it was raining. "You will need a coat and umbrella, madam; the weather has turned with a vengeance."

Doyle gazed out the window at the rain, her bare feet curled under her on the chair. When it rained in Ireland, the shades of green simply became less vibrant. In London, the gray only became grayer. And, she added mentally, it was always raining in this wretched country; any fieldwork needing to be done today would be a miserable slog because of it. Mentally, she shook herself; it was unlike her to be melancholy, especially after the wake-up she'd received.

Acton crossed through the kitchen and dropped a kiss on her head on his way to pack up his electronics, and she asked, "Have we heard whether forensics can put Rourke at the scene of the Solonik attack?"

"Nothing yet—I may have to bring Rourke in for questioning with only Solonik's ID as a basis, such as it is; if I can't shake him, I will have to let him go."

Doyle considered the stormy sky out the window. "Why do you suppose Solonik is protectin' him? We tried to puzzle it out yesterday, with little luck."

Acton put his arms through the coat that Reynolds held for him, and replied almost matter-of-factly, "There is a secret. Rourke would only attempt such a risky attack if he was very much afraid of Solonik, and as Solonik is no longer a threat to Rourke or his organization, he was afraid of what Solonik might reveal."

Doyle knit her brow, following this logic, which seemed sound. "But then, why doesn't Solonik reveal whatever it is?"

Acton took his umbrella. "Because Solonik cannot afford to reveal it, either. It is a mutual secret." He paused before heading to the door. "Have you heard anything useful about Aiki?"

"No," she replied sadly, and explained to Reynolds, "My cab driver was killed yesterday."

The servant considered this in silence. "Another poisoned plant, madam?"

"No; I'm afraid he was simply stabbed. Right outside the building, no less."

"That is indeed a shame," said Reynolds in extreme disapproval. "Not what one would expect at this address, if I may say so." It was clear he was offended by such bad taste.

"This place is worse than the Sailortown Docks," Doyle agreed. "Let's hope bad luck doesn't come in threes, as my mother used to say. If only Aiki could have given me somethin' to go on before he died—a random crime like this is a bear to solve." Clasping her knees to her chest, she sighed. "Aiki mumbled a few words, but no one there spoke French."

"You were *there*, madam?" Reynolds was very much shocked.

"I wish I had been, Reynolds; but I came down after he was wounded, and it was too late." She frowned, trying to remember. "I thought he said, 'Notify Amy,' and that perhaps he wanted me to notify his wife, but her name is not Amy."

The front door shut abruptly, and she looked up in surprise; Acton had left. How odd that he didn't say good-bye.

She prepared for work, and at the door Reynolds held her black coat for her, having notified the driving service that she would need a ride to the Met. I'm to be chauffeured in cashmere, she thought, and wondered what her mother would say about such a thing—she'd have laughed, probably, and called Doyle a mushroom. Times had certainly changed; when she'd first met Acton, she was living a very simple and solitary existence, trying to scrape together a down payment for a small condo and barely keeping her head above water. No question that everything was a million times better now, but she was still trying to adjust to the whirlwind change and her new status in life.

With a small smile, she remembered their quick session that morning, and consoled herself with the fact she had definitely adjusted to marriage—they were finding their way as a couple, and he was letting her see an occasional glimpse of himself, even though he was still very careful around her. No point in quizzing him; he'd only reveal what he wished, but he was trusting her more and more—she could feel it—and because of this, perhaps his symptoms would ease. She still could not be easy about Acton's going to a therapist.

When Doyle arrived at her desk, Munoz was already hard at work next door, so Doyle didn't disturb her—it sounded as though the keys were being pounded in annoyance, so best to stay well away. Williams had sent another message, but she didn't open it—she'd give it another day before they made their peace.

Reviewing the other messages, she saw that Habib had given her an assignment stemming from a lead she'd uncovered whilst she was researching Acton's cold cases. It appeared that several murders over the few months, in hindsight, could be considered the work of a single perpetrator. Due to the nature of the crimes, they could very well be the work of someone in law enforcement, and so the assignment was to be kept as quiet as possible.

Because a serial killer was always cause for concern, Doyle decided she would check the boxes in the Evidence Locker straightaway; she had solved the aqueduct murder by taking a look at the hard evidence, and sometimes her instinct worked best when she handled the various items.

As she rose to leave, Doyle was confronted by Munoz, who had appeared at the entrance to her cubicle. "Hallo, Munoz," said Doyle with false heartiness; Munoz, she could see, was still in a temper, and Doyle yet again marveled that the male of the species seemed to find such a trait so attractive.

"There's no point in even making a complaint," complained Munoz. "Acton is too powerful."

"Whist, Munoz," Doyle retorted, very much annoyed. "You will draw the wrong sort of attention if you make such a complaint. Think on it; the PR people are not goin' to take on someone who's not a team player."

"I wouldn't want to get you in trouble," the other replied grudgingly, although this was not exactly true.

Doyle, as it turned out, had her own sulking to do. "You have nothin' to fear from the likes of me, I promise you. I'll not be in the field much, anymore."

Munoz was instantly suspicious of what should have been good news. "Why?"

Doyle replied honestly, "Our job is dangerous, and Acton would prefer it."

Naturally, Munoz had to find fault with this plan. "You are quitting fieldwork because your *husband* told you to?"

"Of course not." Doyle was annoyed yet again, and threw out her own little dart. "Marriage is about compromise, Munoz—not that you'd know."

"So what is *his* compromise, then?"

Doyle was not about to discuss such matters with anyone, let alone Munoz, and particularly when she had no ready answer. Instead, she retorted in exasperation, "Faith, there's *no* pleasin' you; I thought you'd be happy with less competition."

Munoz, true to form, was going to be contrary, and tossed her hair. "It is ridiculous to take you out of the field—that's the only thing you can do well."

Nettled, Doyle retorted, "That is not fair—I can do a lot of things well."

"I meant *outside* of the bedroom."

Barely hanging on to her temper, Doyle flashed at her, "Now there's a foine case o' the pot an' th' kettle."

Before blows could be exchanged, Habib stepped between them, looking from one to the other in well-bred dismay. Doyle, her blood still boiling, excused herself in muffled tones and stalked down the hallway to take the lift to the Evidence Locker, all the while thinking very uncharitable thoughts. After a few minutes of silent reflection, however, she felt a little ashamed. First Williams, and now Munoz; she was losing her temper more easily than she was used. She would hate to believe it was the result of feeling she was untouchable, like Caesar's wife.

I am behaving badly, she conceded; I must beg everyone's pardon and try not to be so touchy. Father John would say we are always being led, and I must try not to resent being led into people who always seem to bring out the worst in me—it can't be in the grand plan to be constantly spoiling for a donnybrook, and it does not reflect well on Acton, either. It would only confirm everyone's assumptions if his new Irish bride was always brawling like a fishwife—although it would be so nice, just *once*, to take a swing at Munoz. I could take her, she thought with some optimism—although maybe not until I've gained a bit more weight back.

CHAPTER 38

DOYLE SIGNED IN TO THE EVIDENCE LOCKER, AND LOCATED the boxes containing evidence from several recent cases that were now loosely termed the park murders because the killings had occurred in park settings. Because the room was chilly, she wished she had remembered to wear her coat—although she probably would have looked ridiculous in it amongst the dusty shelves. She would buy a less ostentatious coat to keep at her workstation so she didn't hurt Acton's feelings—she could wear the black one to and fro, and he'd be none the wiser.

After spending several hours studying the hard evidence along with the case notes, she felt the familiar prickling of her scalp; there was indeed a pattern, and she began to take careful notes so that she didn't forget her first impressions. Absorbed in the task, she didn't realize how much time had elapsed until she stretched her back and glanced at her mobile to check the time. She had forgotten to text her symbol to Acton, but he had not checked in with her, as he invariably did when she was late or forgot. This was a surprise; perhaps she couldn't get service, here in the bowels of the building. As she walked down the linoleum hallway, she phoned his private line, hoping he wasn't worried about her.

"Yes."

She was a little surprised by his abruptness, considering he knew it was her, and teased him, "I see how it is; you've had your way wi' me this mornin' and now I'm to be neglected."

"I'm sorry, Kathleen; I'm trying to track down a suspect who's agreed to speak with me. I'm afraid it's rather important."

She paused. This was true; and equally true was the fact he was in no mood to speak to her for perhaps the first time in recorded history. "Is everythin' all right?" she asked, trying to stifle a pang of alarm.

"Yes—I will ring you later, once this is straightened out."

"Of course." She rang off, and frowned at the blank screen on her mobile for a moment. Something was afoot; he was preoccupied, and she was uneasy—mother a' mercy, here we go again. As she considered this strange turn of events, the mobile vibrated in her hand; it was Samuels.

"Ho, Doyle, I wondered if you'd heard anything about Solonik's attack—have they found the suspect yet?"

He was actually wondering if she'd heard anything from Acton; Samuels would have the same access to reports that she had. "No, I haven't heard yet, which is probably not good news."

"No," he agreed. "Should we brainstorm for ideas?"

"Absolutely; I'll be right over."

Doyle made her way to Samuels's corner of the basement, feeling that it was the least she could do. Compared to Williams, Munoz, and her fair self, Samuels didn't have much of a portfolio and the Solonik attack was a fine chance to be involved in a high-profile case—she would make good work of her latest resolution to be kinder, and hope it lasted longer than her last resolution to be kinder.

She joined the other DC at his desk, and together they reviewed the Solonik report on-line, which listed all the latest efforts that were being made to track down Rourke, including the addresses of relatives and known associates. He had many relatives, some in Ireland and some in England, which meant a lot of slog work to check in with them—assuming a relative would grass on him in the first place. All agencies had been alerted that he was wanted for questioning, but no leads had been called in, even by paid informants. It was almost incredible, except that it had happened; Rourke had attacked Solonik, walked out of the high security Detention Center, and disappeared—even the CCTV cameras around the facility and in the street were unhelpful. He was good with disguises, thought Doyle; but still and all, it was baffling—where did he go?

"Has Acton mentioned whether there are any other leads? Perhaps this is not up to date."

Doyle remembered her preoccupied and distracted husband, and shook her head. "I think he's handlin' somethin' else; in any event, I haven't heard."

"Too bad."

This was true, which meant that Samuels was trying to gain an advantage by priming her for information the others wouldn't have. She felt a bit sorry for him, and it was a shame she couldn't help him out. To make up for it, she offered, "Acton seems to think that Solonik and Rourke have a mutual secret."

Samuels stared at her for a moment. "Is that so?"

Doyle rose, since she needed to return to her station and begin entering her notes from the other case. "It doesn't make much sense, though; you wouldn't think Solonik and Rourke would be willin' to collaborate on *anythin'*."

Thoughtfully, he eyed her for a moment. "Tell you what; drop me a line if you hear anything—I'd love to help break this one."

She decided not to mention the obvious; that by the time the fair Doyle heard anything, it was usually all over but the shouting. "I will. Sorry I couldn't be of more use."

He expressed his thanks, and Doyle returned to her cubicle, thinking Samuels was a bit odd; if you were hoping to impress the brass by tracking down the Irish kingpin, one would think you'd be out in the field following the leads and hoping for a break, not sitting at headquarters trying to find out what Doyle knew.

As she came down the aisle way, Habib spied her and said in surprise, "DC Doyle; have you not left yet?"

"Left where?" she asked blankly.

He pursed his lips slightly to express his disapproval that she was not well-informed. "Dispatch received a call from a tipster on the Solonik attack, specifically asking to meet with you—it was someone who didn't want to be seen coming in. I could not reach you on your mobile, and so Munoz said she would find you."

With a faint twinge of alarm, she thought of the walk-in who had asked for her—the one who may have been sent by that Savoie person—but decided it couldn't be the same man; Lestrade hadn't been afraid to come into the Met. And this was a very good sign; usually, if an informant wanted to keep a meeting with the police quiet, he was not the usual gate-crasher but instead someone with valid information, hoping to cut a deal. "How long ago?"

"Twenty minutes, perhaps," said Habib. "Where is Munoz?"

With a flash of dismay, Doyle whirled and looked into Munoz's cubicle—she was gone and Doyle was suddenly certain that the other girl had made no attempt to find her, but had gone to meet the tipster herself. Making a monumental effort to moderate her voice, Doyle asked Habib the location of the rendezvous point and discovered it was Greyfriars Bridge, off Battersea.

"I'll go straightaway, sir," she said a bit grimly. She noted that her coat was missing, and added, "Believe me."

Nearly grinding her teeth with frustration that Munoz had not only pulled such a trick, but had left her without a coat, to boot, Doyle debated borrowing someone's jacket, but then decided she didn't want to miss the meeting altogether, and so grabbed her rucksack and left with all speed. It was still raining, and at least Munoz had not taken Doyle's umbrella— although it was probably unnecessary because the flippin' coat had a hood. Come to think of it, the rain may actually be a boon; if traffic was slow, Doyle might even beat Munoz there by taking the tube—it would serve her right.

After sitting uncomfortably amongst the wet and crowded passengers on the tube for a few minutes, Doyle began to calm down, and reflect upon her actions. She was still holding on to her anger at Munoz from their argument that morning and as a result, her reaction was perhaps a bit overwrought. Munoz, like Samuels, had seen a chance to try to break this important case by exploiting Doyle's connection and—to be fair—she shouldn't be angry at Munoz if she wasn't angry at Samuels. In addition, Doyle had been in the bowels of the Evidence Locker, and valuable time would have been wasted in going to fetch her. And Munoz may also feel some residual guilt for her role in squiring Rourke around when he was posing as Sergey—indeed, perhaps the tipster was Rourke himself, hoping to cut a deal and be brought in.

No, Doyle thought almost immediately; Rourke is dead. Surprised, she shifted away from the man thinking lecherous thoughts to her right, and wondered why she was convinced of this, closing her eyes to try to come up with it. After a moment, she gave up; she didn't know why, but she knew—in the way she knew things—that Solonik's attacker was no longer amongst the living.

As she exited at the nearest station to the bridge, she realized that now they may never know why Rourke attacked Solonik, and that in any event, she shouldn't be so jealous and territorial. Munoz was right; Doyle had been investigating interesting and high-profile homicides alongside Acton when she should have been collecting statistics or reviewing CCTV tape like any other first-year DC, and it wasn't fair. By the time she emerged from the stairway, she'd resolved to take a secondary role today, and help Munoz win some acclaim. I am sorry, she offered up, thinking of Aiki and how fragile life was; I have to be remembering what's what.

CHAPTER 39

Doyle approached Greyfriars Bridge, which was deserted. Very few people were about due to the rain, which pattered steadily on Doyle's umbrella. She wondered if Munoz had already spoken to the tipster, or if she hadn't yet appeared on the scene, having been stuck in traffic. Doyle decided to walk out to the center of the bridge so as to be conspicuous in the event the tipster was watching from some concealed position, which was always a possibility.

As she waited there a few moments, shivering in the cold wind, she looked about. There was no one who remotely looked like a tipster in the area. After glancing at her mobile to check the time, she decided to wait twenty more minutes and then stop in a pub for coffee—she shouldn't have come without a jacket, and now she was paying the price. As she put her mobile away, she thought she heard a small sound, coming from beneath her. Leaning carefully over the railing, Doyle peered at the flowing river, brown and churning below her. The light was not good, and she didn't see anything of interest.

But there. A movement. Doyle strained her eyes and made out the outline of a figure clinging to one of the cement supports as the strong current flowed past. She couldn't make out the face, but knew immediately that it was Munoz.

Her mouth dry, Doyle dropped her umbrella and looked frantically in all directions, but there was no one about. She leaned over the railing to look again at Munoz and shouted at her, "Izzy! Can you hear me?"

No response. The girl's arms clung to the cement base of the support, but her face appeared to be nearly submerged in the swirling water—she was losing consciousness. Think, Doyle. Stay calm.

Quickly pulling out her mobile, she texted an exclamation point to Acton's private line; it was their symbol for an emergency, and she had never used it before. She laid the phone on the bridge, propped her umbrella over it, then turned her rucksack upside down and dumped out its contents—even her tablet, which broke apart upon impact with the concrete walkway. Holding the empty rucksack upside down against her chest, she pushed her arms through the straps, and climbed to balance atop the rail, which was slick with the rain. I can't hesitate, even to say a prayer, she thought, or I'll change my mind. Just as she jumped, she could hear her mobile ring.

She aimed to land in the water a few feet into the current, up from the support to which Munoz clung, and with this in mind held the bottom of her upside-down backpack open as she fell through the air, her midsection clenching with the sensation. Hitting the surface of the river with a roaring jolt, she bobbed up immediately, the trapped air in the rucksack making her buoyant. The water was an unbelievably cold shock, and the current began to move her as she frantically flailed her legs so as to grab on to the support. There was a terrible, terrible moment when she had trouble securing a grip on the wet cement and she was almost swept past, but then she flung her arms wide and managed to scramble onto the support next to Munoz, gasping for breath. Nothing to this swimming business, she thought; good one, Doyle.

Her relief was short-lived, however, as Munoz began to sink

into the river, her hands trailing limply on the cement base. Doyle grabbed at her, trying not to lose her own grip on both the rucksack and the support, and just managed to grasp the hood of Munoz's coat. My coat, Doyle amended.

Doyle strained to heave the other girl back onto the support, but the coat was heavy with water and she decided she would have to let go of the rucksack, which was in the way. Thanks to her recent bouts with poison and pregnancy, she was not as strong as she normally was, but she managed to leverage Munoz into a position so that her face was above the swirling water. "Izzy," she gasped. "You have to help me."

Munoz moaned and her eyes fluttered open. Doyle could have wept with relief; she had been afraid, for a moment, that the other girl was dead. "Help me take the coat off—it's too heavy."

Weakly, Munoz obeyed by moving one arm at a time and between them they removed the coat, and let it sink.

"I'm hurt," mumbled Munoz. "Back."

Doyle leaned out, trying to look, but found she did not want to risk her precarious grip on the support and on Munoz. "It's hardly anythin', Munoz, you'll be fine," she said firmly. "The cold water will help."

Munoz's eyes slowly closed again, and Doyle could see the delicate blue veins on her eyelids. "Izzy," she called sharply. "You must stay awake—help is comin' and I can't hold you."

Munoz lifted her head weakly in response, but did not open her eyes and after a moment, her head slipped back again. Gritting her teeth, Doyle closed her own eyes, fiercely concentrating on not letting her hands release their weak grip on the cement as the other girl's weight became heavier and heavier. I can't let her go, she thought in despair; I am so sorry, Michael—I can't let her go.

Through her eyelids, Doyle thought she could see flashing blue lights and opened her eyes again, equal parts incredulous and relieved to see the reflection of emergency vehicle

lights on the water—a rescue crew must be on the bridge. A
few more minutes, a few more minutes. She had to keep
Munoz awake; she could not maintain her grip if the other
girl lost consciousness and became dead weight—and they
were so close, so close to being rescued. "You never gave me a
weddin' present, Munoz," Doyle loudly accused in the other
girl's ear.

"Shut *up*, Doyle," murmured Munoz weakly.

Doyle heard someone shouting. She didn't want to move
her head, but shouted "Help!" as loudly as she could, and
Munoz started from the noise as it echoed along the rafters
under the truss.

"I'll want one of your drawin's," Doyle gabbled. "Of the
Madonna. I'll hang it over my fireplace, I will."

Munoz moaned and began to slowly roll away. "Izzy,"
scolded Doyle desperately, "don't you *dare*."

She started in surprise at a large splash near her side, but
didn't want to turn around to look as the displaced water
landed on her in a wave. An arm was felt, supporting her up-
ward so that she could get a better grip, higher up on the support.

"How are we doing?" asked Williams, slightly out of breath,
from behind her head.

"Ach," panted Doyle, "not so very grand, I'm afraid. Munoz
is hurt."

She could feel Williams lean back to inspect Munoz, and
lean in again. "They'll bring her up with a lift—right now
they're spanning a rope across the river downstream, in case
we let go. Cover your ears." He leaned back and shouted that
one of them was hurt and needed medical. The person on
the bridge had a megaphone and assured him a lift would be
lowered straight away.

Williams returned to his position supporting them from
behind, his arms securely around both girls as the cold water

rushed by. Doyle was shivering uncontrollably. "Sorry," she chattered. "It's s—so cold."

"It is a shame there is no desk nearby," he replied. "We could have sex."

She started to laugh, and so did he, huddled together with Munoz's limp form firmly wedged between them. "I didn't know how I could face you again," she confessed. "I shouldn't have said what I did."

"You definitely got your point across." With a lunge, he reached over to grasp the canvas harness that had been lowered to the water.

"I'm sorry I didn't respond to your messages." She helped him fasten the harness around the unconscious girl. "But there's nothin' I can say to make it better."

They watched anxiously as Munoz was briefly suspended over the water and then, swinging slightly, disappeared above them into the darkness that was punctuated by flashing blue lights.

Williams maintained his grip on Doyle and lowered his head to hers so that they were face-to-face, inches apart. "Promise me something."

"That depends," she answered cautiously. He may have saved her, but that didn't mean she would throw caution to the winds.

"If I promise not to bother you anymore, please don't shut me out of your life."

"That's fair enough," she agreed through chattering teeth.

"I love you," he said simply. "I know I shouldn't, but there it is."

She swallowed and shivered, not knowing what to say and fighting an almost overwhelming urge to cry. He continued gently, "I'll get over it, don't worry."

"I would like us to be friends," she replied, as steadily as she was able. "But it may not be possible."

"I will make it possible."

Then, because he was so sincere and because she figured she wouldn't get the chance for the next fifty years or so, she leaned in and kissed him, even though her mouth was nearly numb with the cold. He returned the kiss, and it was rather nice. It was the sort of kiss she may have had after a promising first date, and she couldn't help but compare it to the first time she'd kissed Acton, when it felt as though they'd set the room on fire.

They disengaged when a harness splashed behind her, and Williams helped fasten her in. He then held her legs carefully so she didn't bang against the support as they pulled her up. The cold wind hit her and she shivered convulsively as she was lifted to the rail where many hands reached for her, including her husband's.

CHAPTER 40

THE RESCUE TEAM IMMEDIATELY WRAPPED AN EMERGENCY FOIL blanket around her as Acton crouched before her, chafing her hands as he looked into her face, assessing. He is having trouble breathing, she thought, so she smiled at him through shivering lips. "Stupid Munoz."

"Are you injured?"

"Not at all; just cold."

Munoz had already been transported away and the medical team from the second ambulance asked Acton if they could examine her. Doyle threw him a stricken look; she had an extreme distaste of being examined as a result of her miscarriage, and there was the small matter of her illegal weapon, wet but intact in her ankle holster.

"Not necessary," said Acton, reading her aright. As the ambulance personnel retreated, he said, "Come into the car. Can you give a statement?" He motioned to Samuels, who joined them, taking out his tablet.

They retreated to Acton's Range Rover and he engaged the engine and turned up the heat. Doyle's shivering was now under control, and she threw off only an occasional shudder. "How is Munoz?"

"Stabbed. Between T-5 and T-6."

"Mother a' *mercy*," said Doyle, stunned. "I couldn't see. It's a miracle she didn't bleed out. "

"The cold water, plus there wasn't sufficient penetration," said Acton. "Her vitals are stable—she should be all right. What happened?"

This, of course, was a good question. "I don't know, Michael. There was a call to Dispatch; an anonymous tipster wantin' to give information on Solonik. I was in the Evidence Locker, so Munoz took it."

The back door opened, and Williams joined them in the car, wrapped in his own foil blanket with his wet hair plastered against his head. Acton said to him, "Well done," and then returned his attention to Doyle.

"I came because I thought I could help," she continued, which was the truth, after all. "When I got here I didn't see anyone, but then I heard Munoz. She was barely hangin' on to the support, in the water."

"Did you see anyone leave? Anything unusual?"

Doyle closed her eyes to concentrate. "No. No one was about. There was no one to shout to, so I texted you and jumped."

Acton paused. "You jumped in the river?"

Faith, thought Doyle; he's going to have an apoplexy, he is.

"Quite a jump," said Samuels admiringly.

"She cannot swim," Acton revealed. This announcement was met by the other two men with the incredulous silence it deserved.

"I caught some air in my rucksack," Doyle explained, demonstrating with her hands. "For buoyancy—it worked really well." Proud of her own ingenuity, she looked at the others for approval, but they seemed unable to respond.

"Let's go home and get you out of these wet clothes," her husband suggested. To Samuels he said, "See if you can find a witness or a CCTV that caught something."

"I want to stay with Munoz," insisted Doyle. "I don't know if anyone is with her."

"She'll be in surgery, and her family has been notified. If you feel up to it, we'll go after you are put to rights." Acton gave more instruction to Samuels and thanked Williams, shaking his hand.

"Yes; thank you Williams," added Doyle sincerely. "I don't know how much longer I could have held on." She would show Acton that they were to be civil, now that they had made their peace.

The others exited the car, and Acton put it in gear and headed for home. He took one of her hands and stroked the back with his thumb; back and forth, back and forth.

"I couldn't help it, Michael; there was nothin' for it."

"No," he agreed. "You did well."

"Then you'll not be regrettin' the loss of my fine coat."

"No," he said. "I will buy you a dozen."

"To be accurate, it was Munoz's fault—she borrowed it without askin'."

This offhand comment, however, received his full and alert attention. He asked slowly, "Was Munoz wearing your coat when she was attacked?"

Doyle saw where this was going, and protested, "Michael, Munoz looks nothin' like me." She added, "Even if you were color blind."

Acton looked forward again. "It was raining; if she had the hood up, someone approaching from behind may not know the difference."

Doyle thought about this, feeling a twinge of alarm. She admitted, "It is true she didn't have an umbrella."

There was a silence. The stroking had stopped. He knows something, she thought. She waited to hear what he was thinking, but he remained silent. She prompted, "Do you think it was done on Solonik's order?" This never-ending vengeance business.

"Perhaps," said Acton neutrally, so that she couldn't read whether this was indeed what he thought. "Was the tip specifically for you?"

"Yes," she conceded, not liking the implication at all.

He made no reply, and she eyed him—Mother of God; the man would drive a saint to sin. "Don't be tiresome, Michael. Do you think this was connected to the turf war?"

He wrestled with it, and finally admitted, "I'd rather not say."

This admission was almost welcome; he didn't want to put her off, but he didn't want her to read a lie. She pointed out reasonably, "If you're thinkin' that I'm a target for some reason, you shouldn't keep it a secret."

"No," he said immediately. "I don't think you will be attacked again."

It was the truth. Well, she thought—here's a relief, although it was a mystery; how could he be so sure?

His mobile vibrated, and he checked the ID, and then picked up. "I'm afraid I am unavailable just now, may I call you back?" He waited for a response then rang off.

She teased him, "Was that your girlfriend?"

He smiled as he drove, genuinely amused. "I have nothing left over for a girlfriend."

"Keep that to mind," she teased him. "Else you'll be embarrassin' yourself."

They arrived home, and Doyle did not pause but stepped immediately into a shower so hot it was painful. Before she did, she could hear Acton begin to explain to Reynolds what had happened, and couldn't control her giggle—Reynolds must think this place is disaster central; best raise his salary or he'll flee in horror.

She let the hot water wash over her and began to feel her toes and fingers tingle. I wonder, she thought, if that knife was meant for me. It was a chilling thought. She also wondered where Acton had been—he'd arrived at the scene later than Williams, although he must have contacted Williams to come to her aid. He was at a distance, then—farther away than the Met. She remembered how terse he'd been when she'd rung him up earlier; lucky it was, that it hadn't been their last conversation on earth.

She turned to rinse her hair and saw Acton looming outside the shower door. He stepped in, and his mouth found hers, gently. She put her arms around his neck and decided this was all that was needed to warm her up completely.

Later, she dried her hair, embarrassed to note that Reynolds was still there and surely must have noted that all other residents were in the same shower. Acton watched her dress, unable to take his eyes from her, and she tried to ease him down. "Are you plannin' on taking a bite out o' the scotch?"

"No," he replied, then amended. "Not yet."

"I don't mind, my friend. I can be the barkeeper."

He smiled. "You don't know the first thing about bar keeping."

"I do know the first thing about you, however."

They regarded each other for a long moment. He was not going to budge, so she gave up trying to find out what he was thinking. "Let's be off to the hospital, then."

They left after explaining to Reynolds that they were going to visit Munoz. Once in the car, Doyle took a long breath. "I'll be needin' a new coat for Brighton—Brighton is goin' to be glorious and much needed, after this little episode." She leaned her head back against the leather headrest. "Between you and me, I'm ready for glorious."

"Yes," he agreed.

Mother a' mercy, she thought in dismay; we are not going to Brighton.

CHAPTER 41

T HERE WAS A GUARD POSTED OUTSIDE MUNOZ'S ROOM, AND Acton showed his ID as a formality. Munoz lay on the hospital bed, propped up on her side and conversing with the others who were in the room and clearly related to her; a middle-aged couple who must have been her parents, along with a young woman—who was unmistakably her sister—and a grandmother, seated closest to the injured girl. They all turned to regard the newcomers, and Doyle was much struck; the group resembled the portraits of the Spanish royal family one saw in museums. Between these people and Acton, thought Doyle, I am a stranger in a strange land.

Doyle went straight to the patient and stood beside the bed. "Munoz," she said accusingly. "You owe me a coat."

"That's not fair; I'm not the one who put a knife in it."

Acton asked, "Did you see the attacker?"

Munoz shook her head. "No, sir—I was coshed first. There was no one on the bridge that raised any alarm; I was taken completely unawares, and Samuels has taken a report."

Doyle leaned to examine her head. "Oh, Munoz," she said in dismay. "They've had to shave some of your fine hair."

"Yes—the doctor said it was a sacrilege." This said with the slightest touch of smugness.

"Another one down," Doyle proclaimed, and Munoz smiled.

The older woman interrupted to speak in a torrent of Spanish, and Munoz answered in kind. Doyle heard her name, and the others stood with one accord and approached her, thanking her profusely; Munoz's mother embracing her fiercely and kissing both cheeks while Doyle blushed mightily.

"They're going to give you a commendation for bravery," said Munoz dryly. "Samuels told me."

Doyle smiled and shook her head. "I'm that sorry, Munoz; it's unlucky, you are."

Munoz threw back her head and laughed aloud, much to the surprise of her family. Her grandmother directed a stream of Spanish at Munoz, who then responded and turned to interpret to Doyle. "My grandmother wanted to offer you a sum of money, but I told her you were married to this rich man whom you stole from me, and she has now withdrawn the offer."

It appeared she wasn't joking, as the grandmother had furrowed her stately brow and now fixed her incredulous gaze on Acton, who stood against the back wall. Before the woman could confront him, Doyle decided they should take their leave, and so she said to Munoz with a smile, "Well, I'm glad you're all right, Izzy."

"I'll start on that project we discussed as soon as I am able."

Doyle found, suddenly, that she had to wipe away tears with the back of her knuckles until Acton put a handkerchief in her hand. "That's grand," she whispered.

"Doyle," Munoz remonstrated. "Don't go soft on me."

After they left, Doyle and Acton sat in the car for a few minutes whilst she cried on his chest, thoroughly wetting his shirt. When the tears stopped, she sat up and had recourse to his handkerchief once again. "Sorry. It's reaction, I think, from seein' her again."

"You're entitled." He started the car. "I've asked Reynolds to prepare something to eat."

"I think," she ventured, "that we are out of fruit pies."

He turned his head to look at her. "Please," he teased, "you've put me through enough today; don't do this to me."

Delighted that he seemed in a teasing mood, she insisted. "Recall that I'm to be gettin' a commendation. It's deservin', I am."

They stopped at a corner convenience store and Doyle assured him she was willing to go in alone. "Although it's not like we're buyin' pornography, Michael, and no one will recognize us, anyway."

He accompanied her with a fine show of reluctance, and she teased him the entire time, threatening to tell the clerk that she was buying the pies for him, and debating what flavors to choose at length. He smiled and touched her, the expression in his eyes promising intimate attention later. She was not fooled, however. I wish I knew what it was, she thought, but I haven't a clue; at least he's not in one of his black moods, and I'm determined not to allow him to start in.

When they returned home, Reynolds informed them that a reporter had asked for Doyle at the concierge desk. "I told him you had already retired, so that he wouldn't be waiting for you at the garage."

"Thank you, Reynolds," she replied, and wondered if it was the same one who had tried to speak to her that day when Aiki came to her rescue. He'd get no story from her, leastways.

They ate in companionable silence, and when they did speak, Doyle noted well that there was no mention of the turf war murders, and no mention of Brighton.

After Reynolds had cleared away the dishes and left for the night, she sat with Acton on the sofa, gazing at the fire and letting her fingers play on his chest. Usually this activity drew an immediate reaction from him—the man was on a hair trigger, he was—but tonight he seemed lost in thought. Doyle rested her head on his shoulder and hoped he would be done thinking soon, she was tired. Small wonder, she thought; another crackin' foul day.

She didn't realize she had fallen asleep until she was awakened by his hand moving on her breast. Sleepily assessing, she realized that she was lying with her head in his lap, and he was drinking, his hand beginning to wander. She picked it up and brought it to her mouth to kiss it. "I might actually be too tired, Michael," she murmured. "Can you proceed without wakin' me up?"

She could feel him smile, and his hand moved to caress her cheek. "You are something."

She knew he referred to the bridge-jumping. "I truly didn't have a choice. All's well that ends well, I suppose."

He made a sound to indicate this was a gross understatement, and she could feel his chest rise and fall as he took a deep breath. Thinking it an opportune time to do a little probing, she asked, "Where were you this afternoon—when you were so short with me on the phone?"

"I thought we had established I was visiting my neglected girlfriend."

"She should find another callin', poor thing."

His hand found her jaw and turned her head so he could meet her eyes. "You know I don't even look at other women."

"Oh, I know," she said with emphasis. It was a little daring; they rarely spoke directly of his neurosis.

He leaned back into the sofa, satisfied, and took another drink. Unimaginable that he should have an affair; he was focused on her like a laser beam. She duly noted, however, that he had avoided answering the question. He would not tell her unless he wanted to, and he clearly didn't want to; hopefully he wasn't plotting more retribution murders.

"Rourke is dead," she announced.

His hand stilled. "Is he indeed?"

"Bank on it," she teased. They rarely spoke directly of her abilities, either. "Is Solonik under lock and key?"

"Solonik is under lock and key." He said it with great satisfaction.

"Cheers, then." She tapped the bottom of his glass with a finger, wishing she knew what he was thinking about; he had feared the attack on Munoz may have been meant for her, but then assured her she was in no danger. It was a puzzle, and her husband's puzzles always seemed to end up being cataclysmic.

"I would say that you are wide-awake, wouldn't you?" The hand moved back to her breast and she giggled.

CHAPTER 42

Upon arriving at work the next day, Doyle was met by Habib, who was agog but hiding it well. "DC Doyle," he said. "The detective chief superintendent wishes to see you at your earliest convenience."

The commendation, she thought with resignation; this is going to be a tryin' day. Just when my last bout of celebrity had elapsed, along comes another. "I will see him straight-away, sir."

"How does Munoz?"

She paused, feeling a little sorry for him. He's like Williams, she thought; it's hopeless and they know it, but they can't help themselves. "I saw her last evenin' and she was in fine form, sir; they think there will be no lastin' damage. She will be back and we will be shoutin' at each other in no time."

He was delighted to hear it. "I sent some flowers from our team—I did not presume to visit."

Just as well, thought Doyle, dreading to think what the Spanish royal family would make of Habib. She made her way to the rarefied atmosphere of the DCS's office, and his assistant phoned to inform him of her arrival. The DCS's assistant was very businesslike and friendly, unlike Acton's assistant, who was probably auditioning to take Doyle's place at this very moment. Not that Acton would notice, she thought, and felt better. They had a lengthy and wordless lovemaking session in front of the fire last night, which had the added benefit of making Acton forget that he wanted to drink some more. He had fallen asleep on the rug with her lying atop him; definitely no energy left over for a girlfriend, she thought in satisfaction.

The DCS ushered her into his office and offered her coffee, which she refused for fear she'd disgrace herself by spilling it on his fine desk. He was very pleased and congratulatory, and she was asked to recite the story again for his benefit. She began to wonder if she would retell it so much that she would forget the actual memory, and just remember the story. No, she decided; I will never forget how it felt when Munoz started slipping away as long as I live.

"Any leads on a suspect as yet?" he asked.

"I don't believe so, sir, which is amazin', considerin' it was afternoon, and one would think someone would have seen somethin'."

He told her she would receive a commendation at next month's awards ceremony, and he had contacted the newspaper to run a story.

"Oh," said Doyle, trying to hide her dismay. "There's truly no need, sir."

"It's great PR," her superior explained firmly. "The public loves it when female PCs defy death. And there's the Acton angle, also."

She nodded miserably. As a clincher, he added, "And you are photogenic, besides—a good face to show the public."

"Thank you, sir," she replied, not sure what one said to such a thing. Acton had once given her a compliment about the bone structure in her face, but she hadn't really been paying attention.

"The reporter will be in contact; give him whatever he needs—it will be nice to have some positive coverage for a change."

"Yes, sir."

As she returned to her cubicle, Doyle rang up Acton to ask his advice. He couldn't countermand the DCS—could he?— but they could at least get their story straight. God forbid she relayed the truth; that she and Acton had no courtship at all, but had eloped from a crime scene where her estranged father was one of the victims. Mother a' mercy but it was a recipe for disaster; she tended to talk too much when she was nervous. Snabble it, my girl; less is more.

Acton did not pick up the call; that morning he had tucked a note under the sole remaining fruit pie that said he would be in meetings all day. She was disappointed, but she didn't try to call his private line, she had to stop being such a baby and face the music.

An hour later, the reporter phoned her desk and she reluctantly agreed to meet him for coffee at the deli. There was also a text from Williams, asking how she did. She responded immediately, keeping up her end of their bargain. One good thing about the whole ordeal, she thought; I'm no longer quarreling with Munoz and Williams. She mentally girded her loins and went out to meet the reporter.

It was the same one that had tried to speak to her before, and he identified himself again as Kevin Maguire. As he needed a haircut and wore a worn corduroy jacket, anyone would have immediately guessed he was either a reporter or a teaching assistant. Doyle sat down warily; Maguire had a reputation for being hard on the police and sympathetic to criminals.

"We meet again," he began with a rueful smile.

She couldn't help smiling in response. "I'm sorry; I just hate this."

"You have no protectors, today."

"I've been ordered to cooperate, so here I am." She suddenly had an idea—perhaps some good could come out of this misery. "My protector—the cab driver from last time, re-member?—was murdered a few days ago."

He was immediately sympathetic. "I'm so sorry."

"Perhaps you could run a photo and a small story, askin' if anyone saw anythin'."

"Tell me what you know." He jotted down notes while Doyle recited the story of Aiki's death, and the widow and child he left behind. She concluded, "The cab company will have his photo."

"You were friends?"

"Yes," she said simply, and suppressed the pang of grief.

He turned the page in his notebook. "Now tell me about yesterday."

Doyle recited the story once again, omitting the detail about the borrowed coat.

At its conclusion, the reporter leaned back in his chair—he was very pleased, she could see. "You jumped off Greyfriars Bridge into the Thames, even though you don't know how to swim. Extraordinary."

"It wasn't such a risk, truly," said Doyle reasonably, "what with the rucksack, an' all."

But the man continued to enthuse, "With this kind of story, every reader will pause and wonder if they could have done the same thing. It's a compelling connection—a great human interest story."

"Oh," said Doyle.

"And you saved your colleague," he checked his notes, "Detective Constable Isabel Munoz."

"Yes; Munoz is a very fine detective," said Doyle. "We are great friends." She hid a smile and had the immediate impression he knew she was saying it tongue in cheek.

He glanced at her with a glint of humor, but dutifully wrote the quote down, and then asked in an offhand manner, "What was it, were you rivals for Acton?"

"Everyone is a rival for Acton," she replied in a dry tone,

then stopped, horrified. "Please," she begged, "don't write that I said that."

He looked up at her, still smiling, "Come now—that's a hell of a human interest story, too. The public loves him; he's got a title, he's single, and as far I can tell, wasn't seeing anyone at all until he married you out of the clear blue."

Fiona, thought Doyle. Thank all available saints and holy angels he doesn't know about her.

"So—there were plenty of girls putting it to the touch, so to speak?"

"Mr. Maguire," she asked, "—are you married?"

"No," he admitted, smiling. He knows where I am going with this, she thought.

"Acton and I are very private people. Any story about my winnin' a make-believe competition for him will not speed me toward my next anniversary."

He eyed her thoughtfully. "Then give me something else. How did you meet?"

"At work," she said carefully; she was not going to make another mistake.

There was a pause. "Most people tell me more than I want to know when I ask how they met."

Doyle found she could not even construct a plausible story. "I'm afraid I'd like to be keepin' the details private."

He leaned forward on his elbows, suddenly all business. "You know, I will ask around and I may hear some stories that are not true. It would be better just to set the record straight."

Blackmail, she thought. "I won't," she replied firmly. "Do your worst."

He chuckled and closed his notepad. "I serve the public, ma'am."

CHAPTER 43

AFTER MAGUIRE LEFT, DOYLE REMAINED AT THE DELI, DRINK-ing coffee and dejected. Why couldn't she guard her tongue? Her tendency to be flip often earned Acton's silent disapproval—just wait until he heard this one. I have to warn him, she thought, and nearly groaned aloud; he'd be repenting of his foolish marriage, he would. She remembered last night, his eyes intent on hers as he moved against her in the firelight, and decided perhaps there was a chance he wouldn't.

Nothin' for it, she thought, but finished off the last of her coffee to gather her courage before she attempted the call. Samuels wandered by and saw her at her table near the window. "Doyle," he greeted her cheerfully. "Are you recovered?"

"As you see," she answered easily. "Have you found any leads?"

"Not much," he admitted. "Dispatch says the caller was a woman, but we can't conclude the attacker was the tipster, with this Solonik bunch. We're trying to check female known associates, but it is possible the attacker thought Munoz was the tipster, and wanted to silence her."

This indeed seemed plausible, and gave Doyle pause as this meant the tipster would be reluctant to come forward again, which may have been the intended result. "What sort of weapon?"

"Small blade, only five inches or so which was lucky—any longer and the damage would have been fatal. Not serrated. Holmes seemed to have a good idea of the type of knife, when he saw the report."

"He's seen the report already?" Doyle thought of Acton's crowded schedule. "That's quick work, Samuels."

The other man smiled in appreciation. "Thanks—it was a chance to shine and I grabbed it. He was anxious to see the report, and had me bring it by your flat, just now." He paused and said appreciatively, "Nice view."

"Yes, it is that," agreed Doyle. She was distracted, trying to assimilate the surprising information that Acton was at home. Were his meetings cancelled? And yet, he hadn't answered her call. After thanking Samuels for the information, she excused herself, claiming work obligations.

She walked out to the sidewalk and paused, thinking. She could call Acton again, on the private line if necessary, and start a conversation with him so as to assess what was going on. Her instinct, however, was making her very uneasy. She remembered the intensity of the lovemaking last night; remembered that Acton had left a note rather than tell her in person that he'd be unavailable at meetings today—apparently so that she wouldn't know he was lying. Wretched man; the game's afoot, she thought, and abruptly decided she was going home for lunch. As she made her way to the St. James's Park tube station, she knew with complete certainty that whatever it was, he was doing it to serve her—everything always did. But he had no compunction about compiling a body count in the process and she couldn't seem to convince him to rethink this strategy.

She arrived at the flat to see Reynolds, cleaning the kitchen wearing yellow rubber gloves and an apron. Unlikely Acton was still there, then.

"Hallo, Reynolds," she said easily. "Is Acton still about?"

The servant paused, and looked at her impassively. Ah, she thought; he's uneasy. Now what?

"No, madam," was all he replied, and Doyle admired his ability to say as little as possible to avoid possible repercussions; she wished she had the same talent.

"He was about, earlier, though," she prompted, taking off her jacket.

Reynolds looked at her consideringly, and Doyle took pity. "I hate to be puttin' you in the middle, Reynolds, but I need a truthful answer, if you please."

Surprisingly, Reynolds mused, "I cannot imagine that he would do wrong by you."

"No," she agreed, trying to hide her dismay. "He would not, no matter how it looks." They regarded each other, and she chose her words carefully. "Sometimes, Acton needs to be saved from himself." Reynolds nodded, and seemed to understand exactly what she meant. He's very sharp, she thought; I wonder how much he knows or has guessed, and I wonder if that's a good thing.

The servant was still weighing his options, so Doyle played her trump. "You owe me, Reynolds."

The man peeled off his gloves. "Lord Acton was here, and asked that he not be disturbed and that I not mention he was in to anyone, whom I took to mean you, madam."

Doyle considered this, furrowing her brow. "What was he about? Did he make any calls?"

"A young policeman delivered some paperwork and left. Lord Acton then removed something from the safe, and made a call."

"And," prompted Doyle, waiting to hear whatever Reynolds was omitting with a sinking feeling in her midsection. Samuel's report was not delivered by e-mail, but by hard copy which was easier to keep confidential. The guns were in the safe, and Reynolds was reluctant to tell her the rest. Saints and angels, she thought, tamping down panic; another flippin' crisis.

"He did not wish me to overhear, but it is hard to avoid," the servant explained apologetically. "I could not make out words, only the tone. It sounded as though he was speaking to a woman—very friendly, if I may say so. There were many assurances." He regarded her impassively, his expression wooden.

But Doyle was not thinking about infidelity, she was furiously trying to figure out who Acton was attempting to beguile. Solonik's woman? Rourke's? She had no idea; she did not know enough. The tipster had been a woman, and that must be who it was. Doyle racked her brain, but the only woman she could think of in connection with the turf war cases had already been murdered.

Reynolds cleared his throat. "Then there is the matter of the photograph."

This caught her full attention. "What photograph, Reynolds?"

"Yesterday Lord Acton asked me to review a photograph. He asked that I not mention it to you."

Honestly, she thought; I have to take up drinking, I can see the merit.

"It was of a woman," said Reynolds, who then hastened to assure her, "Not a very attractive woman."

Ah, here was a clue. "What did she look like?" Then, without waiting for an answer, she realized there was a more pertinent question, "And why would he show it to you?"

"He asked if it was the woman who was at the door that day—Marta."

Doyle stared at him, completely astonished. "He showed you a photo of *Marta?*" This made little sense; was Marta involved in the turf war? Had one side or the other set her up as a spy in their household? Perhaps she was still alive—Doyle had only Acton's word for it that she had killed herself. Why would he lie? No—on second thought, he wasn't lying when he'd called to say that Marta was dead. Doyle closed her eyes to concentrate. Think, Doyle. Acton would advise you to try to make sense of it without any preconceptions. If Marta were not, in fact, dead, Acton would not be calling her and being friendly, he would be murderous—they had no doubt that the poison was by Marta's hand. He'd not be trying to beguile her, he'd be throttling her. So why did Acton need Reynolds to confirm that indeed it had been Marta at the door? Marta was dead; it was moot.

Unless it wasn't.

Her eyes flew open. As calmly as she was able, she asked Reynolds, "What did the woman in the photo look like?"

"She had dark hair, tall—and was a bit *embonpoint*, madam."

"Reynolds, please speak in understandable terms."

"A bit heavyset," he amended.

This described Marta. "How old?"

"Not yet forty, I would guess."

Not Marta.

"And," he continued, "She was being given some sort of award, at a ceremony."

Doyle reached out involuntarily and grasped his arm. "Holy Mother of God," she breathed, and just caught herself just before adding, "Caroline."

CHAPTER 44

DOYLE SAT DOWN AND TRIED TO STEADY HER BREATHING FOR A few minutes before she phoned Acton. He didn't pick up his business line. She called his personal line. It rang twice, and then he answered.

"Yes." Terse again, he was. Caroline was there, then.

"I'm sorry to bother you, Michael, but I had an interview with a reporter from the London World News and I think I said the wrong thing. I wonder if you could use your influence with the editor again."

"Let me try. I will phone you back later."

"Grand," she replied, and rang off. Staring at her mobile, she tried to think it through. It must have been Caroline who was working with Marta—and perhaps Acton's mother—to poison the fair Doyle. It made sense, once you got past the shock of it; Caroline was unhappy Doyle had married Acton, she knew her way around poisons, and knew Marta—she was the perfect suspect. And she'd been trying to get Doyle to meet with her alone—even come to her flat, without telling Acton. Perhaps the object hadn't been murder, but only to induce an abortion; either way, Acton's fury would have no bounds.

Doyle wondered how he was made aware. He had warned Doyle that Caroline did not mean well by her, but surely he hadn't known at that time she was the poisoner—had he? She gave herself a mental shake; best lose no time in useless speculation, but act to stop the next retribution murder on what was Acton's apparently inexhaustible list; she had no doubt Caroline was slated to die. He must have convinced the woman that he knew what she had attempted and had forgiven her. Perhaps he also assured her that he would set Doyle aside; that would explain the friendly tone and assurances Reynolds had spoken of—it would also explain how he knew Doyle was no longer in danger.

She wondered where they were; Caroline was to speak at a conference—was it today? She couldn't remember; she truly needed to start paying more attention to things. She couldn't track Acton's GPS device as he did hers; he had disconnected it. Fingering the mobile, she debated ringing up Caroline on a pretext, but immediately discarded the idea; Acton would know what she was doing in a second, and would simply reschedule.

Although she'd been there once before, she pulled up the McGonigal address on Acton's laptop and jotted it down to figure out how to get there on the tube—it was her best chance. As Reynolds helped her back into her jacket, she said, "I'll try to keep you out of it."

"I would appreciate it, madam," he replied, and saw her out.

Doyle arrived at the building, and dug around in her wallet for the passkey Caroline had given her, inserting it into the security slot at the elevator. Caroline was a brilliant woman, but she was apparently dumb enough to believe Acton would be interested in her, which was a bit incestuous as her friend Fiona had been Acton's mistress, if you could call it that. Munoz is right, Doyle thought, thoroughly confused; everything is always about sex, and I am completely oblivious to it. And murder is not always murder—only it *truly* is, even if I'm the last person left who thinks so.

She walked quietly to the flat's entry door and pressed an

ear against it, but couldn't hear anything. Debating, she tried to decide whether she should go in or knock first—she would hate to burst in and surprise Timothy at lunch. She knocked. "Caroline, are you there? It's Kathleen Sinclair."

No answer, but Doyle knew, in the way that frightened Habib, that they were both within, and she could feel her heartbeat accelerate—Acton didn't know she had a key. She waited a few minutes, so that they would think she had left, and then she quickly inserted the passkey and entered the room, closing the door behind her. Her attention was immediately drawn to the tableau at the table, where Caroline was seated next to Acton, leaning on her elbows—they were drinking some sort of alcoholic beverage in glasses with ice. Acton's gaze was fixed on Doyle, betraying no surprise. Caroline, however, was frowning in disbelief, as though she was seeing an apparition. No one spoke.

Doyle found her voice. "May I come in?"

Acton said in a tone that brooked no argument, "No. You must go home and wait there. We will talk later."

"Stupid, skinny *bitch*," said Caroline in accents of such loathing that it made Doyle involuntarily flinch; it was apparent she was quite drunk.

Doyle met Acton's eyes, but they were hard and impenetrable, and the black mood hovered, ominous and threatening. "Can we have a non-discussion about this?" she asked softly.

"There is nothing to not discuss."

"He doesn't want you, you stupid, *stupid* bitch." Caroline was enjoying herself immensely, and swayed slightly. She was more than drunk, and Doyle concluded he had put a drug of some sort in her drink.

"Michael," asked Doyle with complete sincerity, "how many more people are goin' to come crawlin' out o' the woodwork, tryin' to kill me to get to you? In round numbers, if you please."

"Don't you dare call him 'Michael,' " Caroline chided, slurring her words. "You don't even know him. Fiona knew him. I know him. You are only a *stupid* Irish bitch."

"Caroline," Doyle cautioned, "you are not doin' yourself any favors, here."

"Cheers, Caro," said Acton, lifting his glass so that she responded. They took another drink. He then said to Doyle, "You must go home, Kathleen; Caroline and I are having a drink together."

It occurred to Doyle that she was the only rational person present, and this being the case, she should at least make a push. "Michael, you cannot," she said firmly. "It's a Commandment."

"Skinny *bitch*. What the—what the hell are you talking about? Go 'way, he doesn't want you."

Acton's eyes met Doyle's. "She killed your baby."

"As if she was worthy to have your baby, Acton—can you *imagine?* With her dirty African cab driver, thinking he could tell *me* what to do. *Me.*"

Doyle stared, completely shocked.

"You were to die a slow and agonizing death," Acton continued as though Caroline had not spoken.

"Stupid, skinny *bitch*."

"I was to watch you die."

"Yes," Doyle acknowledged; all valid points—it truly didn't look very good for Caroline when you toted them up like this.

"I would not have wanted to outlive you."

Doyle could feel the prickling of tears. Caroline would have completely destroyed them; there would have been nothing left of their little family-to-be. Nonetheless, murder was murder. "Michael, please don't do this."

"Acton, tell the skinny bitch what you told me—make her go away and never, *never* come back."

"Don't cry," he commanded Doyle.

"I'll try." Doyle wiped her cheeks with the palm of her hand—he didn't do well when she cried and she was afraid it could prompt him to finish it. "We are called to forgive, Michael."

"Whore. Stupid *whore.*"

"You can forgive this?" He sounded genuinely curious.

"I am supposed to try," she said honestly. "It's not an easy thing, seekin' redemption instead of retribution. But it's a better thing."

"Not in this case." He withdrew a small caliber gun from his jacket pocket, held it to Caroline's right temple, and fired.

Doyle jumped, and then put her hand over her mouth as Caroline slumped over, the blood spray pattern showing bright red on the wall. Acton looked up at Doyle. "Be careful going home; I will be there as soon as I can."

CHAPTER 45

Doyle didn't take the tube, but walked all the way home. It had started to rain again, and she forgot to bring an umbrella, but in her current mood it didn't matter much. She rang up Reynolds, standing under an awning so her mobile didn't get wet, and told him he should make himself scarce. "Might be a donnybrook," she explained. "If there's to be mayhem, best have no witnesses."

Reynolds expressed his willingness to stay if he could be of any support, but Doyle assured him she did not need reinforcements. Continuing on her way, she found the long walk in the rain very therapeutic, and was feeling better as she entered their building wet, cold, and bedraggled. It could be worse, she rationalized—I think he shot her because I was getting to him. Not much of a victory, but we'll take what we can. She knew he would clean up the scene so it would appear Caroline committed suicide after drinking and taking pills—how fortunate she had publicly spoken of suicide at lunch the other day. Not that there would be an investigation, of course; it was an open-and-shut case of suicide in a locked apartment—only she and Acton would know that the destroyer had in turn been destroyed.

The concierge showed commendable restraint in not making a disparaging comment about her appearance, but instead asked her very kindly if the police had made any progress in Aiki's murder. She was tempted to say that yes—as a matter of fact, justice had been very swift and very sure. Instead, she said only that it seemed unlikely they were ever to know.

Piecing it all together, she made her way to the private lift, dripping water on the fine marble floor. Caroline was poisoning her, and careful to poison only what Acton wouldn't eat. But then she must have heard from her brother that they were aware of the poisoning attempt, and had panicked a bit, trying to kill any witnesses who could place her at the flat for no apparent reason; Reynolds, who had seen her at the door, and Aiki, who must have challenged her in some way—although how Aiki would have known that Caroline meant to do her harm was unclear. We saved one of them, Doyle thought as she made her way to the flat's front door; I wish we'd managed to save both.

Doyle stepped into the flat and was immediately aware that Acton had not yet returned. She peeled off her wet clothes, showered in blessedly hot water once again, and then pulled on a robe, feeling a bit numb and wondering what she would say to her husband when he returned. Another retribution murder, she thought, gazing out at the rain with her chin in her hand; and this one much closer to home. I wonder if he found out whether his mother was involved, and I wonder what he will do if she was—it is becoming distressingly clear that I don't have as much influence as I thought; at least in matters vengeful. With a mental shake, she called Habib to report in and was relieved to discover that he seemed not to have noticed she'd been absent most of the day.

"Munoz is going home from the hospital tomorrow," he reported happily.

"That's grand, sir." A dedicated man, she thought; I wonder if Habib would lay waste to most of greater London for Munoz.

She realized she hadn't given Munoz a thought all day, and immediately phoned her. "Munoz, how goes the recovery?"

"Well. They tell me the thickness of the coat probably saved my life."

"Aren't you the clever one, then—and light-fingered, to boot."

"I'll get you another."

"Don't—I never liked it much, anyway."

There was a pause. "You know what I want to say."

"Then spare us both, Munoz."

"Right. They can't find anything wrong with me—although the doctor is trying, so as to keep me here."

"He'll have to arm wrestle with Habib."

"Wonderful. I do need to find myself a decent man."

"Is there to be a scar? You may have to settle, if that is the case."

"A scar will only add to my mystique. You'll see."

"I don't doubt it for a moment, Izzy; they'll be linin' up, hopin' to get a glimpse of it."

Munoz laughed, well-pleased, and Doyle rang off. Acton was still not home, which made her a bit uneasy. To pass the time, she opened up her tablet to review her messages and saw an e-mail from Maguire, the reporter, along with an attachment. Mother a' mercy; Acton had not had a chance to try to intervene on the article, being as he was too busy running amok. With some trepidation, she opened the message to see that Maguire relayed his thanks for her participation, and referenced the attached article. After closing her eyes to invoke the aid of any available saints, she opened it, and began reading. The article gave a factual and slightly sensationalized account of Munoz's rescue and asked the public's help in coming forward with any useful information concerning the attack. Another paragraph explained that Doyle was to be recognized by the CID for her bravery. The article concluded with the summation that she had been a PC for two years, a DC for two, and that she had recently married Chief Inspector Acton, as though it were a footnote. Directly below the article was another one, showing Aiki's photo and asking the public for information concerning his attack.

Doyle lowered her head and pressed her forehead against the tablet in profound relief. Thank You, she offered up; and thank Maguire for having mercy. Lifting her head, she immediately wrote back to him, expressing her admiration for the well-drafted article. She could be tongue-in-cheek, too.

Rising, she wandered over to the window to contemplate the view as the lights faded, and debated whether she should text Acton. It was likely he had gone somewhere to drink, perhaps his office, and she may be needed to gather him up—she didn't want him to get into a state. She typed, "Shall I give you a lift?" and sent the text.

The reply came almost immediately: "With Tim. It may be a while."

Of course, she thought; poor Timothy would be shocked and bereft. And naturally he would call Acton, to support him in his loss. They would wonder together how Caroline could have done such a thing, and suffer remorse that they were unaware of her deep unhappiness. I am not cut out for this, she thought; I was never any good at deception.

She began biting her thumbnail, and wondered uneasily if the scene had been processed by the police yet. There may be questions about how Caroline had come to have an illegal weapon; suspicions raised. Another message came in on her mobile.

"Are you all right?"

Now, there was an innocuous question that was nevertheless loaded with meaning. "Yes," she replied. "Am I needed?"

"Yes. But not here."

Despite everything, she smiled at the message. Acton, Acton, she thought; what am I going to do with you?

She decided to make an exception to her policy; if anyone

deserved a drink it was she, after the last two weeks. Or months. Taking an inventory of the liquor cabinet, she noted there was scotch, vodka, and brandy. After having tasted Acton's, she didn't much care for scotch and she thought vodka a bit extreme, so brandy it was. She poured out a small amount in a glass and diluted it with water, then sat at the table and watched the lights, sipping tentatively. Horrid, she thought, and desisted—how anyone could drink this stuff was beyond her. She thought of Williams, keeling over after his two pints of Guinness, and on a whim she texted him.

"Hey."

He answered immediately. "Where did U go?"

"Home. A crackin' foul day."

"Sorry. Can I help?"

She looked at the screen for a moment. "No, but thanks." Another dedicated man; best not encourage him.

"Note that I M behaving myself."

She smiled. "Note that I am not coming to cuffs w/U."

"Good 4 us."

The reference to an "us" gave her pause; she must be tipsy to be engaging with him again; she should keep him at arm's length for a bit. To conclude the session, she texted, "C U to-morrow."

He was reluctant to sign off. "No leads yet on Munoz or cab driver."

And there wouldn't be; Acton would see to that. "A shame. Must go."

"Cheers."

She rang off, wondering if they could ever get back to normal, whatever normal was for them.

CHAPTER 46

DOYLE SAT AT THE TABLE WITH HER FEET CURLED BENEATH HER and waited; thinking of nothing in particular, until Acton finally appeared, looking weary as he came through the door. The ultimate in a dedicated man, she thought as she turned her head to watch him approach. I have a surfeit of champions, whether I wish them or no.

His sharp eyes were upon her, assessing, then he ran a hand over her head and picked up the brandy bottle. "What's this?"

"You've driven me to drink, my friend. It was only a matter of time."

He said mildly, "I'll join you," and went to the liquor cabinet to address the scotch bottle; she noted that he took the brandy bottle with him.

"How is Timothy?"

"Bad," he replied shortly, and poured himself a tall glass of scotch. He didn't want to talk about it, which was no surprise, and so instead she asked the question she had been wondering all evening.

"How did you know?"

He glanced over at her as he took a seat at the table. "Caroline knew our new domestic was a 'he' and not a 'she'; so she must have been the one at the door when Reynolds answered."

Doyle stared in surprise at the simple explanation. "You are *somethin'*, Michael."

Acton took a healthy swallow from his glass and leaned back in his chair, his gaze resting on its contents. He was alert and wary, despite his relaxed pose, and she decided that it served him right; she truly should be railing and throwing things if she had any self-respect at all. On the other hand, this certainly felt like a discussion, which was a promising sign. He must be remorseful—or, she amended, at least remorseful about putting her though it. She doubted he harbored a flicker of remorse for all the various and sundry murders.

He continued, "Aiki tried to tell you."

"*Aiki* did?" She was at sea.

"Yes; you described what he said, but you misunderstood. He was saying '*votre amie.*' It means 'your friend' in French."

"Oh—I see. That would clinch it; I suppose, after Reynolds verified the photo."

He lifted his gaze to hers, and immediately she realized her error—the wretched brandy was goofing her up. "I browbeat him into the admission, Michael; I knew somethin' was up, and I came home for lunch to discover what it was. Please don't be angry or fire him; he so loves saying 'Lord Acton.' "

Acton considered. "Do you think we can trust him?"

She nodded. "I do. Believe me, you will be the first to know if he puts a foot wrong; we can't have another snake livin' in the chicken coop."

"There is no one," he pronounced slowly, "who can turn a phrase quite like you."

"I'm a corker," she agreed.

Cradling his glass, he bowed his head. "Reynolds should not have disobeyed me." He paused. "And now he may piece together what has occurred."

Doyle hadn't thought of this, but remained unalarmed. "Unlikely," she insisted. "I'm the only one who pieces things together." She paused. "Aside from you, of course—you take the palm."

"You are extraordinary."

She had the feeling that he was referring to her current state of restraint as much as her intuitive ability, but what else could she do? She loved the man, and at least it all made some sense, finally. Cautiously, she tried to keep this fragile discussion going. "And I suppose Marta didn't truly kill herself."

He nodded. "Timothy must have told Caroline about the poisoning, and she killed Marta so as to silence her and give us a likely suspect at the same time—the case would be closed." He paused, contemplating what was left of the scotch in his glass. "Caroline was unhappy we married."

"Yes—already aware of that, Michael."

"Are you unhappy we married?"

Ah, she thought; here we go. "No, I am not unhappy we married—I think it is the best and greatest thing I have ever done." She took a sip of the brandy because she'd forgotten how foul it was, and then added fairly, "thus far." Dropping her head, she traced her finger in a water drop on the table. "Although I will admit that some days are better than others."

He leaned forward and covered her hand with his. "Do you remember when you told me that you had no choice but to jump off the bridge?"

"Yes." She lifted her face and understood what he was trying to tell her. "I see."

"I am sorry." The truth rang like a clear bell, and his relief was palpable. "I will do whatever is necessary so that—so that this is not so difficult for you."

But this was the wrong tack, and she made a sound of frustration. "You are not to be careful around me, Michael—I hate it, remember? Just—let's just try to make certain there aren't any more days like today." She met his eyes. "Although nothin' will make me change my mind, Michael—truly." Fingers crossed, she thought; living with this man was not for the faint of heart.

He made no response, but she was heartened—he was allowing her glimpses within, and even though he hated to speak of it, they were making progress; they were sorting out how they were to deal with each other. In the end, this was surely not much different than what every other new married couple had to do. Except for the forensics, of course. "Will there be an investigation, do you think?"

"No."

"How can you be so certain, Michael?" She allowed her voice to reveal her uneasiness.

"I am very good at what I do."

This was inarguably true. And it would never cross anyone's mind to suspect him in the first place; it would take some very serious digging to come up with evidence of Acton's dark doings, and no one would even think of trying. "Then we should be havin' no more problems like this one."

"I hope not," he agreed.

It was the truth, and she was relieved; in the back of her mind was the unspoken concern that he enjoyed this—that it was a symptom of his condition. Things could get very dicey if he was going to start wreaking revenge on anyone who bumped into her on the sidewalk. "I suppose our trip to Brighton is postponed, then?"

"Yes. I'm sorry, Kathleen; I'm to help Timothy with the funeral."

She sighed philosophically. "I'll help you do it; you don't speak RC very well, after all." She wondered if he would ever make a real confession—Father John would fall out of his chair.

They sat in silence for a few minutes, and then she asked, "Have they found Rourke's body, yet?"

"Not as yet." He lifted his gaze to hers, curious. "Any ideas?"

"No," she confessed. "I'm afraid it doesn't work like that." Since he'd given her a glimpse, she'd return the favor. "Any leads on motive?"

Acton leaned back and crossed his long legs at the ankles; he was able to relax, now that he knew she wasn't going to brain him with a joint stool. "I think so—we discovered some encrypted e-mails that indicate the Rourkes and Solonik were in league together, agreeing to cut each other in on a new contraband operation."

Doyle blinked in surprise. "Holy Mother—truly? That seems unlikely, they are sworn enemies." Then she remembered his theory. "A mutual secret, just as you thought—neither the Rourkes nor Solonik could allow their people to learn they'd been conspiring against them with the enemy." She remembered Habib had said something to this effect—speculating that Solonik's refusal to identify his attacker stemmed from a business decision, and not necessarily a tribal allegiance. "What was the rig they wanted to run, do you know?"

"Solonik runs a contraband operation, and the Rourkes were going to siphon money off their track earnings to fund a mutual operation on the side—it is unclear exactly what it was."

"Skimmin'," quoted Doyle, her brow clearing. "Our Mr. Thackeray was right." She paused because her scalp was tingling, and she wasn't sure whether it was just the brandy. "Thackeray also said there were an unusual amount of horse trailers, going in and out."

Acton slowly pulled his legs in and sat up. "Did he indeed?"

With some excitement, Doyle played her trump. "Remember the wary walk-in—the one with the fancy French watch— he said he was a driver; they must be smugglin' contraband in the horse trailers. It would be a simple way to regularly transport somethin' almost anywhere in the country without raisin' suspicion."

"Savoie," Acton mused.

Doyle blinked, as this seemed a non sequitur, and just when she was solving the case like a house afire. "What?"

Acton tilted his head, contemplating the view out the window. "No wonder Solonik wanted assurances; they were both trying to cut in on Savoie."

But Doyle was having some trouble keeping up. "Remind me who Savoie is, Michael—another kingpin?"

He glanced at her, debating what to say, and she was reminded that he had his own little black market enterprise on the side, which she was not to know about. "Savoie is a major international player, and very dangerous. I imagine he caught wind of the Solonik-Rourke plan, and to warn them off, deposited Rourke's body at Newmarket." He paused, and added almost unnecessarily, "Savoie is not someone you cross."

"Neither are you," Doyle pointed out, thinking of Barayev's grisly corpse. "And here I thought it was you that had Rourke killed."

But this was a discussion too far, apparently, and instead of responding, he pulled his mobile and called Williams to let him know that the body of the missing Rourke would no doubt also be found on Newmarket heath near where his brother's body had been found, and that a search team should be sent in the morning.

"Another retribution murder," she observed as he rang off. "Faith, you need a spreadsheet to keep track."

Acton leaned back again, well-satisfied. "I will look into this in the morning—the horse-trailer theory seems very sound; if we play our cards right, we may be able to bring in even more players, once we see how the operation works."

Yes, she thought; whether or not you approved of Acton's methods, there was no arguing that all the evildoers had been thoroughly thwarted—or killed, one or the other. "The DCS should give Thackeray a commendation—or at least deputize him; he twigged the whole case, he just didn't know it. I wonder why Solonik was there in the first place."

"He no doubt felt that such an out-of-the-way place was a safe venue to meet with Rourke."

Doyle had to smile at the irony. "Far from it, as it turned out." She thought about it for a moment, and then wondered aloud, "If Solonik thought the Rourkes had killed his brother-in-law, why would he even agree to meet with them?"

Acton set his glass down. "Solonik never thought the Rourkes were responsible for killing his brother-in-law."

Yes, of course; she'd forgotten that Barayev was killed in retribution for Owens shooting *her;* Acton would have made certain to let Solonik know this—no point in going to all the trouble of a retribution murder, one would think, unless the target was aware it was a retribution murder. You almost felt sorry for Solonik, who—as it turned out—had nothing to do with Owens shooting her, and must have been bewildered by Acton's wholesale vengeance-seeking.

But any stab of sympathy quickly dissipated; after all, the Solonik-Rourke allegiance may well have been hatched as a way to team up against Acton as much as against this Savoie character, and there was no question Solonik deserved to be in prison. A good riddance, she decided; but Acton could not go on as he was—perhaps therapy was not necessarily a bad idea.

"Is it time for bed?" Her husband's gaze rested on the décolletage of her robe, as apparently this night's crime-solving was fast coming to an end.

"It is," she agreed. "This day cannot be over fast enough."

His arm around her waist, Acton led her to the bedroom. "Tell me of your interview with the reporter; what was your concern?"

"It turned out to be nothin', Michael; I just panicked a bit. I talk too much when I'm nervous."

"Is that so?" he teased.

"The reporter is a wily one, though; best to avoid him. He's determined to make us a page-seven story." She glanced up at him sidelong. "Not that anyone would believe it."

"Nonsense," he said, pausing to kiss her. "Nothing to see, here."

Keep reading for a sneak peek
At Acton and Doyle's next adventure
MURDER IN HINDSIGHT

CHAPTER 1

DETECTIVE SERGEANT KATHLEEN DOYLE WAS FRETTING; FRETting and stalling until Detective Chief Inspector Acton could make an appearance whilst she tried to appear calm and composed in front of the Scene of the Crime Officers. As a newly-promoted DS, she should maintain a certain dignity and display her leadership abilities, even though she was longing to bite her nails and peer over the hedgerow toward the park entrance. The various Scotland Yard forensics personnel were impatiently waiting because Acton was delayed, and Doyle had a good guess as to why he was delayed. One of these fine days, someone else may make the same guess and then the wretched cat would be among the wretched pigeons—although the mind boggled, trying to imagine Acton being called on the carpet by Professional Standards. Pulling out her mobile, she pretended to make a call just to appear busy.

"I'll lose the light soon, ma'am." The SOCO photographer approached, cold and unhappy, and small blame to her; Doyle was equally cold and unhappy, but with better reason.

"Ten more minutes," Doyle assured her, holding a hand over her mobile so as to interrupt her pretend-conversation. "Then we'll move forward—whether DCI Acton makes it or no." She wanted Acton to have a look before the corpse was processed and removed, but she could always show him the photos.

The woman immediately plucked up. "No hurry; we can wait, if the DCI is on his way."

Has a crush on him, the brasser, thought Doyle. Join the club, my friend; the woman probably had some private photographs she'd be all too happy to show Acton in her spare time. The SOCO photographer used to treat Doyle with barely-concealed contempt, but her attitude had improved remarkably after the bridge-jumping incident. A few months ago, Doyle had jumped off Greyfriars Bridge into the Thames to save a colleague, and was now a celebrated hero. All in all, it was a mixed blessing, because Doyle was not one who craved the spotlight and now she was perceived as sort of a female version of St. George—except that she'd rescued the dragon instead of the maiden, when you thought about it.

Irish by birth and fey by nature, Doyle had an uncanny ability to read people, and in particular she could recognize a lie when she heard it. This perceptive ability had launched her career as a detective, but it also made her reclusive by nature—it was no easy thing, to be able to pick up on the currents and crosscurrents of emotion swirling around her. The SOCO photographer, for example, was lusting after the vaunted chief inspector but bore Doyle no particular ill-will for being married to him, since she was the heroic bridge-jumper and thus above reproach.

With a nod of her head, the photographer gestured toward the victim, being as she didn't want to take her hands out of her pockets until it was necessary. "Is there something special about this one, then?"

There was, but Doyle did not want to say, especially before the loose-lipped SOCOs who were notoriously inclined to blather when in their cups—it came from wading knee-deep in guts all the livelong day. So instead, she equivocated, "There are a few details that are worrisome, is all. I wanted the DCI to have a quick look."

As it appeared to be an ordinary case of a bad 'un coming to an only-to-be-expected bad end in this part of town, this pronouncement would ordinarily hold little water, but because the photographer was anticipating a chance to bat her eyes at Acton, no demur was raised. Doyle was reminded that on the aqueduct case, this particular photographer had withheld evidence at Acton's request, and wondered at such foolish devotion. Then she recalled that it was a case of the pot and the kettle—Doyle herself was an aider and abettor, after all—and so she tempered her scorn. Although she was married to him, Acton was in many respects a mystery to her as few were; he abided by his own notions of justice, and was not above manipulating the means to achieve the ends he desired—not something one would expect from a well-respected DCI at the Met. But the fact that no one would expect it was— ironically—the very reason he got away with murder on certain memorable occasions; his reputation acted as a shield. Any suggestion that the celebrated Lord Acton was running illegal weapons, dispatching villains, or manipulating evidence would be met with disbelief and derision, as well he knew. In the meantime, his better half was left to hang on to his coat tails and try to curb his wayward ways—it was no easy task, and Doyle reluctantly rang off from her pretend-conversation so as to decide how best to proceed without him.

After peering over the hedgerow yet again, she blew into her hands because she'd forgotten her gloves, and reflected that the cold was actually a blessing because the recently departed wouldn't be further decomposing whilst they cooled their heels—she truly shouldn't delay for much longer, or the senior investigating officer might think they'd all gone for a pub crawl.

"Here he comes, ma'am," the photographer chirped happily, and with a great deal of relief, Doyle looked up to see that Acton was indeed approaching; his tall, over-coated figure emerging from the evening fog. In such a setting he appeared larger-than-life, and small wonder that female underlings harbored a crush, or that the younger detectives at the Met called him "Holmes" behind his back. He was a local legend, which only made her fret all the more whilst she entertained the bleak conviction that the whole thing was about to come crashing down around their heads.

"DS Doyle." He nodded to her. "Have you an ID?"

"I do indeed, sir." They kept up a professional façade when they were dealing with each other at work, but she met his eyes and felt the chemistry crackling between them like an electrical charge. No one could fathom why the great Chief Inspector Acton had married the lowly likes of her, and literally on a moment's notice. She could fathom it, however, and did—sometimes twice a day. Thus far in their short marriage they were very happy together, despite the occasional crisis. "He's twenty-three years old with a record of petty thefts and drug-dealin'—nothing major—but he was a suspect in an arson homicide about eight years ago." She paused significantly, and Acton met her eyes with interest. He then stepped carefully over to the body, lying next to the hedgerow, and she followed to crouch down beside him and contemplate the victim's remains for a silent moment. The victim had been shot in back of the head, and there were no signs of a defensive struggle.

She continued, "No sign of robbery, and he was armed—had a .38 revolver tucked into the back of his belt." That it was illegal went without saying; guns were carefully controlled in Britain, but the black market flourished, particularly among the criminal classes. Lowering her voice, she indicated with a finger, "The entry wound is angled, and there's no visible residue, so it's at mid-close range—no more than a foot or so. Another shot from behind, but not a professional hit."

He began to pull off his leather gloves by the fingers. "Allow me to lend you my gloves."

"You mustn't," she warned. "I'll never learn, else."

"Your fingers are white."

"Are you *listenin'* to me?"

"Yes." He glanced up at her. "He used a different weapon, this time, and shot from the opposite side in an attempt to obscure his identity."

"I think so," she agreed, mollified that he was paying attention and had come to the same conclusion as she had. "He's trying to disguise it, but it's the same killer. And the victim has another cold case connection."

They rose, and Acton stood next to her, his breath making a cloud in the chill air.

In a low tone, she ventured, "Perhaps you should button your coat, my friend—and try not to be breathin' on anyone."

There was a pause. "Is it so obvious?" he asked quietly.

"Only to me," she assured him. "Was it completely wretched?"

"I've been admonished not to discuss it with you, but the answer is yes."

"Grand," she observed dryly.

He continued in a neutral tone, "I am asked a great many questions about my mother and about you."

"Whist, Michael," she scoffed. "As if that has *anythin'* to do wi' it."

He chuckled, which was a good sign, and she chuckled with him, not caring what the impatient SOCO team would think to see the CID detectives amusing themselves over the remains of the decedent. Acton had begun therapy for an obsessive condition, the object of his obsession being her fair self. He had developed a fixation for his first-year colleague, and by the time Doyle had become aware of it, he'd convinced her to marry him—which she had, in a pig's whisper, which only spoke to the state of her own mental faculties. To make a try at a normal life he was seeing a therapist, hoping to learn techniques to control his symptoms without necessarily disclosing the reason. Apparently, the therapist had not been misled.

"So you've been servin' yourself some self-help," she concluded. After his sessions, Acton would drink impressive quantities of scotch. He was not one to refrain, even under normal conditions, but it seemed to Doyle that the therapy was only making matters worse.

"We're losing the light, sir," the photographer ventured from a respectful distance.

Thus reminded, Acton called the SOCO team over and began giving instructions; particular care was to be given to physical evidence at the site, although there was little to hope for, with the ground so cold. Because the killer was using a variety of murder weapons to disguise his involvement, any footprints or trace evidence they could scrounge up might provide a means to link this murder to the others; by all appearances, they were dealing with a serial killer.

While they watched the forensics team go to work, Acton lifted his head to survey the area and observe the placement of the CCTV cameras. "Tell me about the cold case that is connected to this one."

"Unsolved double murder by arson. Our victim here was the chief suspect, eight years ago, but there was little evidence and he had a lot of sympathetic press coverage, bein' so young." There was a pause.

"Eight years; a strange sort of vigilante, who abides for such a length of time."

"Aye, that," she teased solemnly. When Acton drank, his tone and language reverted to House of Lords, and so she reverted to hardscrabble Dublin so as to counter him.

Amused, he turned to meet her eyes and said sincerely, "This was very good work."

She shrugged, nonetheless pleased by the compliment. "Lucky, more like. And give yourself some credit; it all came of you throwin' me off the cases." Acton had been concerned—and rightly so—that Doyle was in danger when they were investigating the Kempton Park racecourse murders. He had taken her out of the field, and instead placed her on thankless and uninteresting cold case duty, locked in the CID basement and looking through dusty boxes of unsolved homicides. Thoroughly frustrated and resentful, she had nevertheless used the time to review and index Acton's cold case files, and had noticed a link between a recent string of apparently unconnected murders and some of the unsolved cold cases. Her intuition came to the conclusion that someone was murdering killers who had previously escaped justice—a vigilante was at work. This latest victim would appear to confirm her theory.

A PC who was monitoring the cordon came over to have a word with Acton. "Sir, there is a reporter who would like to have a word."

Doyle caught a quick flash of annoyance from her husband, but there was nothin' for it; if you tried to avoid the pests, it would only make them think you were hiding massive police abuse. Cooperating with the fourth estate was a necessary evil, especially in this day and age, but on the other hand, Acton was not one to suffer fools. This attitude worked only to enhance his standing with the public, who followed his career with avid interest—not that he cared or noticed. He signaled for Doyle to accompany him, and so she followed him as he went to address the reporter, a woman who stood with her arms crossed against the cold despite wearing a fine cashmere coat—reporting must pay well. She was from the London World News, a paper that had often been critical of the Met. Recently, however, an uneasy truce had been achieved and the detective chief superintendent had cau-

tioned them that the Home Secretary desired as much coop-
eration with the press as possible. Doyle was nervous; Acton
was very self-possessed and she doubted that anyone else
could tell that he had been drinking, but if the interview did
not go well she'd have to create some sort of distraction—
perhaps another pretend phone call.

The reporter seemed a very competent woman in her
midthirties, brimming with confidence, Doyle could see;
someone who would never forget her gloves on such a day.
Holding out a hand to shake his, she threw Acton a friendly
smile that held a touch of flirtatiousness, not an uncommon
occurrence as the SOCO photographer was also attempting
to sidle up next to him on the pretext of waiting to be dis-
charged. You're not his type—neither of you, Doyle thought;
his type was shy redheads who nonetheless tended to fly off
the handle on occasion. She was resigned, though; Acton was
titled, handsome, rich, and unattainable, a combination that
was apparently fatally attractive to the general female popula-
tion. Male, too, she amended, remembering Owens, the detective trainee who had harbored an unhealthy obsession for
him. She was lucky Acton was literally crazy about her; there
was a lot of temptation lyin' about.

Acton didn't introduce her, and so Doyle stayed back, monitoring the conversation between the two and wondering if
she had the wherewithal to step in, if the need arose. Judging
by the questions, however, it didn't appear that the reporter
was yet aware of the pattern that pointed to a serial killer, and
so Doyle relaxed a bit. As the scene had been cordoned off in
a public place and there had been a delay in waiting for
Acton, no doubt the press had merely caught wind of it and
had come to see if there was a story. Serial killers were tricky;
although there were times when the public should be warned
there was such a killer afoot, in cases like this, when it seemed
unlikely the killer was aware they had twigged him, discretion

was the better option—all the better to set up a trap and seizure.

In a provocative gesture, the reporter threw back her head and laughed at something Acton said, which inspired the photographer to interrupt with barely-concealed jealousy. They were both making a dead run at him, but he appeared completely oblivious to it, which was commendable, being has his wife was making a mighty effort not to interject a smart remark. Instead, said wife comforted herself by recalling that she'd carried off the palm, and thus managed to curb the urge to knock both their heads together.

At this point, the reporter deigned to notice Doyle. "Why, you're the bridge-jumper, aren't you?"

Doyle acknowledged that indeed, she was the bridge-jumper.

The woman shook her head. "I have to say—I don't think I could have done it."

Doyle remembered that Kevin Maguire, the reporter who had interviewed her from the same paper, had told her it was a great human interest story because everyone who read it would pause and wonder if they would have run such a risk. Apparently, he was right. "Please give my regards to Mr. Maguire," she said; the man had done her a favor and Doyle was grateful.

"Will do," the woman agreed, and with one last glance under her lashes at Acton, she left.

After giving instruction to close down the scene, Acton and Doyle walked back toward Acton's Range Rover, parked a block away. He was quiet, and she broke the silence. "You should probably go straight home, my friend."

"Come with me."

She could see that he was in need of the cure—it was her experience that a good, hearty serving of ungentle sex tended to bring him out of the dismals. "I can't," she explained regretfully. "I'm slated to help at the clinic, and I'm past due already."

He ducked his head for a moment, and then looked at her with an expression she knew very well. "Don't stay late."

"I won't. Don't be startin' without me."

"Not a chance," he replied.